BOOK 3

PEACEKEEPERS
OF SOL

RAVEN'S COURSE

BOOK 3

PEACEKEEPERS
OF SOL

RAVEN'S COURSE

GLYNN STEWART

FAOLAN'S PEN
PUBLISHING
faolanspen.com

This edition published in 2020 by:

Faolan's Pen Publishing Inc.

22 King St. S, Suite 300

Waterloo, Ontario

N2J 1N8 Canada

ISBN-13: 978-1-989674-23-9 (print)

A record of this book is available from Library and Archives Canada.

Printed in the United States of America

1 2 3 4 5 6 7 8 9 10

Second edition

First printing: December 2020

Illustration by Sam Leung

Faolan's Pen Publishing logo is a registered trademark of Faolan's Pen Publishing Inc.

Read more books from Glynn Stewart at faolanspen.com

CHAPTER ONE

"Welcome to the bridge, Ambassador Todorovich. *Shaka*'s crew stands by to assist you in any way we can."

Sylvia Todorovich acknowledged Captain Adriano Chavez's courtesy as she glanced around the destroyer's bridge. The tall blonde diplomat was used to larger warship bridges, but her usual partner and his ship were under repair.

She was more attached to the battlecruiser *Raven* than she would admit—and that was *before* mentioning the other warship's commanding officer. *Shaka* was not only a smaller ship than *Raven* but an older one, built over a decade earlier at the height of the war against the Kenmiri.

"I hate to imply that your ship is only a taxi, Captain," Todorovich told the destroyer's CO as she stepped onto the command dais at the center of the bridge, "but if you are required to do more than fly me around today, something has gone very wrong."

Lieutenant Colonel Chavez—the United Planets Space Force had kept the title of *Captain* out of its rank structure, leaving it solely as the courtesy title of a starship commander—grinned unabashedly at the diplomat.

"Well, we got you here safely enough, so we're doing all right as a taxi service," the dark-skinned officer told her. "We've made first contact with Blue Stripe Green Stripe Orange Stripe. A fighter wing is on their way out to escort us in to the Convoy."

Sylvia nodded sharply, studying the displays around her as she settled precisely into the observer chair. *Shaka*'s bridge was a simple U-shaped room with sixteen people in it, including the ambassador. The observer seat normally folded into a wall and had no acceleration tank of its own.

If *Shaka* needed to use her full acceleration, Sylvia would need to retreat to her quarters to immerse herself in the tank required to survive the twenty pseudogravities that would leak through. As with the destroyer's weaponry, though, if the engines had to be used at full power, she'd done something wrong.

"Do we have any scans of the Convoy itself?" she asked Chavez.

"Negative," he replied. "Ra-Twenty-One isn't a system we know well, but we've at least been here before. My guess is they're here."

He indicated the larger of the two gas giants on the displays. There were also four rockier worlds, but they more closely resembled Mercury or Mars than Earth. Nothing in Ra-21—the twenty-first system the United Planets Alliance had scouted in what they had labeled the Ra Province of the Kenmiri Empire—was habitable or even valuable to most people.

"If the Convoy is on the far side of the gas giant, we wouldn't be picking up more than loose electromagnetic radiation...which we are seeing at Ra-Twenty-One-Epsilon and not at Ra-Twenty-One-Zeta."

"Ser, Em Ambassador, we have our fighter escort on scopes," the destroyer's tactical officer, a Black woman who was probably not as young as she looked to Sylvia, reported.

Once you reached Sylvia's mid-forties, everyone under thirty started looking like a child.

"On the main screen, give the Ambassador and me a tactical readout," Chavez ordered calmly.

There were no holograms on a warship bridge, but Sylvia was

long used to that. She'd been a wartime diplomat, after all, sent into a hostile empire to make alliances with the rebel factions known as the Vesheron.

The six starfighters on the big display were pretty standard: spheres with rockets on each of their cardinal aspects. They were bigger and better armed than the standard UPSF equivalent, though they also lacked the one key advantage the UPSF had over their enemies.

"No real threat here," Chavez said with a wave of his hand. "Our gravity shield can absorb their missiles without any problems."

"Really," Sylvia said sharply. The gravity shield was universal to UPSF combat spacecraft, even their starfighters using it to survive the overwhelming firepower possessed by the Kenmiri and the Vesheron that had revolted against them.

"Do you, Captain, possess some intelligence on who has the anti-gravity resonance disruptor missiles that hasn't been shared with the Diplomatic Corps?" she asked. "Because my understanding is that we have no idea who supplied the disruptor missiles to the Kozun."

And those missiles were why Sylvia was aboard *Shaka* instead of *Raven*. In the hands of the Kozun Hierarchy, they'd overwhelmed *Raven*'s gravity shield, leaving the battlecruiser defenseless in the face of the Hierarchy's forces.

Raven had survived—but another UPA ship hadn't.

"I...do not, Em Ambassador," Chavez admitted stiffly. "I just... I didn't think that the Drifters were likely to be in possession of an advanced technology like that. They're just nomads, after all, aren't they?"

Sylvia shook her head at the UPSF officer.

"You won't think that once you see the Convoy itself," she told him. "But before you make any more assumptions, let me remind you that every missile in your magazines was based on a reverse-engineering project we ran in a lab we rented from a Drifter Convoy—and a good chunk of the missiles you hauled into Kenmiri space in the war were outright *bought* from Drifters."

"It's...easy to forget that, Em Ambassador," Chavez said. "Do you think it's likely that those fighters have disruptor warheads?"

Sylvia studied the starfighters decelerating to match *Shaka*'s course.

"Probably not, if only because they weren't waiting for us," she told him. "We didn't exactly tell them we were coming."

Sylvia, like *Shaka*, was assigned to the Peacekeeper Initiative, a special project of the United Planets Alliance to try and stabilize the Ra Sector now the Kenmiri Empire no longer existed. They'd deployed postal outposts throughout the portion of the Sector they'd made contact with, small prefab stations with a small crew and a stockpile of skip-capable courier drones to keep everyone in contact with each other.

Blue Stripe Green Stripe Orange Stripe had appeared on the perimeter of the zone the Initiative was in contact with several weeks earlier. The UPA could have sent a drone, but it wouldn't have been far ahead of *Shaka* itself...and Sylvia knew things Chavez didn't. Like that the UPSF was reasonably certain at least one Drifter Convoy was responsible for the Kozun Hierarchy's possession of resonance disruptor weapons.

"Fighters are in formation," the tactical officer reported.

"We are being sent a course for Epsilon," an older man, the destroyer's coms officer, said. "ETA is just over an hour."

"Plug it in and let's see what we find," Chavez confirmed. "Any instructions yet?"

"Nothing detailed," the coms officer replied.

"We'll be rendezvousing with one of the Guardians," Sylvia told the captain with a concealed sigh. "I will meet with a Protector-Commander who will decide whether *Shaka* and I represent a threat to the Convoy.

"In the last years of the war, that would have been a formality. Now..." She shook her head. "I don't think we'll have any problems, but with the Vesheron alliance shattered, we have no guarantees of access anymore."

Sylvia had been aboard Drifter Convoys before, though not Blue Stripe Green Stripe Orange Stripe itself.

"And after that?" Chavez asked.

"Hopefully, I'll be able to meet with one of the Ancients," Sylvia told him. "My chief of staff will meet with a Quartermaster with our shopping list, but our main mission is political. That means I need to speak to the people in charge."

The Ancients weren't always the oldest members of the Convoy as they had once been, but the title remained. The Council of Ancients ran the fleet...and that meant that Sylvia needed to talk to them if she was going to get them to do what she needed.

SYLVIA COULD TELL who on *Shaka*'s bridge had seen a Drifter Convoy before and who hadn't in the moment the destroyer crested the horizon of the gas giant and the contacts started to propagate on the sensor reports.

They'd seen half a dozen ships already by that point, but those were escorts, the standard Kenmiri light warship. Everyone in the former empire had escorts, either stolen from Kenmiri docks or built to Kenmiri templates.

As they came over the gas giant, *hundreds* of icons began to appear on the displays. Small ships. Big ships. Everything in between.

Chavez himself was stunned to silence along with his officers. Two of the noncoms clearly had seen a Convoy before, one of them meeting Sylvia's gaze long enough to wink at her before getting back to his work.

"I knew they were a nomadic fleet, but that's..."

"I make it six hundred and forty-three contacts," the tactical officer replied. "Looks like sixty warships, a quarter of them Guardians."

"It's a three-stripe Convoy, Captain Chavez," Sylvia pointed out.

"That means a minimum of *both* five hundred ships and five million people. If Blue Stripe Green Stripe Orange Stripe had fewer ships or fewer people than that, they'd be a *four*-stripe Convoy."

"We've confirmed our destination, ser," the communications officer reported. "As the Ambassador suggested, it's one of the Guardians. Looks like the biggest."

"Set your course," Chavez ordered. He leaned back in his chair and looked at Sylvia. "Anything I should be worried about?"

"We don't know this Convoy in particular," Sylvia said. "They were deeper in Kenmiri space than most of our operations and weren't one of the ones we leaned on to supply Golden Lancelot. With subspace coms, the Drifters were more unified than anyone suspected. Without them…"

She shrugged. Golden Lancelot had been the final solution to the Kenmiri war, a term chosen with deadly historical propriety afterward by the officers and spacers who'd carried it out. The UPSF, combined with their Vesheron allies, had launched a campaign of precision attacks across the entire Kenmiri Empire and killed every single one of the Kenmiri's Kenmorad breeding caste.

Without the Kenmorad, the Kenmiri were a dying race. They had abandoned entire worlds to concentrate their remaining population into eight of their original twenty provinces—and the former Vesheron expected that remnant to shrink over the next eighty years until there were no Kenmiri left.

But the Kenmiri's return salvo had been devastating. The subspace communicators every known race had relied on for faster-than-light communications had turned out to be using an artificially stabilized segment of subspace. In revenge for their destruction, the Kenmiri had disabled the stabilizers.

The Grand Alliance of the Vesheron had collapsed into infighting within hours of the loss of that instant communication. Sylvia didn't know how the Drifters' fragile inter-Convoy unity had handled it, but the UPA had lost a lot of friends to the Kenmiri's final blow.

"Remember that the Guardians are modular warships," she finally said. "You know more about what that means for them as combatants than I do, I hope."

Chavez chuckled.

"I'm hoping not to underestimate them again," he agreed. "My understanding is that each of those Guardians is more dangerous than a Kenmiri dreadnought, if not as tough. And, well..." He shrugged. "*Shaka* couldn't fight a dreadnought, let alone something nastier."

"Then let's follow instructions and go say hello as they ask," Sylvia told him. "We are, after all, here to ask for a favor."

CHAPTER TWO

SHAKA'S SHUTTLE SLIPPED THROUGH A SEA OF BEHEMOTHS. Most of the ships in the Convoy made the hundred-and-forty-meter-long destroyer look like a toy, which left the twelve-meter shuttle looking like nothing.

Most of the ships were freighters, refitted to act as flying arcologies holding everything from hydroponics to living quarters to factories. Some of the largest ships were flying refineries or mobile, self-lit agriculture domes.

Drifter Convoys were self-sufficient in a way the Kenmiri had prevented many of the planets they controlled from being. Arrayed around the edge of the Convoy were the ubiquitous Kenmiri-style escorts and gunships, but the core of the Convoy's defenses were Guardians like the one their shuttle approached.

It was a misshapen vessel a kilometer and a half long and half a kilometer high. Several of its components had clearly started as other ships, welded together by a mobile production setup that could never have built a single ship of this scale.

The asymmetrical hull glittered even to the unaided eye with the power of its energy screens. Those shields were normally imperceptible in the visible spectrum, but the power of the Guardian's defenses changed that.

"There, there and there," the Chief Petty Officer in charge of Sylvia's escort murmured, pointing at particular parts of the outline.

"What's there?" Felix Leitz, Sylvia's chief of staff, asked. The heavyset man had his own tasks on the Drifter Convoy, though he would accompany Sylvia today.

"Look, Em Leitz," the Chief said, pointing. "You can see the turrets for her plasma guns. Her silhouette is visibly shaped by the extra reinforcement around the batteries."

"*Shaka* would probably survive a full salvo from that thing's guns," Sylvia said. "*Probably*. But they're overpowered even compared to a Kenmiri dreadnought's. It wouldn't take more than one blowthrough to end our little destroyer."

"Any battle with a gravity shield is a question of odds," the Ground Division noncom confirmed. She grinned, bright white teeth flashing against dark skin. "Given that *Shaka* would be running from that behemoth, not fighting it, I like our odds."

Sylvia smiled thinly and glanced at the woman's name tag. DAKARAI ARENDSE.

"Chief Arendse, have you seen a Guardian in action?" she asked.

"I haven't," Arendse admitted. "I'm GroundDiv, ser, not a spacer. I've seen Drifter commandos in action, though, and if their ships are half as competent as those terrifying masked bastards..."

"My understanding is that their ship crews are more competent than their ground troops," Sylvia pointed out. "The ground troops are small escort detachments, after all. The ships are the life of the Convoy."

The war against the Kenmiri had had three sources of capital ships: stolen Kenmiri dreadnoughts, capital ships from El-Vesheron powers like the UPA, and the Drifter Guardians. The Guardians had rarely been deployed, since the Convoys had maintained at least the appearance of neutrality until the very end, but their involvement had been critical in multiple battles.

Getting them involved had been one of Sylvia's jobs.

"We don't want to fight these people," Sylvia said quietly. "Can you make certain, Chief Arendse, that your people give no offense? The Drifters are used to dealing with different cultures...but not always on their own ships."

"My people will stick close to you and Em Leitz and keep their mouths shut and guns holstered," Arendse promised. "I hope that'll be enough."

Sylvia nodded her approval.

"It should be. And on this ship...Felix, here, *I* am the only one who says *anything*. That clear?"

Her chief of staff nodded.

"As crystal, Em Ambassador," he confirmed. "We can't risk screwing up this mission."

Sylvia nodded firmly to him and Arendse as the shuttle adjusted its course, the acceleration shivering across the passenger compartment as they slowed to the docking bay.

"Let's get this show on the road."

THE SHUTTLEBAY they landed in could have been on any ship in the former Kenmiri Empire. It would be a while before anyone was building anything that was dramatically different from the ship types favored by their former overlords—and even when they started doing that, components like shuttlebays wouldn't change much.

An honor guard was waiting for Sylvia, and she buried an atavistic shiver at the paired lines of black-robed-and-masked soldiers. All of the Drifter soldiers were shrouded in bulky black cloth that concealed their race and build.

For this duty, they all wore identical plain masks under their hoods. Small gold marks at the chin of the masks served as rank markers for those with the knowledge to look, but nothing else distinguished twenty soldiers that could easily have come from twenty species.

They were *probably* all Ashall, the group of humanoid races that included Terran humanity, but the robes could cover a few of the bipedal non-Ashall aliens, too. That was the point, after all.

The Protector-Commander waiting at the other end of the honor guard was at least more obviously Ashall. Their robes were still bulky enough to conceal gender and race, but they were smoother and more shaped to the wearer's form.

Their mask was white and gold, the individualized patterns marking it a Face Mask instead of the honor guards' Duty Masks. A double length of gold chain held a full-sized plain steel dagger on the middle of the Protector-Commander's chest, the mark of their rank.

"Ambassador Sylvia Todorovich of the United Planets Alliance," the Protector-Commander greeted her in fluent Kem. The main language of the Kenmiri, Kem had become the de facto trade language of the former Empire and the surrounding worlds. "Be welcome amongst Blue Stripe Green Stripe Orange Stripe. I am Protector-Commander Third-White-Fifth-Gold, commander of Blue Stripe Green Stripe Orange Stripe's defenders.

"You are known to me by reputation, Ambassador, but duty demands that I ask what brings you to my Convoy."

Sylvia approached to a carefully measured two meters and bowed to the Protector-Commander, her people pausing sensibly behind her.

"I appreciate your trust and welcome, Protector-Commander Third-White-Fifth-Gold," she told them. "We approach Blue Stripe Green Stripe Orange Stripe on a dual mission, ser. My companion here, Felix Leitz, has been authorized to trade precious metals for technology and supplies needed by the United Planets Alliance's friends in the La-Tar Cluster. If you will permit, he will speak with the Quartermasters of the Convoy on trade and commerce."

Third-White-Fifth-Gold bowed their mask in acknowledgement.

"But you, Ambassador, are not here for trade," they said. "What do you seek?"

"I must speak with the Council of Ancients of Blue Stripe Green Stripe Orange Stripe," Sylvia said formally. "I am here on behalf of the La-Tar Cluster and the United Planets Alliance on an errand of peace. We would ask that the Ancients of Blue Stripe Green Stripe Orange Stripe aid us in ending the war between the La-Tar Cluster and the Kozun Hierarchy."

It was impossible to read expressions through the mask. That was the point—all of the Ashall shared certain microexpressions that could be learned. They were hard to learn and hard to read, but even harder to conceal. Wearing masks barred strangers from reading the Drifters' moods and intentions.

But Sylvia suspected that Third-White-Fifth-Gold was amused from the slight sardonic tilt of their head.

"I have heard about this conflict, yes," the Protector-Commander conceded. "I am inclined to grant access to the Quartermasters, Ambassador, but access to the Council of Ancients is more difficult to earn."

"I understand this," Sylvia replied. "But I believe we share a common interest here, Protector-Commander. Your Convoy are traders, travelers between star systems bearing goods and news. A war, even if both sides wish to avoid harming you, is a risk to your people. Neither the La-Tar Cluster nor the Kozun Hierarchy are your enemies. Both could be valuable trading partners to Blue Stripe Green Stripe Orange Stripe, but their conflict renders the area around their systems dangerous to you."

"The Kozun have more than one conflict ongoing," Third-White-Fifth-Gold told her. "They have clashes on many sides, but it is the UPA that draws their ire the most. You speak of a conflict between the La-Tar Cluster and the Kozun Hierarchy, but the Kozun speak of a war between the Hierarchy and the UPA."

Sylvia smiled. It was a thin, sharp expression. Most of her expressions were. She was one of the few who *had* learned to control her microexpressions, and her face was as much a tool and a weapon as her voice.

"The United Planets Alliance has signed a treaty of mutual defense with the La-Tar Cluster. Through that, units of the Peacekeeper Initiative have engaged Kozun units in defense of the Cluster. The only *war* ongoing, however, is between the Kozun and the people they invaded. Our involvement is entirely in the defense of the Cluster."

The La-Tar Cluster was five worlds, four factory planets and an agriworld, that the Kozun Hierarchy—once unfriendly fellow Vesheron, now dangerous ex-allies—had invaded. Sylvia had been aboard *Raven* to negotiate with those worlds and had helped Colonel Henry Wong, *Raven*'s captain, convince the Cluster to stand together and help Wong drive the Kozun from their worlds.

"I can see how you view matters," Third-White-Fifth-Gold said. "But it is not in the interests of this Convoy to get involved in a war between our former allies."

"Even to help bring it to an end?" Sylvia asked. "We do not wish the Cluster to conflict with the Kozun. We would see a peaceful trade between our former allies and our current friends."

"After all that has passed between you and the Kozun?"

The Drifter clearly knew more about the fight at La-Tar than Sylvia had expected. The UPSF had lost an Initiative destroyer there to antigravity disruptor warheads in Kozun hands. There was a small but vocal component of the UPSF that wanted revenge, but the political will wasn't there for a real conflict.

"We are not at war with the Kozun," she repeated. "We protected an ally, nothing more. That ally is prepared to protect themselves, even to take the war to the Hierarchy if they must, but peace is better for everyone."

"Especially the United Planets Alliance?" Third-White-Fifth-Gold asked.

Sylvia sharpened her smile and was rewarded with a small, almost invisible recoil on the part of the Protector-Commander.

"If the Kozun Hierarchy believes they are at war with the United Planets Alliance, they have forgotten how the UPSF makes war," she told him. "They have a dreadnought and a few dozen escorts. Two carrier groups would probably be overkill against their entire fleet.

"So, if we were *actually* at war, we would send three."

The shuttlebay was silent, and Sylvia wondered what her escort was making of her *diplomatic* approach to matters. She knew Drifters, though, and it was easy to get lost in byzantine bullcrap negotiating with them.

She'd spend that time when she spoke to the Council, but there was no point to it with the Protector-Commander. She needed a decision from him *now*, so she would push.

And since most soldiers only had so much patience for that same bullcrap, she suspected it was working.

Third-White-Fifth-Gold laughed behind their mask.

"Come, Ambassador," they told him. "Join me for a drink while I arrange your appointments. I am curious as to how your efforts in this Sector have fared."

"Gladly. I must remind you, though, Protector-Commander, that nothing is free," she replied. "That kind of intelligence costs more than a drink."

CHAPTER THREE

The garden ships at the center of the Drifter Convoy were, Sylvia suspected, far less defenseless than they looked. Nonetheless, the ships with their massive transparent domes were hidden away behind every other ship in the Convoy.

That made them the safest place in any Drifter Convoy and the home of the political leadership of the fleet. *Shaka*'s shuttle wasn't even allowed to approach the garden ships. Sylvia made her trip to her audience aboard a Drifter shuttle, though her GroundDiv escort was permitted to come with her.

More black-masked-and-robed soldiers greeted her as she left the shuttle, escorting her into the main area of the garden ship.

Even for Sylvia, a child of actual planets, the garden ships were stunning to look at from the inside. The core transparent dome was two kilometers across, and every square centimeter of the surface area was covered in plants.

The vast majority of the vegetation was edible, and even the decorative plants provided oxygen for the rest of the Convoy. The most efficient food crops from the ten thousand stars of the Kenmiri Empire had been gathered there to serve the Drifters.

Passageways lined in more decorative—though likely still fruit-bear-ing, Sylvia suspected—trees cut through the dome toward the center.

Glow lamps were suspended above them, each sector getting different amounts of light, heat, humidity...every part of the climate and ecosystem of the immense starship was controlled to the utmost degree possible, and there would be decks upon decks of hydroponics beneath them as well.

Here, the Convoy was far enough from the local star that the glow lamps were necessary. In a different system, the garden ships would be orbiting closer to the sun and positioned to use natural light to reduce their power draw.

Each ship of the Convoy attempted to be self-sufficient, but the garden ships made up for any shortfall while also providing food surpluses the Convoy could trade. They were custom-built, each one a unique and stunningly impressive achievement.

The center of this particular ship's dome was a circle of trees that rivaled the California redwoods some of her ancestors had imported to Russia's Epsilon Eridani colony. The giants on Eridani were only a century and a half old...but without knowing how quickly *these* trees grew, Sylvia had to guess that they were at least as old.

Which meant the ship she was standing on had been built at least that long before. The Drifter Convoys had been around for a long time.

She was led through that ring of trees into a shaded circular amphitheater that descended toward a central stage. The benches weren't full, but the dark red robes of the occupants said all she needed to know.

While Sylvia was certain the Drifters were perfectly willing to shift robes and masks to confuse outsiders, the colors and styles all meant very specific things. She doubted they would do so without purpose, so those dark red robes told her she was looking down at the Council of Ancients of Blue Stripe Green Stripe Orange Stripe.

"Approach, Ambassador Sylvia Todorovich of the United Planets

Alliance," the robed Drifter standing on the central stage instructed in Kem. "You have requested an audience with our Ancients."

They gestured at the figures seated on the benches around them.

"We have gathered to hear your words. We do not do this for every supplicant, Ambassador, but the deeds of your people have earned this respect. You will be heard."

Sylvia gestured for her guards to wait at the circle of trees and proceeded forward. Each bench was a shallow step down from the one above it, the metal of their construction a reminder that they were aboard a spaceship.

As she approached the central stage, she realized that only about half of the figures on the benches were actually there. The rest were holographic projections, the virtual presences of Ancients on other ships scattered through the Convoy.

Most of the Ancients, aside from any other role the Convoy put on them, also served as captains of their own ships. They were busy people—but they had made time for her.

Sylvia concealed a smile. Blue Stripe Green Stripe Orange Stripe was making a big deal of the favor they were doing for her, but there was another read to it: they *knew* how much the UPA could do for them.

Or...do *to* them.

SYLVIA JOINED the Drifter on the central stage, looking up at the small crowd around her. Blue Stripe Green Stripe Orange Stripe's Council of Ancients had thirty-two members. One of them was Protector-Commander Third-White-Fifth-Gold, seated at one of the farther benches.

That was probably a sign of their lack of seniority in the Council.

"Has the Protector-Commander briefed this Council on the request the United Planets Alliance has sent me to deliver?" she asked.

"You wish us to intercede between the La-Tar Cluster and the Kozun Hierarchy," the Ancient on the stage with her summarized. "The intent is clear, though the details of what you would have us do remain unknown.

"So, too, do the details of how our Convoy would benefit from this arrangement, beyond the unquestionable indirect value of peace," the politician continued.

Sylvia studied the stranger's mask carefully, committing it to memory. Even if the Ancients didn't give her names, the patterns of blue whorls across a silver mask that the Drifter wore would be unique. Only Duty Masks were shared, and no Ancient would wear a Duty Mask to a gathering of the Council.

"I presumed that it would not be necessary for me to give the full details to the Protector-Commander to be granted access to this Council," she told blue-whorls-on-silver. "If this Council is prepared to consider it, I will lay out the proposal in full measure."

Kem was not a liquid language at the best of times and the formal phrasing preferred by the Drifters made it even more stilted. Sylvia knew the dance, however, and she knew she needed to give the Ancients the appearance, if not the truth, of complete control of this meeting.

"Very well," blue-whorls-on-silver told her. "You may present to this Council."

"Thank you," she replied. She turned slowly to take in the entire Council. There was no way she could see all of the Council members at once, which had to be intentional. There was more than enough space for all of them to sit in one quadrant of the amphitheater.

"I presume you are all briefed on the nature of the La-Tar Cluster and their conflict with the Hierarchy, but I will summarize," she told them. "The Kozun invaded La-Tar, the agriworld that fed the worlds of the Cluster, nine months ago.

"They withheld the food supplies from La-Tar to force the surrender of the four industrial worlds surrounding it. A UPSF vessel was in negotiations with one of the Cluster governments and was asked to intervene.

"While our ship did engage the Kozun in combat, La-Tar was liberated by ground troops provided by the rest of the Cluster's worlds. La-Tar now sits at the center of an economic and military alliance dedicated to the mutual security of five worlds.

"That alliance distrusts and fears the Kozun Hierarchy and has asked for UPSF help maintaining their independence," Sylvia noted. "We have agreed to this, but we have no desire to make war on the Hierarchy. We also do not believe the Kozun wish to fight the La-Tar Cluster again, but pride and eager triggers have prevented any attempt at communication so far."

She looked around again, carefully meeting the drawn-in eyes of the masked faces around her.

"We ask that Blue Stripe Green Stripe Orange Stripe use your ships to make contact with the Kozun Hierarchy and establish the terms on which the Hierarchy's leadership would negotiate with the Cluster's leadership.

"The United Planets Alliance believes, firmly, that if we can get empowered representatives of both states into a room, the differences and conflicts between them can be negotiated to a resolution that requires no further conflict or bloodshed."

The room was silent for several moments, and Sylvia shrugged and continued.

"Such a conference will also require a neutral third party providing security to allow both sides a sense of safety. We accept that the United Planets Alliance does not qualify and would ask that Blue Stripe Green Stripe Orange Stripe act as the guarantor for these negotiations.

"We would expect payment for that service to be split with the Kozun and hence to be negotiated later, but we are willing to provide payment for acting as a go-between with the Hierarchy," she concluded.

"And what did you have in mind as payment?" blue-whorls-on-silver, who still had not introduced themselves, asked.

"I am prepared to make payment in refined palladium or refined iridium," she told them. "That has traditionally served as our highest medium of exchange with the Drifter Convoys, yes?"

The Drifters traded in two things, as Sylvia understood it: refined metals from which they could build ships and electronics, and technological data with which they could make better use of the materials they had.

"It has," the Ancient confirmed. "We will discuss this in private, Ambassador." They gestured back up the stairs she'd come down. "If you return to your escort, they will see you to a waiting area."

"I appreciate the Council taking time to hear my words and consider my proposal," Sylvia told them. "I will await your response."

THE WAITING area was the closest thing Sylvia had seen to what she'd normally call a garden on the "garden" ship. She suspected most of the pleasant-smelling flowering plants around her still produced edible fruit, but the main focus of the small space had been on beauty.

The Drifters had even laid out a selection of drinks for her and her people, though Chief Arendse's testing quickly warned them that all but two had either cannabinoid- or opioid-analogs in the mix.

Since Sylvia had no intention of negotiating when high or drunk, the pitcher of water was almost empty when a robed official returned to guide her back to the Council of Ancients.

She once again reached the center stage, joining the speaker on the stage and looking up at the crowd around her.

"Blue Stripe Green Stripe Orange Stripe is prepared to act as your intermediary in this matter," blue-whorls-on-silver told her. "We have a condition and a price."

"I will hear them, on behalf of the United Planets Alliance," Sylvia replied.

"Our condition is that you and your vessel remain with the Convoy until we have heard from the Kozun," the Drifter speaking for the Council said. "We have no desire to spend time chasing down an appropriate contact point for you. While we understand the negotiation is between La-Tar and Kozun, we are acting as an intermediary for the United Planets Alliance.

"Is that clear and acceptable?"

"It is both," Sylvia said calmly. She'd be more out of touch than she liked, but *Shaka* had enough skip drones on board to provide reasonably solid communications with La-Tar and the Peacekeeper Initiative base in the Zion System.

"And your price?" she asked.

"We will require the technology of the gravity shield," the Ancient told her.

Sylvia laughed. She would have faked it even if she *hadn't* thought the Drifters were joking, so letting the emotion out was safe in this case.

"Even if I was permitted to trade that technology, which we both know I am not," she said, "we also both know that this task is not of nearly sufficient value to call for a prize of that magnitude. I am prepared to pay in refined metals, not in strategic systems."

She couldn't see the Drifter's face behind their mask, but she could see enough of their body language to guess they were amused.

"That is as expected," they conceded. "We will carry out this task for seven tons of refined palladium."

Sylvia smiled thinly.

"You are still aiming rather high, do you not think?" she asked. "Three tons."

"Six."

"Five."

"Done."

She nodded firmly and offered her hand. This was something the

Drifters shared with Americans, the firm handshake as a close to the deal. Blue-whorls-on-silver shook her hand firmly.

"We presume your destroyer has the materials?" they asked.

"She does," Sylvia confirmed. "And for the deals my companion is closing with your Quartermasters. I will return to *Shaka* and we will await confirmation of the success of your mission."

"We will send over food and other supplies to make certain you are not strained by the delay," the Ancient assured her. "This will take some days at least."

She nodded her understanding. *Shaka* would be fine for the twenty or so days she understood a round-trip journey to Kozun would take, but the gesture was meaningful as well.

If the Drifters fed them, they were guests—and that meant something in almost every culture she'd encountered.

CHAPTER FOUR

"JUST WHAT IS THAT AND WHAT IS IT DOING ON MY FLIGHT deck?"

Colonel Henry Wong was more amused than the sharpness of his tone indicated, but the captain of the battlecruiser *Raven* was also truly unsure what he was looking at. The...*thing* was sitting in the middle of the small flight deck that handled his eight starfighters, and it could not have looked less like it belonged.

"That's a starfighter, boss," Commander Samira O'Flannagain, his Commander, Air Group, told him. The gawky woman with the Ophiuchi accent adjusted her red braid as she turned to look at her captain. "A brand-spanking-new one, straight from an assembly line on Luna all the way here."

Henry inspected the craft as he approached, shaking his head. The dark-haired Chinese-American Colonel was shorter than his CAG, though they both wore the same black turtleneck uniform. *His* uniform had a white collar, marking him as the captain of a United Planet Space Force starship, but both of them had the raven-with-quill-pen shoulder patch of *Raven*'s crew.

"Starfighters are spherical, Commander," he said drily. "I've flown enough of them to know that."

The craft in the flight deck was saucer-shaped. The SF-122 Falcon starfighters the deck had held before had been flattened spheres, but this was barely taller than the pilots would be.

Stepping up to the fighter, he assessed that it was the same three-meter diameter as the older fighter and would fit in the same hangers and launch tubes. The straighter sides meant it didn't lose as much volume as he'd have thought, but something had to have been given up...

"I'm guessing less fuel capacity," he said aloud. "Which makes this the fabled SF-One-Thirty Lancer?"

"*Fabled* is the right damn word, ser," O'Flannagain confirmed. "I first heard about a GMS starfighter almost ten years ago. Stopped expecting to see one on my flight deck five years ago, but...well, we got the new simulators a year ago and I made sure my people were all qualified."

Henry vaguely recalled a conversation around that point. He'd almost certainly even received a notification that the fighters were aboard, but *Raven* was just exiting a six-week intensive repair. There were a *lot* of messages in his inbox.

"Fill me in," he ordered the CAG as he circled the starfighter. "I'm sure I have a technical briefing buried in my inbox somewhere."

He could pull it up on his internal network, but that hardware was never *quite* the same as learning things the old-fashioned way.

"Stripped out the engines almost entirely," the woman told him, touching the fighter with a fond expression. "Six light jets at the cardinal points; that's it. Only capable of about five gees under reaction thrust and not for long.

"Main engine and the gravity shield operate out of the same projectors," she continued. "My understanding is that in a bigger ship, they'd use different gravity projectors, but this is a starfighter." She shrugged. "Gravitational maneuvering system basically leaves the ship in free fall down an artificial gravity well.

"She's rated for three kilometers per second squared, fully compensated. With reduced fuel and no need for an acceleration tank, they managed to sneak a cabin with a kitchenette and a *bed* into her."

"Seriously?" Henry asked. "I guess that makes sense."

He shook his head. The UPSF's Fighter Division had fought the war with starfighters that could get to 1.5 KPS^2, half again the maximum thrust of their starships but still barely edging out Kenmiri capital ships.

Their Vesheron allies had better engine technology, stolen from the Kenmiri, and had regularly outmaneuvered Terran starfighters. Of course, Terran starfighters had gravity shields and the Vesheron ones *didn't*.

The GMS was the long-promised alternative use of gravitic projection, the technology the UPA had mastered and neither the Kenmiri nor Vesheron had. And with that acceleration…

"You'll be able to outfly anything else in space," he told her. "I'm impressed."

"I haven't had a chance to take one of them out for a spin yet, but they also have one more feature I've fallen in love with," O'Flannagain told him. "It's *almost* as important as the coffeemaker!"

She gestured for him to join her as she hooked a mobile stepladder over to her.

"Climb up, boss," she instructed.

Bemused, Henry obeyed and found himself on top of the flat disk of the spacecraft. O'Flannagain joined him, walking over to the most obvious feature of the disk: a man-sized groove running from one edge to the other.

"What does this look like to you, ser?"

"Missile mount," Henry said instantly, but his eyes narrowed as he studied the size. "That is not the size of a fighter missile."

"No, it's not," his CAG confirmed. "That's a full-sized missile, ser. We'll be able to draw our birds from *Raven*'s main magazines.

And vice versa—we've stocked the flight-deck magazines with full-size missiles, though there's no cross-loading systems."

"We'll fix that with the next generation of ships, I presume," Henry murmured. He'd been involved in the discussions around several of the SF-122's predecessors, and the fact that they couldn't spare the mass for full-size missiles had been a perennial nightmare.

"How?"

"Amount of mass falling into the gravity well the GMS creates is irrelevant," O'Flannagain told him. "So long as the birds fit in the bubble, we're good to go."

Henry nodded and then the dark-skinned Chinese-American smiled at his CAG.

"So, given all of that, is the fighter wing ready for deployment?"

O'Flannagain drew herself up straight and sharply saluted.

"Ser, yes, ser!" she barked. "I could use live flight time on the Lancers for my people, but we had the swap-over well planned. If *Raven* is ready to go, ser, we're ready to go."

"We'll find the time for those exercises, probably en route," Henry told her. "I have a meeting with Admiral Hamilton this afternoon, and I was hoping to tell her everything was green and ready to deploy."

"Getting twitchy away from the action, ser?" his CAG asked. "Or away from the ambassador?"

He waved a warning finger at his subordinate.

"Are you ever going to *stop* trying to matchmake, Commander?" he said.

"In the general situation or the specific, ser?" O'Flannagain replied, then laughed. "Though, to be fair, the answer is the same for both: no, not really."

"Why didn't I cashier you, again?" Henry asked, but he was chuckling as he did.

"Because I keep hauling the entire ship out of the fire, ser," she said. "And I've got your back. Down to hell and up to the other one, wherever you lead us. Enjoy your meeting, boss. The fighter wing is ready to go."

LIEUTENANT COLONEL TATANKA IYOTAKE was waiting just outside the flight deck, the broad-shouldered Lakota officer looking as tired as Henry felt.

"XO," Henry greeted him. "Report."

"You told me to meet you here," Iyotake replied. "What do you need?"

"A report on the ship's status," Henry said. "While I head to the airlock. Walk with me, Iyotake?"

"Of course, ser." The executive officer fell into pace beside Henry. "All of our damage is repaired. All weapons systems, defenses, power plants and heat radiators are online. Sensors are still in testing, but I expect them to clear those tests with flying colors by the end of the day.

"*Raven* is ready for action in all aspects, ser."

"Good." They walked in silence for a moment. "O'Flannagain confirms the fighter wing as well," Henry told his right-hand man. "That's the news I wanted to give Admiral Hamilton. Nobody liked having half of the Initiative's battlecruiser strength laid up like this."

The Peacekeeper Initiative was only grudgingly operated by the United Planets Space Force, a sop to the consciences of the officers and spacers who'd committed genocide and collapsed a tyrannical interstellar order.

The Kenmiri Empire had much to answer for, but not least among its crimes was how the Empire's worlds had been set up to fail without the Kenmiri. Their retreat to their inner worlds had left a chaotic disaster behind them, one that Henry and many other officers felt responsible for.

Henry himself had killed the last living Kenmorad, a realization that still haunted his dreams despite the best efforts of his therapists.

The state of the worlds the Kenmiri had abandoned felt like it was his personal responsibility.

But the UPA wanted to reap the dividends of peace and focus on their own worlds. The Peacekeeper Initiative was busy in the stars of the Ra Sector, but *Raven* was one of only two battlecruisers in Admiral Sonia Hamilton's command.

"She's ready to get back into action and so are the crew, ser," Iyotake assured him. "Any idea what the mission will be?"

"La-Tar, for certain," Henry replied. "The Hierarchy has been quieter than we like. Until and unless Todorovich's mission is successful, we have to assume they're planning for a new invasion."

"Do you think that mission will succeed?" his XO asked.

"If it was anyone else, I'd say not a chance in hell," Henry admitted with a chuckle. "But it's Todorovich. I give her better than even odds of actually sorting out a peace agreement."

The ambassador's absence bothered him in a way he couldn't quite put his finger on. He'd got used to having the civilian around to bounce ideas and plans off of, in a way he couldn't truly do even with Iyotake...and yet that still didn't feel like it was all of it.

He shrugged mentally. It would sort itself out in his head eventually. He'd learned that over the years. He hadn't made it past fifty as a wartime officer by dwelling in his own head.

"I want you to double-check with Song and Kuroda," he told his XO. That was Commander Anna Song, his chief engineer, and Lieutenant Commander Kouseke Kuroda, his logistics officer. "Make sure we have everything we need aboard in terms of supplies, parts, et cetera, et cetera.

"I want to be able to move within twenty-four hours if the Admiral has orders for us."

"I'm ninety percent certain we're already there, but I'll confirm with everyone," Iyotake promised. "Anything else, ser?"

Henry chuckled.

"Nothing that comes to mind, though I'm sure you're already on three other things I haven't mentioned," he said. Iyotake was a good

XO. That meant he was on a list that Henry didn't really want him to be on: the list of officers that were almost certainly going to get promoted off *Raven* in the next six months.

Henry had signed a *lot* of recommendations for early promotion since *Raven* had returned to Zion with a broken wing and a far-too-long casualty list. It was going to leave some serious holes in his crew—but neither his people nor the UPSF were served well by holding his officers back.

They reached the airlock leading into the main station of Zion's Fleet Base Fallout and Iyotake stopped, snapping a sharp salute.

"I'll get to work, then, ser," the younger man promised. "*Raven* will be ready to deploy on our orders; you have my word."

"That's just doing your job, Lieutenant Colonel," Henry pointed out. "It shouldn't need your word."

"Yes, ser, of course, ser," Iyotake said crisply—but he was returning Henry's grin. "Keep me updated on what the Admiral has to say, as appropriate."

"I'll fill you in when I get back," the captain promised. "Into the belly of the beast I go."

He respected Sonia Hamilton and he'd worked with her for *years*—she'd commanded the carrier a much-younger Henry had flown starfighters off of when the Kenmiri had first entered UPA space—but even he wasn't going to pretend meeting with the woman was going to be easy.

CHAPTER FIVE

The Zion System was the far end of the United Planets Alliance in many ways. It was the closest territory to the former Kenmiri Empire that they officially claimed—and where humanity's first encounter with the insectoid conquerors had been when they'd invaded the small religious colony out there.

Base Fallout had all of the repair yards and supply depots necessary to support the seventeen-year-long war against the Kenmiri, though most of them were mothballed now. A battlecruiser and a flotilla of destroyers were permanently based there under Vice Admiral Zhao Xinyi.

In one of the usual oddities of military bureaucracy, Base Fallout was also home to the Peacekeeper Initiative, under the command of Admiral Sonia Hamilton. Henry Wong was significantly junior to Zhao Xinyi, but he wasn't in Base Fallout's chain of command—and Admiral Xinyi wasn't in the Initiative's chain of command.

That made Henry Wong, as the senior Colonel, Admiral Hamilton's second-in-command. He'd spent a large amount of his time while *Raven* was being refitted aboard the main station of Base Fallout, conferring with the Admiral.

Hamilton's flag lieutenant had a black coffee waiting for him when he arrived, passing the steaming beverage across her desk.

"Did you get the latest updates on the agenda?" Lieutenant Jelena Kukk asked him. The swarthy young woman was half Henry's age at most, and he had to wonder when junior officers had started being quite so young.

"I did," he confirmed. They'd arrived in his internal network while he was in the elevator, and he'd skimmed them. "I'm noticing a complete lack of detail around this 'Operation Yellow Bicycle.'"

The UPSF randomly generated operation names, which ended up with some very strange-looking combinations. Golden Lancelot had been the genocidal campaign against the Kenmiri. Hopefully, Yellow Bicycle would be somewhat less psyche-shattering for the officers and spacers who carried it out.

"I know the name and that's it, ser," Kukk admitted. "The Admiral got a drone update this morning from Earthward, so I'm guessing it's to do with that, but...I'm not sure what official operation would be impacting us."

"Me either," Henry conceded, taking a large gulp of the coffee. "Am I the last?"

Hamilton tried to keep most of her meetings small enough to fit in the six-person breakout meeting room attached to her office on the base. It was almost impossible, though, for her to keep most of those meetings from filling that room.

"Admiral Xinyi got added to the meeting at the same time as the Operation Yellow Bicycle item got added to the agenda," Kukk told him. "I'll be holding down the fort until she gets here. Boss said to send you right in, though."

There were two people who'd originally been scheduled to be in the meeting with Henry and Hamilton, which meant he was the last out of the core Initiative group. Adding Base Fallout's commander... something was going on.

"Bring more coffee when you come in to take minutes?" he suggested.

"Always, ser," she promised.

ADMIRAL SONIA HAMILTON was a sparsely built woman in her early eighties. Age hadn't slowed her down yet in Henry's experience, and the gaze she leveled on him as he entered the utilitarian meeting room was sharp.

"You're late," she snapped.

"The meeting is scheduled to start in forty-two seconds," Henry replied precisely. "I am the last of the original attendees to arrive. I am not late."

He'd tolerate a lot from Admiral Hamilton. She'd sent a medical team to his quarters and ordered him onto medical leave in response to actions that another flag officer might have seen him cashiered for.

The UPSF being what it was, he'd probably have got the medical team at least. She still could have ended his career. She hadn't.

For that reason alone, Henry Wong would deal with Hamilton's sharp edges.

"Sit down," she ordered. "We may as well wait on Xinyi before we get started, anyway. It will be useful to bring her up to speed on our operations before we deal with the scorpion Command sent us."

Henry swallowed his curiosity with another gulp of coffee as he took his seat across from the Admiral. He traded nods with the other two officers in the room, both Lieutenant Colonels.

Veer Priddy was a native of the Sandoval colony in the Procyon System, a child of the European Union. She was petite, green-eyed and platinum blonde—and the officer who acted as Admiral Hamilton's whip hand. She was the Peacekeeper Initiative's operations officer, responsible for making sure their dozen starships ended up where they needed to be when they needed to be there.

Aetius Nicolosi was, despite his name, an American like Henry. He had the swarthy skin and dark eyes of his southern Italian ancestry and he was the yin to Priddy's yang. Where Priddy was responsible for sending ships out, Nicolosi was, as logistics officer, responsible for making sure they had what they needed to get there and do their jobs.

"That scorpion would be Yellow Bicycle?" Henry asked.

"It would," Hamilton agreed. "Priddy will update everyone on where we are, and then I will brief everyone on just what Command is doing. It's the weirdest half-bullshit excuse for giving us what we *need* without giving us what we *want* I've seen...and I've seen sixty years of military bullshit."

Henry buried his smile beneath more coffee, emptying his mug and setting it down.

"*Raven* is fully repaired, resupplied and rearmed," he told the Admiral. "We even have the new starfighters aboard. I'm guessing we're tasked as a test deployment?"

"If you mean you're the Force's guinea pigs, yes," Hamilton agreed. "Some of the senior officers in FighterDiv are twitchy about giving up their rockets, so the deal was struck that the Initiative would get the first batch of One-Thirties. I figure you're more likely to end up in a fight than anyone else, so you got them first.

"*Jaguar* will get her set when she returns from her current sweep. I'm sure Colonel Sharma will appreciate them as much as you do."

Henry chuckled softly.

"Unlike Colonel Sharma, *I* could fly one," he pointed out. "Though if I were to do so in combat, you'd have to cashier me."

"Yes," Hamilton said bluntly. "Though you were easier to train that into than some of our *other* independently deployed battlecruiser skippers."

She tilted her head as she finished speaking, an unconscious tic that marked her receipt of a message to her internal network.

"Admiral Xinyi is here," she told the officers. "Let Kukk know if you want something other than coffee, people; it's time to get to work."

ADMIRAL XINYI WAS A TOWERING woman with heavyset Mongolian features. She took her seat with the careful precision of a large and physically powerful person who didn't want to break anything.

"I appreciate you joining us, Vice Admiral," Hamilton said in an unusually soft and courteous tone of voice for her. "While only part of the meeting is going to be immediately relevant to you, I believe you will find the background of our current status useful."

"Even Vice Admirals jump when full Admirals say tiu," Xinyi observed calmly. "I am only peripherally aware of the Initiative's operations, so an updated background briefing will be valuable, given what I understand of Yellow Bicycle."

Hamilton grunted and gestured to Priddy.

"Lieutenant Colonel, can you update us on the status of the Initiative's outreach operations and current deployments?"

"Yes, ser," Priddy confirmed.

Orders from her internal network brought a three-dimensional map of the Ra Sector and the nearest UPA stars up above the table. The Ra Sector, like the other former Kenmiri provinces, was exactly five hundred stars in a roughly cubical region of space.

Its Kenmiri name was completely unpronounceable to humans—and had turned out to be the name of their sun god. Since humanity had labeled the region "Ra" before learning that, Egyptian gods had ended up being the basis of the naming system the UPA used for the provinces.

"In many ways, the Initiative's current sweep and penetration into the Ra Sector is more complete than our scouting of the region during the war," Priddy noted. "Our focus then was on routes into the other provinces to make contact with the Vesheron, and on the three Kenmiri colonies themselves.

"We had only visited sixty of the systems in the Ra Sector at the end of the war, designated Ra-One through Ra-Sixty, though we know local names for about half of those stars now.

"Since the formation of the Initiative, we have only visited about forty of the previously scouted systems but have visited just over one hundred new systems," she continued. "We have made contact with six different industrial-agriworld clusters and twenty-six individual planets, including the Beren homeworld."

"All of the clusters have made some progress in reestablishing trade links," Nicolosi added. "The Kenmiri left them no choice, but thankfully, they've mostly been more successful than our projections."

"Which does not mean *successful*," Henry said grimly. He'd read the reports.

"No," Priddy agreed. "We're looking at around fifty million dead on the worlds we've contacted alone since the Kenmiri withdrawal. That's including deaths in various conflicts over resources, as well as starvation and deaths due to medicine shortages."

Henry barely managed to conceal a shiver, and the chill in the room was perceptible.

"We cannot take responsibility for that," Hamilton said bluntly into the room. "I know we can draw a direct line from our actions to the Kenmiri's to those deaths, but I remind you: *we* did not set up those clusters and then take away the ships required to keep them running.

"I won't deny our part of the guilt, nor our guilt in the genocide of the Kenmorad, but we are *not* responsible for the innocents killed in the systems of the Kenmiri Empire or due to the direct choices of the Kenmiri Remnant."

Priddy nodded, the Sandovalan officer swallowing hard against the very guilt Hamilton spoke of.

"Of the twenty-six inhabited worlds we've contacted, nineteen—including all five worlds of the La-Tar Cluster—now have postal outposts in orbit with skip-drone magazines," she told them. "Right now, all of those outposts are sending their drones here, which is resulting in a hub-and-spoke model for reliable communications—but those communications *exist* and have already enabled new deals that have stabilized food supplies in all six of those clusters."

"Part of the stabilization has also been deals with our own trade cartels and interstellar corporations," Nicolosi said. "We had some starting difficulties getting our traders and shippers interested in trading outside our borders, but once we were past them, the success of the early ships has resulted in an explosion of interest."

"We were given a budget for humanitarian operations as well as a budget to provide incentives for people trading with those worlds," Hamilton said. "I bribed the six largest trade cartels to carry out the first runs, but once they'd made a couple billion apiece, everyone else was suddenly eager to get involved."

"There may still be excess deaths over what there should be," Priddy said, her voice sad, "but most of the fundamental shortages are now under control in the clusters we're dealing with. Through those clusters, we also now have at least basic intelligence on the remaining systems of the Ra Sector."

"How many systems are we talking here?" Xinyi asked. "My focus was always on the Kenmiri worlds."

"Three Kenmiri worlds, eleven five-world dependency clusters, and seven homeworlds," Priddy reeled off instantly. "We haven't made direct contact with the Kenmiri worlds or with the homeworlds other than Kozun and Beren. The indirect information we're receiving suggests much what we expected, though: the homeworlds are fine and the Kenmiri colonies have fallen into the hands of their slave populations.

"In the long term, the Kenmiri colonies may end up being the most successful of the abandoned worlds," she told them. "They have fully diversified economies and advanced technological industries in a way even the homeworlds don't."

The Kenmiri had treated the homeworlds of the various species they'd conquered with relative kid gloves. They'd imposed external rule and harshly punished resistance, but had mostly allowed them to continue with relatively normal, if forcibly insular, economies and societies...except that every few years, the Empire had drafted several million people to help build the agriworlds and industrial planets.

"What's relevant to today's discussion is how much of all of that is under Kozun control," Hamilton interjected. "Rumor tells us that they aren't the only homeworld to become expansionist in the Ra Sector, just the most aggressive and successful."

"La-Tar would have been the fourth dependency cluster to fall under their control," Priddy reported. "The Tak and Sana homeworlds have been conquered by the Kozun as well. Vague rumor, filtered through trade with the Kozun, is that they're currently at war with an alliance between the Eerdish and Enteni homeworlds."

"At the same time, they are pressing on at least one other cluster," Hamilton told everyone. "Admiral Kosigan's people at Intelligence believe that the Hierarchy has bitten off more than it can chew in multiple directions. Their analysis suggests that the Voices have to be desperate to clarify their borders on at least one side and to find ways to stabilize their existing territory."

"Meaning that they will likely take Todorovich up on her offer of a conference," Henry concluded.

"You know Mal Dakis better than anyone else here," Hamilton pointed out. "Intelligence is basing at least some of that analysis on your own reports on the man."

Mal Dakis was the First Voice of the Kozun Hierarchy. Now a secular leader and a high priest—theoretically the chosen prophet of the Seven, the Kozun Gods—he had once been a moderately religious but dangerously fanatical Vesheron leader.

And in that role, he'd received support from the UPA battle-cruiser Henry Wong had been executive officer of. There were other UPA officers who knew Mal Dakis as well as he did, but he wasn't sure there were any who knew him better.

"Mal Dakis is..." Henry considered carefully. "Pragmatic. Don't get me wrong, he *believes* in his gods. He didn't declare himself a Voice until his people had already been calling him one for years and he felt he had no choice.

"Everything he has done has been to enhance his power base and to protect the Kozun. He will do whatever he feels is necessary to do both of those things," Henry said. "He doesn't care if that is to decimate a planetary population to convince everyone to fall in line...or swallow his pride and negotiate the best surrender he can. *Whatever is necessary.*"

"That's Admiral Kosigan's opinion as well," Hamilton said. "Which means we are almost certainly going to have that peace conference, which raises the interesting questions that have resulted in the plan for Operation Yellow Bicycle."

"Does anyone in this room except you know what that means?" Henry asked.

Hamilton laughed coldly.

"Wait a moment, Colonel; I'm getting to the point."

She took over control of the holographic display and zoomed it in on the vaguely defined crimson area marking the Kozun Hierarchy.

"The Kozun Hierarchy is one of two groups we've encountered that deployed disruptor warheads against UPA ships," she noted. "In both cases, the ship in question was *Raven*. In the first case, however, the attack wasn't even in the Ra Sector—but the missiles used at La-Tar show clear development based on the weapons used by the pirates in the Apophis Sector."

A long finger pointed at the Kozun System, the Hierarchy's central point.

"Intelligence believes that the Kozun, like those pirates, were provided the disruptor warheads by a third party. Since we do not know where Blue Stripe Green Stripe Orange Stripe has been in the last two years and we know the Drifter Convoys host some of the best research-and-development facilities outside the Kenmiri Remnant..."

She shrugged and bared her teeth in what could charitably be called a smile.

"Command has the Drifters as an aggregate entity as one of the most likely sources for both the disruptor warheads and the stolen grav-shield-penetrator warheads used at the Gathering," she told them all. "While Blue Stripe Green Stripe Orange Stripe is not at the top of the list for the previous encounters, there is a high likelihood they provided the weapons to the Kozun."

"But why?" Xinyi asked. "The Drifters underwrote the entire Vesheron war effort."

"The Drifters were the only non-Kenmiri who were allowed to act as merchants under the Empire," Henry said quietly. "They knew they were giving up that monopoly by helping destroy the Empire, but that doesn't mean they're going to stand aside as our trade cartels muscle their way in. Or anyone else's, for that matter."

"Exactly," Hamilton confirmed. "We believe that the Drifters are attempting to neutralize all potential threats, both direct and mercantile, to the Convoys. Their inability to engage grav-shielded ships is unacceptable to them, so they have found proxies to move against us.

"Which brings us to Yellow Bicycle," she concluded. "If the Drifters wish to prevent the UPA from expanding our trade routes through the Ra Sector into the Apophis and Hathor Sectors and beyond...they will want us to continue our conflict with the Kozun. Doing so would pin down at least two potential threats to their economic primacy."

"You think they're going to use the peace conference as a trap?" Henry asked.

"Admiral Kosigan thinks so, and he managed to get Yellow Bicycle through High Command," Hamilton told him. "We're losing Battlecruiser Group *Lioness* shortly. Her recall orders are already on their way. She's to return to Base Fallout and join Admiral Xinyi's command."

Xinyi nodded confirmation of that. *Lioness* and her escorts had replaced the battered *Raven* at La-Tar, standing guard over the UPA's new ally as the Kozun probed the border.

Now that *Raven* was back online, recalling her made sense. She'd never been formally assigned to the Initiative.

"*Lioness*'s status, posted outside the UPA but not part of the Peacekeeper Initiative, appears to have been part of the inspiration for Yellow Bicycle," Hamilton continued. "We're not being reinforced, but a carrier group is en route to the Zion System.

"Those ships are being accompanied by a significant logistic detachment and will avoid all contact with inhabited worlds...but will position themselves one skip away from the peace conference," the Admiral concluded. "Ambassador Todorovich will send her update drones home via the system they are waiting in, and if the Drifters do anything to take advantage of the situation, a fleet carrier and two battlecruisers will be in position to skip to her rescue."

Henry pursed his lips as he considered the situation. A full carrier group was a powerful force, one capable of engaging entire squadrons of Kenmiri dreadnoughts. If the Drifters didn't know it was there, the three capital ships and almost two hundred fighters of that group would overwhelm them.

Being a full skip away, though, meant at least a twenty-four-hour turnaround. The Icosaspace Traversal System wasn't a short-range faster-than-light drive. It could only usefully jump between stars. If the right kinds of stars were in play, the skip length could be as low as eight hours, but they were unlikely to find a link quite so convenient.

"Timing could be tricky," he warned.

"I know that," Hamilton agreed. "So does Admiral Kosigan, but it's the best we can do. We can't hide a carrier group in the same star system as the conference, after all."

"I presume Ambassador Todorovich will be attending the conference aboard *Raven?*" Admiral Xinyi asked.

"That depends on what she negotiates with the Kozun," Henry admitted. He would *prefer* to escort the ambassador himself, but he was biased—both in that he believed she'd be safest aboard *Raven* and in that he wanted to see Todorovich again.

She was a good friend and sounding board, and he missed her.

"Details of the plan will get sorted as we move forward," Hamilton said. "One key component to all of this is that Carrier Group *Scorpius* will not be assigned to the Peacekeeper Initiative. The Initiative officers on the scene, whoever they end up being, will operate independently from Commodore Barrie and Rear Admiral Cheung Jian Chin."

Henry swallowed his emotional reaction to hearing just *who* their support was going to be. The separation of authority would be important, he supposed, if they put him and *Scorpius*'s captain in the same star system.

Commodore Peter Barrie, after all, was his ex-husband.

CHAPTER SIX

Henry was pulled into Hamilton's office when the meeting was over, fresh steaming coffees already waiting on the desk as the doors sealed behind them.

"You going to be trouble?" she asked bluntly.

"Because Peter is in command of my backup?" Henry said. "No. I'm not fond of the idea of calling my ex-husband for help, but I know my damned job, ser."

"I know. Needed to make sure." She grunted. "I'm glad to have *Scorpius*, even with that. A fleet carrier is a fleet carrier right now, but both of her battlecruisers are *Corvid*-class."

Raven's class of battlecruiser remained the newest and most powerful ships in the UPSF's inventory. A fleet carrier was still more dangerous, but the basic design for the big ships hadn't changed since early in the war. Their upgrades had been focused on their fighter wings.

The *Corvids*, on the other hand, incorporated everything the UPSF had learned in seventeen long years of war.

"Three *Corvids* and a fleet carrier should handle whatever the Drifters or Kozun throw at us, ser," Henry agreed.

"You'll be getting an eyes-only technical briefing for you and your chief engineer before you leave the system," Hamilton told him. "We snuck some upgrades into *Raven*'s repairs, ones we're trying to keep quiet."

"From who?" Henry asked. They'd have to tell Song if they'd made changes to his ship—and he suspected his engineer was going to be *pissed* if they'd snuck changes in without telling her. He wasn't entirely happy himself!

"Everyone," his superior said with a laugh. "They're not officially approved yet. A bunch of my people went through the data Song gave us and had a bunch of different ideas on counteracting the disruptor warheads.

"You've got fifty more resettable breakers in the grav-shield projector setup than you had before. The shield will fail in smaller sections and be turned back on more easily—and you have more spare projectors as well.

"Heat and power limits mean you can't run a much more powerful shield than you had before, but it should stand up to the disruptor warheads more effectively." Hamilton waved a hand in the air as she drank her coffee. "The briefing will explain it better than I can; my eyes glazed over when they made their presentation."

"You ordered my ship modified in secret based on something you didn't understand?" Henry asked sharply.

"I *understand* what it does just fine, thank you," she snapped. "The technical details aren't truly relevant to me...or you, for that matter."

"Fair, ser," he conceded.

"You said *Raven* is ready to go," she continued. "How quickly?"

"Twenty-four hours or less, depending on support," Henry said instantly. "Orders?"

"Paperwork will follow," Hamilton told him. "I'm sending you back to La-Tar. That's where Todorovich is sending her drones right now, and I do want you on hand once we know the terms of the gathering."

"Plus, we want a battlecruiser in La-Tar in case the Hierarchy gets clever."

"Plus, we want a battlecruiser in La-Tar in case the Hierarchy gets clever," she agreed. "You're keeping two of *Lioness*'s destroyers. They *are* being handed over to us permanently. They're *Tyrannosaurs*, not new ships, but they're effective enough."

"I wish we'd kept *Lexington*," Henry said.

"We barely had the carrier for a week," Hamilton said with a snort. "Escort carrier or not, Command wants the carriers home and saving fuel, not gallivanting around the Ra Sector, burning cash."

"And yet they're sending us *Scorpius*."

"I think Kosigan and Saren are worried about the Drifters," the Admiral noted. Admiral Lee Saren was the CO of SpaceDiv, the uniformed commander of the UPA's actual space fleet. "They're the people who were most integrated with the Kenmiri before their collapse. We're not sure what they want...and they probably have a better idea of the UPA's location and layout than we think they do."

Henry grimaced. The UPSF hadn't exactly tried to keep the location of their home stars secret, but they hadn't been handing the information out, either. It hadn't been relevant to most of their allies.

And since Zion was thirty light-years from the edge of the Ra Sector, that meant that most of the UPA's former allies didn't even know where to *look* for them. That was part of what made the government's isolationist policy possible.

But if the Drifters were actually an enemy, at least some of them *did* know where the UPA's populated systems were.

"So, we need to know, one way or another," he said.

"If everyone is aboveboard, no one will ever officially know that Admiral Cheung left UPA space," Hamilton told him. "If they're not...well, you'll have the best backup we can possibly provide."

"If I'm leaving tomorrow, how close is *Scorpius* behind me?" Henry asked.

"They're due to arrive in about forty-eight hours," Hamilton told him. "I wanted you at La-Tar ASAP anyway...and I figured you wouldn't mind avoiding that reunion."

CHAPTER SEVEN

Henry loved *Raven*'s bridge in many ways. It was sufficiently different from the bridge of the battlecruiser he'd commanded at the end of the war to serve as a shield against the memories and nightmares of the genocide.

It was an oval two-story space eleven meters long and six meters wide. Including the upper balcony and the support consoles around each senior officer, it was designed to hold forty-eight people in five sections: Communications, Navigation, Sensors, Weapons and Engineering.

Two-sided screens divided the central pit from the support sections, physically isolating the captain and officer of the watch from the support teams while mirroring all of the information into the captain's line of sight. The screens were transparent enough to provide visibility to his crew—and the holoprojectors a civilian ship would have used were too fragile for a ship at war.

On the screens behind him, the bulk of Base Fallout drifted away from them as *Raven* accelerated toward the skip point.

"All departments, check in," he ordered calmly. He didn't even need to send a command to the systems of the captain's chair, with its own screens and computers, for it to relay that to everyone on the bridge.

"CIC is online and fully functional," Tatanka Iyotake confirmed instantly over the network. The Lieutenant Colonel would often be the occupant of either the watch officer chair or one of the observer seats in the main command bubble. His battle station was in the Combat Information Center, running support for the entire bridge crew from a space that could act as a secondary bridge if something happened to Henry and his command crew.

"Engineering reports power and engines are green," Lieutenant Mariann Henriksson reported. The engineering officer was one of the most junior section heads on the bridge, mostly because there was very little for the EO to *do* most of the time. Ninety percent of the time, the EO acted as a relay between the chief engineer and the captain, relaying information the chief didn't have time to pass on themselves.

The rest of the time, the EO spent their time desperately collating damage-control data from across the ship to keep both the captain and the chief engineer informed while the chief spent her time trying to fix the warship.

"We're back to twelve missile launchers, a gravity driver, and two battle lasers," Commander Okafor Ihejirika reported, the big black man's tone cheerfully relieved. "I didn't realize how much I could miss having all of our weapons until we were down a quarter for so long. Tactical and guns are green."

"Sensors are green," Lieutenant Cornelia Ybarra, the assistant tactical officer, and the woman in charge of the Sensors Department, reported. "No unexpected signatures here in Zion."

"I'd hope not," Henry murmured. "Admiral Xinyi would have *words* for her people if we were the first to spot something here!"

"Communications are clear; we are linked into the drone cycle to La-Tar," Lieutenant Commander Lauren Moon reported. There was no need for her to worry about *Raven*'s drones while they were on their way to one of the systems with a postal outpost, not unless there were an emergency.

A skip drone was leaving Zion for La-Tar and vice versa every twenty-four hours. It would take days for the drones to make their trip each way, but a continual cycle of the robotic spacecraft was now in place. Their news from Zion would get older and their news from La-Tar would get fresher as they made their journey, but they'd be getting news from both places.

The skip drones took the same amount of time to skip between systems as a starship, but they could accelerate at almost a thousand kilometers per second squared compared to Raven's point five when traveling between skip points. They made the trip in about seventy percent of the time.

"Navigation is online, and our course is set," Commander Iida Bazzoli reported, the platinum-blonde navigator's attention focused on her consoles. "We'll hit the skip point out of UPA space in nine hours toward Ra-One."

Henry nodded.

"Execute, Commander Bazzoli," he ordered. His internal network then opened channels to the two officers who *weren't* automatically linked to the bridge.

"Thompson, O'Flannagain," he greeted his GroundDiv and FighterDiv commanders. "Status reports?"

"GroundDiv is rearmed and reinforced back up to strength, which you know," Commander Alex Thompson told him. "I have a meeting with Kuroda in twenty minutes to talk about coordinating with the MPs for the trip.

"I presume that if something else comes up that requires a company or three of boots, you'll let me know."

Henry concealed a smile. Despite everything—and the La-Tar campaign had called for some hard, close actions and heavy losses on the part of the GroundDiv detachment—Thompson remained an eager young officer.

He knew Thompson was seeing the ship's counselors and approved. The UPSF regarded mental injuries on the same level as physical injuries. They needed to be addressed and treated as best as possible—and in an age when every military officer had a computer network in their head, the UPSF had options other ages might not have had.

"If we don't schedule a time to test-fly these birds, my people are going to go rogue on me," O'Flannagain said once Thompson was done speaking. "The stats, metrics and simulators say they're amazing, but we haven't got all of them out into real space yet."

"Take a look at Bazzoli's route and pick three systems we have at least sixteen hours in," Henry ordered. "We need to make sure you aren't observed—the GMS birds are going to be a surprise to everybody, and I want to keep them under wraps—so Ihejirika will need to sweep each system ahead of time.

"But we should be able to find a system where we can kick you out into space for a few hours to test them out. No one wants you to be flying them in a crisis on pure sim time."

Henry unconsciously touched the pair of red-enameled wings on his own chest. He would need to get his own realspace flight hours soon enough to keep those. So long as he remained a qualified pilot, the uniform violation inherent in their color would be ignored.

Given what the red wings represented, he'd probably get away with wearing them even after his pilot qualifications lapsed, but he wasn't going to do that.

Staying qualified as a pilot was as much a part of respecting the pilots who hadn't come back from the first campaign against the Kenmiri as painting the wings red. Of the pilots who'd flown in that campaign, only thirty had survived...and most of *those* were dead now.

It had been a long war.

"ALL DEPARTMENTS, REPORT READY FOR SKIP," Henry ordered calmly. Between the two-sided screens surrounding the command pit, the repeater screens on his chair, and his internal network's interface with the starship, he knew the status of the departments.

But verbal confirmation made sure nothing was missed—and the Book called for it anyway.

His officers' responses were as rote as the question, repeats of the responses he'd asked for when they first left Base Fallout.

"We are on target vector and approaching the skip point now, ser," Bazzoli reported once the chorus had died down.

"Understood," Henry acknowledged. "Commander Bazzoli, you have the ship."

He could feel the tensions as everyone on his bridge prepared themselves for the blow. The skip drive was never a pleasant ride. It was named for the metaphor used to describe the effect: they were a three-dimensional rock skipping across the surface of a twenty-dimensional lake.

And no rock enjoyed the sensation of hitting the surface of that lake.

"Shutting down main engines," Bazzoli continued. "Power to icosaspace impulse generators. Transit in one hundred seconds."

An alert was automatically going out to the internal networks of every member of Henry's crew, warning them to make sure they were seated and that their gear was secured. It wouldn't be the first skip for anyone aboard the battlecruiser, but humans were forgetful creatures.

Some people even claimed they could get used to the sensation of a skip. Henry hadn't met any of them himself, but he'd heard about them.

He didn't believe them.

"All hands, this is your final skip alert," Bazzoli said sharply, Henry's internal network confirming her words were going out across the starship. "Entrance in ten seconds. If you aren't strapped in, get strapped in *now*."

A skip had to be between stars, and a ship traveled faster the larger the stars were. Zion was a red giant and so was RX-54R3, their most immediate destination. That meant they were making a twenty-two-hour skip that would take them fifteen light-years. From RX-54R3, they'd skip to another numbered star and then to Ra-1.

It was a nine-day journey to La-Tar, a sign of just how far away from the former Kenmiri Empire the UPA truly was.

"Skip...now," Bazzoli announced.

Raven had internal compensators that allowed her to accelerate at fifty gravities without pulverizing her crew. Those compensators couldn't keep up with the speed of the change as *Raven* bounced through seventeen dimensions her crew could only barely recognize.

The moment of impact was always bad. Without the compensators, humans would need acceleration tanks to survive skip entry. With them, it merely felt like someone had dropped three large men on Henry...from beneath him.

Raven fell up. Then down. Then alternated through seven different versions of sideways. Each shift was enough to leave Henry's inner ear screaming objections.

It lasted twenty seconds—or a few eternities, depending on your opinion. Then it finally stopped, and Henry slowly breathed a sigh of relief. Things still felt slightly odd, even with the compensators and artificial gravity plants doing everything they could to create normality aboard the ship.

"All hands, hear this," Bazzoli said into the PA. "Skip insertion complete. Initial skip complete. First secondary skip will be in four hours, thirteen minutes. Set your alarms."

CHAPTER EIGHT

Sylvia was bored.

She wouldn't *dream* of letting her staff or *Shaka*'s crew realize that for even one second, but their limbo-esque status with the Drifter Convoy was frustrating. After their initial visits, they had been politely but firmly informed they were to remain on *Shaka* unless they had new business.

That meant she was left sitting in the guest quarters of a destroyer, watching six hundred Drifter ships go about their daily business, ignoring her.

"Em Ambassador?" Captain Chavez greeted her from the door of her tiny office. "May I come in?"

"Certainly. How may I help you, Captain?"

Chavez gave her a salute he technically shouldn't and leaned against the wall opposite her desk. There was a chair concealed in a compartment on that wall, Sylvia knew, but she suspected Chavez was more comfortable standing than trying to fit himself into the collapsible seat.

"I was hoping you could give me an idea of how much longer we're going to be here," the Spanish officer told her. "We've been sitting here for over a week, and some of my people are getting antsy. I can run virtual exercises all I want, but so long as we just...sit here, well."

"I understand, Captain," Sylvia allowed. "Unfortunately, I can't say for certainty. One of our drones could get to Kozun in just over seven days, but a ship..." She shrugged. "*Shaka* would take twelve. My understanding is that a Drifter should take ten."

"They have Kenmiri compensators," Chavez allowed. "We don't."

Sylvia nodded. *Shaka* could accelerate at one kilometer per second squared if her crew went into acceleration tanks against the twenty pseudogravities that leaked through. A Drifter ship—or any Vesheron vessel, for that matter—could reach the same acceleration with full compensation.

The Kenmiri had been known to push their ships to one point one KPS^2 in combat, but even they had recognized that as risky. Few Vesheron powers would risk losing one of their ships. None of them could replace ships as readily as an empire of ten thousand stars had been able to.

"Why don't we?" Sylvia asked Chavez. There was no urgency to their conversation, which made it a perfect time to ask random questions that bothered her. "I *know* we dragged samples of everything the Kenmiri had back to the UPA."

One of her more challenging tasks during the war had been to negotiate with several Vesheron for the UPA to take possession of a wrecked-but-potentially-repairable Kenmiri dreadnought, after all. The UPA had access to samples of everything from energy shields to plasma guns to compensators.

"Same reason we don't use their energy shields, as I understand it," Chavez told her. "They interfere with the grav-shield. Our compensators aren't as good, but if we use theirs, the gravity shield loses an unacceptable level of efficiency."

Sylvia nodded her understanding. The gravity shield was humanity's key advantage over everyone else they'd encountered outside their borders, but it was also a fragile technology in several ways.

"So, somewhere back home, someone is working on reinventing a whole bunch of Kenmiri technology so it works with the gravity shield," she guessed.

"Almost certainly, but they don't brief destroyer captains on that," Chavez told her. "But as to my question...twenty days until we hear back?"

"From when they left, which was eight days ago," Sylvia confirmed. "I'd expect that it will take at least two days for the Kozun to make up their minds, so we'll be here at least fourteen more days, Captain.

"Is there anything we can do to make your crew less...restive?"

"If I could arrange an R&R schedule to send people off-ship somewhere, that could help," he admitted. "We're orbiting alongside one of the most impressive spacegoing civilizations I've ever seen, but we're stuck on our own ship."

"Those ships are their homes, their factories, their farms," Sylvia pointed out. "They're not generally willing to let strangers tramp all over them."

"I know," Chavez agreed. "My grandmother was Roma. From the stories she told—legends, thankfully, at this point—they would never let anyone inside their wagons without good reason."

"I'll ask," Sylvia promised. "It will be good for both of our peoples, I think, for *well-behaved* UPSF crew to visit and see what's on their ships. I'll speak to the Protector-Commander."

If nothing else, making the request gave *Sylvia* something to do.

SYLVIA WAS surprised by how easily she was able to get in touch with Third-White-Fifth-Gold. She contacted their flagship and asked to speak with them, expecting to have to make an appointment.

Instead, she was immediately connected to the Protector-

Commander, their Face Mask glistening in the light of their office as they gazed levelly at her.

"Ambassador Sylvia Todorovich," he greeted her. "I will admit, I expected your people to make contact at least twenty hours ago."

"We are twelve days from the earliest I would expect your messengers to return," Sylvia observed. "Why would you expect us to make contact?"

"I know how long my warriors would tolerate sitting and doing nothing," Third-White-Fifth-Gold said. "I believe that the discipline of your arms is as strong as ours, but distraction serves better than idleness."

"That it does," Sylvia agreed. "You know us well, then, Protector-Commander."

They shrugged.

"I know warriors, Ambassador, and people," they told her. "Much is common across all races, be they Ashall or Unseeded. Limbs and eyes and organs define much...but much, I find, is a constant of the condition of sentient life."

Ashall meant *Seeded Races*. No one knew quite what that meant —except, perhaps, the Kenmiri—but the term covered a slim majority of species known to the UPA. Every one of those species could pass for human—and vice versa—given carefully selected clothing.

That was part of why the Drifters were as cloaked as they were, after all. It concealed everything about them—including their species.

"I see," Sylvia said. She didn't disagree with them, either. Her own experience said much the same—even the Enteni on La-Tar, aliens whose eyes were inside massive mouths, were recognizably *people* in their actions and choices.

"Then you have guessed that I wish to negotiate some relaxation opportunities for the crew of my escort vessel," she told the Protector-Commander. "I have no desire to risk the safety of the Convoy or even the goodwill of your people. Anything you and your Council are prepared to offer would be welcome."

"We have an opportunity available now that we did not have

when *Shaka* first arrived," Third-White-Fifth-Gold told her. "The casino vessel *Trust in Fortune* has returned to the Convoy from a sojourn to the Tak System.

"*Trust in Fortune* is designed to handle significant numbers of strangers in a controlled manner," the Protector-Commander concluded. "While her normal customers are, frankly, wealthier than I expect your crew to be, I am sure we can arrange some level of group discount or prepaid credit between us."

Sylvia let her face settle into a sharp and disapproving look—even as she concealed a smile internally.

Of course the Drifter's suggestion for R&R was going to end up costing her more refined metals. Blue Stripe Green Stripe Orange Stripe was going to profit from this encounter in every way they could.

That was how nomadic merchants *survived*, after all.

CHAPTER NINE

"Sensor sweep complete. Ra-One is clear of any active spacecraft," Ihejirika reported. "We are utterly alone out here except for a single skip drone headed to Zion."

"Have we confirmed that drone's bona fides?" Henry asked.

"Really, ser?" O'Flannagain asked from the flight deck. "Do we even know anyone else with skip drones?"

"Not yet, but that *will* change," Henry replied. "It's too obvious a solution to remain unique for long."

O'Flannagain was right that he was probably being too paranoid about the realspace maneuvers she wanted to put her new fighters through. He wished there'd been time to test the SF-130s in Zion or even the numbered systems between the UPA and Ra Sector.

Their stops in each of those systems had been too short to both confirm the system was clear and get a useful amount of exercise time in.

"Drone is definitely ours," Moon reported, the tall and heavyset Martian communication officer sounding amused. "On her way from the station at Beren."

"Understood," Henry acknowledged. "Commander O'Flannagain, you are cleared to commence your exercises. I want all of your birds back aboard in ten hours, an hour before we skip. Understood?"

"Yes, ser," she said crisply. "Rocking and rolling."

Readiness icons started flicking to green on Henry's repeater displays immediately, and he grinned.

"Was the Commander already in her starfighter, ser?" Ihejirika asked in amusement.

"O'Flannagain wasn't," Henry told him. "But it looks like most of her pilots were."

He sucked a breath in through his teeth as the readiness icons solidified. Of the eight SF-130 Lancers on his flight deck, five were glowing solid green, "ready to launch." The other three were flashing amber.

These fighters hadn't even left the hangar bay yet and a deep foreboding settled onto Henry's shoulders.

"O'Flannagain?" he asked.

"I see it too," she said grumpily. "Techs are on their way. Initiating launch of the fighters that are clear."

"Understood," he told her. "Carry on, Commander. The fighter group is yours."

There was a double meaning to that phrase that he knew his CAG understood: she could do whatever she wanted with the fighter group...but she was also entirely responsible for it being a combat-ready force when he needed it.

ONCE IN SPACE, the five working fighters blurred on Henry's sensors as their gravity shields came up. Those shields were stronger than on the old fighters too, he noted. The shear zone was twelve thousand gravities versus the old fighters' ten thousand.

The difference wasn't *that* much—there wasn't much that could survive hitting a zone of space three centimeters across with a ten-thousand-gravity well. Tidal forces made a mess of missiles, plasma beams, even lasers that crossed that shear zone.

A twenty percent stronger shear zone did reduce the number of hits that would get through. It brought the new-generation starfighters up to nearly the same level as the UPSF's destroyers on their main defense.

The first enemy to run into the Lancers was going to have a rude awakening when they started to hit the fighters—almost as rude as the one the Kenmiri had suffered when they first met the UPSF's shielded starfighters.

The initial maneuvers were tentative, the pilots testing the limits of the new craft and comparing them to what they'd seen in the simulators. A sixth starfighter—this one O'Flannagain's, Henry noted absently—joined the exercises before they started doing anything complicated.

Once the hotshot CAG joined her pilots, the tempo of the maneuvers began to accelerate, and Henry had to nod in approval as he watched his people put the new starfighters through their paces.

"That's funny," Ihejirika noted.

"What is?" Henry asked.

"At low acceleration, up to about one KPS-squared, they're harder to pick up than traditional fighters," Ihejirika told him. "No reaction plume, combined with the usual dispersal effect of a gravity shield.

"But once they're at one point five or above, the shield itself is putting off a *lot* of heat. The combination of increased power generation and space-warping effects..." The tactical officer grunted. "I don't think they're going to be easier to hit, not when they're pulling three kilometers a second squared of accel, but they're a lot easier to find."

"Henriksson, any words on our two hangar queens?" Henry asked his engineering officer. The deck personnel were FighterDiv and technically didn't report to Song's engineering department, but

Henriksson was the best person to ask about the deck with O'Flanna-gain in space.

"Looks like Lieutenant Commander Turrigan's fighter is down for the count," Henriksson admitted. "Chief Lin believes they can get the other bird in the air in an hour, but number four is in full emergency shutdown.

"They think there might be a flaw in the reactor casing that passed all tests short of full live power-up," the EO concluded. "It happens; that's why there's fail-safes for it. Power plant safely shut down; everyone is fine. It's just a pain."

"Pass that on to O'Flannagain," Henry ordered. "Her people should be focusing on getting the birds up, not giving her reports."

"Yes, ser."

He turned his attention back to the fighters in the empty space around his ship. The pilot in him couldn't help but thrill at their maneuvers. The last time he'd flown in combat, his fighter had barely been able to get up to one KPS^2—and that had been with him in an acceleration tank.

His people were now dancing in circles around the battlecruiser at three times that acceleration, and he knew they were strapped in at most. The Lancer *had* acceleration tanks and the pilots were expected to use them in combat as a safety precaution, but with the first truly reactionless drive available to humanity in play...the next generation of the GMS starfighters might not bother.

It would depend on how the Lancers worked out.

Part of *that* calculation, though, was how many of them turned out to be hangar queens. Henry turned back to the readiness icons. One continued to flash amber but one had turned completely red.

If one in eight Lancers failed to launch every time, well...that was going to be a very big problem for the people who wanted to replace every fighter in the UPSF with them.

CHAPTER TEN

The La-Tar System was both much the same as it had been when Henry had last seen it and completely different. Six months wasn't enough time for planets and stars to change in any noticeable way or even for major new space stations to take shape.

It was enough time for regular traffic to start up. When Henry had first visited the system, the food transports intended to feed the four industrial worlds that relied on La-Tar had been stuck in a single lump in orbit.

Now, a dozen similar starships hung in low orbit, a busy stream of shuttles lifting food up from the surface—and presumably delivering the products of the industrial worlds to La-Tar's population.

Henry had no idea how the economics of that was going to shake out in the long run. The factories on the industrial worlds had been partnerships between the Imperial government and Kenmiri corporation-esque private entities. Neither of those entities existed in the region now, but someone was presumably running the factories that were still online.

In the long run, only the warships scattered around the system in a protective pattern would remain in government control. Right now, though, food and necessary goods were probably being handled by the governments themselves.

"Looks like the Cluster managed to come up with some new warships," Ihejirika noted. "I make it eight escorts backing up our destroyers."

"That's more than the Cluster had to begin with," Henry agreed. "But my briefing said that they got the skip drives repaired on the damaged units a couple of the worlds had in orbit—plus Tano rushed four new ships out."

Tano had been the world the UPA had first reached out to *because* they were the one with skip drive factories and orbital shipyards. They'd built most of the food transports the Cluster was still relying on and had now built two waves of warships.

The first wave was long gone, destroyed in the desperate defense against the original Kozun conquest of La-Tar.

"So, all of their ships are here again?" Ihejirika asked.

"Plus four from their allies, which makes it two more ships than they had last time the Kozun came," Henry pointed out. "Plus four of our destroyers and one of our battlecruisers."

There'd been about six days between *Lioness* leaving and *Raven* arriving, but the Kozun shouldn't have had time to learn about that and take advantage of it—and clearly hadn't.

"We have an incoming transmission for you, ser," Moon told Henry. "From... *Arbiter* Casto Ran?"

Henry concealed a smile.

"I see our old friend didn't manage to dodge that promotion," he observed. "Who exactly was going to be appointed as the Cluster's interim head of state was still in flux last I'd heard, but the odds were on Casto Ran."

Casto Ran had been the Lord Nominated of the Skex System, a role with notable similarities to the old Roman concept of *dictator*. Skex had been the last system they'd recruited for the liberation of La-Tar...and Casto Ran had made a permanent alliance his price for joining.

That alliance had turned into a loose political confederation over the last six months, one that needed an interim leader. And the title of Lord Nominated came with an assassin-enforced end date.

"I'll take it on my internal network," Henry told Moon. He didn't want to leave the bridge just yet, and his network could easily provide a private virtual meeting.

The Tak politician and soldier appeared in front of Henry as the bridge faded away in favor of his preferred virtual meeting space. To someone from Earth, the Chinese-style temple might clash with the Rocky Mountains behind him, but Arbiter Ran wouldn't know that.

And the virtual space was a clone of a temple near where Henry had grown up in Montana, anyway. Just because it clashed to many people didn't mean it didn't exist.

"Arbiter Ran," he greeted his host in Kem. "It is good to hear from you again."

"Welcome back to La-Tar," Casto Ran greeted him. Ran had pale red skin, weathered by age and radiation, with a small forest of sensory tendrils on his head instead of hair. In Ran's case, those tendrils were pure white, a sharp contrast to the rest of his skin.

"It is always reassuring to be reminded that the UPA means what they say when they promise to protect us," Ran continued. "*Raven* is fully repaired?"

"She is," Henry confirmed. "And I see you got promoted?"

"My term as Lord Nominated was almost up, and I was looking forward to going back to being a mere fleet commander," Ran replied. "It appears that I am once again denied that. I agreed to a term of two La-Tar years."

That was twenty-seven months, Henry's network informed him.

"With or without assassins?" Henry had to ask. A Lord Nominated served for a specified term—and if they didn't step down at the end of that term, they were assassinated by killers who'd spent that entire term familiarizing themselves with the Lord's security.

Ran laughed.

"Without, I believe, though I did promise not to run for the role of my replacement," he noted. "I suspect my role is going to be exactly what the title says: playing arbiter in arguments between system governments.

"I am not certain anyone is going to want it."

"You might be surprised," Henry said. Most people didn't quite seem to realize how much *work* was involved in being in charge of something. Even one ship was a lot. He couldn't imagine running one star system, let alone five.

"Likely," Ran conceded. "This was not entirely a social contact, Captain Wong. We have a situation of some concern, and I would like to impose on the UPA forces in the system to assist us."

"We are here to guarantee the sovereignty of the La-Tar Cluster," Henry said. "I can justify quite a bit inside that mission, if it seems reasonable to me."

"You know the Satra System," Ran told him. "Your people designated it Ra-Fifty, I believe."

"I do," Henry confirmed. "I have not visited it myself, but it was definitely on our minds when the Kozun were retreating."

It was the first system along the short route to Kozun itself. When the Kozun forces had withdrawn from La-Tar, they'd skipped to Ra-50—Satra.

"We have two ships in Satra," Ran said. "It is more of our force than I like sending forward, but a single ship is vulnerable in ways that two are not."

"I understand." That made sense to Henry, though it suggested that even more of the Cluster's ships were in La-Tar than he'd thought.

Skex only had five escorts. Ratch had two, neither of which had been skip-capable when Henry had last encountered them. Tano had built four that he knew of. The entire Cluster only mustered eleven escorts and no true heavier warships.

Yet. Tano was expanding their yards and Skex was building new ones. All four industrial worlds had orbital defenses and starfighters, too, defenses that La-Tar lacked.

Still, that put ten out of eleven active warships in or next to La-Tar.

"We have seen the occasional Kozun scout through the system, but we had, until recently, regarded Satra as otherwise completely secure," Ran said. "We...can no longer do so."

"What happened?" Henry asked.

"For as long as we have had vessels posted in Satra, our sensor technicians have been seeing what we thought were glitches in the software," the Arbiter told him. "While we have had few solid contacts, the continual presence of these vague detections forces us to conclude that there is something there.

"We now believe the Kozun have a concealed facility of some kind in the Satra System and are using ships with an unknown-to-us level of stealth technology to maneuver around Satra and keep an eye on our activities. The corvettes we have seen are picking up the information from the facility, as a skip cannot be concealed."

"I am not aware of any technology that can reliably hide a starship," Henry replied slowly. His new reactionless fighters were harder to detect, as they lacked a drive plume, but they were still far from invisible.

"Neither am I," Casto Ran agreed. "I commanded starships for the Vesheron for half my life, Captain Wong. I have never seen or heard of anything like what we are encountering in the Satra System. But we are definitely encountering *something*."

"And you want me to go to check it out," Henry guessed.

"In company with several of my own ships, yes," Ran confirmed. "Admiral Zast is assembling a task force around one of our carriers. The use of starfighters should enable a large number of scan angles that should unveil whatever is hiding from us."

Henry paused his direct display to conceal his moment of concern. The La-Tar Cluster's "carriers" had been a brilliant solution to bringing extra firepower to the liberation of La-Tar, but the retrofitted freighters were still fragile and slow ships...carrying fighters that were just as fragile.

But Ran was correct in that starfighters would help them narrow down a station or ship someone had managed to hide.

"I will have to meet with the destroyer commanders here before I commit to anything," he told Ran. "But I see no reasons why *Raven* should not be able to assist in this mission. We await news from Ambassador Todorovich's mission, in any case."

"We hope for her success," Ran told him. The Tak's tone suggested *his* hopes were low, but that was his job. Pessimism was part of the job description for running a five-star-system nation, Henry was certain.

"I have faith in the Ambassador," Henry replied. "But even with an explicit peace agreement, we do not want a Kozun scouting outpost next to La-Tar."

"We do not," Ran agreed.

"We will speak again once *Raven* is fully in orbit and I have consulted with my fellows," Henry promised. "Or should I reach out directly to Admiral Zast?"

"Let me know when you can assist and I will arrange a meeting," Ran told him. "We appreciate your help as always, Captain Wong."

CHAPTER ELEVEN

Henry woke up from his dreams bolt upright, breathing rapidly as his internal network flashed an alert. For a few moments, he sat on his bed, staring blankly into space, then sent a mental command to bring the lights up.

He sat cross-legged on the floor, leaning back against the bed as he worked through his breathing exercises. Once he'd calmed his body, he carefully ran through the vague memory of the nightmare.

This was an old one with a few new twists, a memory of one of the more horrific scenes of his time with Mal Dakis. A small group of mid-level officers in the Vesheron faction had tried to make a deal with the Kenmiri, to betray the rebels and their Terran allies to the Empire.

Mal Dakis had found out and trapped them. The six leaders had then been crucified in the main loading bay of the asteroid base they'd all been operating out of.

In the past, Henry hadn't known any of those officers, *and* they'd all been given a lethal dose of painkillers before being put on display. In his dream, the victims had still been alive—and they'd included both Sylvia Todorovich and Kalad, his old Kozun friend who'd commanded the retreat from La-Tar.

He was reasonably sure that Sylvia was still alive, even if the last report from *Shaka* was several days old. Kalad, on the other hand... she had not expected to survive returning to the Hierarchy. Refusing would have doomed her mate and child, so she'd gone back to face the penalties of failure.

So, Kalad was joining his dead in his nightmares. Henry couldn't blame his subconscious for that. He ran through the dream scenario again in his mind, facing it and letting it flow over him. He had a lot of practice with that now.

He'd lost a lot of friends and subordinates in the war. He'd lost a marriage—consummated with the immortal certainty of young men and then sacrificed on the cold realism of old soldiers. He'd spent months under medical supervision to make sure he didn't commit suicide...and he was far from the only one.

The psychic wounds of war and genocide were torn deeply into the soul of the United Planets Space Force. That was why he was there, in La-Tar, trying to keep strangers safe.

With a long exhalation, the dark-skinned Chinese American officer rose from the floor and crossed to his desk. He wasn't going to get back to sleep, which meant he may as well go over the files for his new officers.

He was meeting the destroyer captains in the morning, only a few hours away. He'd have been *better* if he could have rested, but he could tell when that wasn't happening.

⋁

"TAKE A SEAT, PEOPLE," Henry ordered the four officers waiting for him. "I appreciate you taking the time to meet with me."

None of the four were physically present. The four destroyers were all within ten thousand kilometers of *Raven*, allowing for real-time transmission. The holograms were as solid and present as if the Lieutenant Colonels had shuttled over.

"We await your orders, ser," Lieutenant Colonel Heléna Orosz told him. The pale woman commanding *Glorious* was the youngest of his four destroyer captains, an Earth-native officer responsible for the most advanced of the escort warships.

"I have reviewed Captain Rahmi's standing orders for your assignment in the system," Henry said. "I see no reason to change any of them at this moment, so I won't be issuing any immediate orders.

"This is an introductory meeting for us to touch base," he continued. "I know Captain Spini from my last visit here." He nodded to *Hadrosaur*'s captain, the Indian man returning the gesture.

"If you have any concerns about our position or situation here, now is the time to raise them. From my conversation with the Arbiter on our way in, I expect to be moving *Raven* out in company with Cluster forces shortly.

"We are also on standby, waiting for an update from the diplomatic mission attempting to find a peaceful solution to this conflict," he reminded them. "While *Raven* is officially posted to La-Tar, there is a reason you four are assigned to the La-Tar station as opposed to a Cruiser Group *Raven*.

"The nature of the Initiative and our limited hull numbers require you all to maintain a certain degree of independent posture. While you answer to me as the senior officer while I am present, I expect my duties to have *Raven* outside of the La-Tar System on a regular basis."

He looked around the four virtually present officers.

"If you have any concerns, any questions, about our mission or our situation, now is the time to raise them."

"We are supposed to be a peacekeeping force, ser," *Albertosaur*'s captain said slowly. Lieutenant Colonel Omobolanle Abiodun was an immense African with swirling tattoos inked across their face. Henry didn't know quite what the tattoos meant, but he understood them to be related to Abiodun's culture's traditional third gender.

"Our position here in La-Tar is not a peacekeeping role," Abiodun continued. "This is a defensive position with clear rules of engagement and an expected enemy. This seems...contrary to our role."

"It's part of the role, unfortunately," Henry replied. "I agree, Captain. However, sometimes, keeping the peace requires us to get in the way of people trying to fight wars. We do not and cannot recognize the use of force for conquest as a legitimate tool.

"If the Initiative is to stand behind that statement, we must back it up with the necessary tools. That means we have to be prepared to defend systems that have been the target of violence.

"We will attempt to find peaceful solutions, and if at all possible, we want to avoid the UPA getting drawn into a real fight with the Kozun or anyone else. But...protecting these people is very much part of our mandate.

"Our task is to keep the peace and restrain the warlords rising from the Kenmiri's ashes. We can't do that without fighting anyone—and the best way to avoid a fight sometimes is to make it very clear you're ready to have one."

He grimaced.

"I *hope* that our presence here acts as a deterrent and keeps the Hierarchy from repeating their attempt to conquer these systems. If it doesn't...well, we fight."

Abiodun nodded silently.

"I appreciate you establishing that, ser," Straton Nosak, the fourth destroyer skipper, said. "It helps us know where we stand and what to tell our people. No one signed up for the Initiative because we *didn't* think we needed to do something out here."

Even the crews of the two destroyers pulled out of Cruiser Group *Lioness*, Nosak's and Abiodun's commands, had been assembled from volunteers. Not that they'd needed to make much adjustment to *Stegosaur* or *Albertosaur*'s crews. They'd basically volunteered as a body.

"Once we have the situation with the Kozun resolved, this all should become much smaller-scale," Henry promised them. "We weren't expecting to stumble into a war out here, after all. All of our missions were *supposed* to be making contact with single planets or maybe a dependency cluster at the most.

"Ambassador Todorovich and I were out here to make contact with just Tano," he said. "We all saw how that turned out!"

"These are good people," Spini added softly. "They never deserved to be slaves, and I don't think I have it in me to stand by and see them enslaved again."

"None of us do, Parvan," Abiodun assured him. "We all volunteered for this."

"We are under your orders, ser," Orosz told Henry, "but we're all here for a reason. I have no concerns about our positioning in this system."

"Good," he said. "Now. Supplies? Weapons status? Morale issues? Anything I need to know about or that you need backup on?"

Both the UPA and the fledgling defensive forces of the Cluster were based on the old Vesheron logistics pipelines—which meant everyone's missiles were clones of the Kenmiri weapons. The Cluster could easily replenish almost every munition Henry's people needed.

CHAPTER TWELVE

"It is a pleasure to meet you in person again, Captain Wong," Zast told Henry as he stepped off the shuttle, her Kem smoother than he remembered. The old Tak—she was older than Casto Ran by a significant margin, he suspected, with liver spots that stretched up onto her head-tendrils—took his hands in hers in a strange two-handed gesture.

"I hear that you are having some unusual problems in the Satra System," Henry said. "The Arbiter asked me to provide some support."

"He came aboard shortly ahead of you," the Admiral told him. Zast had been a food freighter captain before the Kozun invasion and had helped organize the relief fleet that had fed the industrial worlds, picked up their troops and then liberated La-Tar.

In exchange, she was now the senior officer of the La-Tar Cluster Defense Fleet.

"I have a few officers who will be hologramming in, but it will not be a large meeting," she told him. "*Sunshine* has been upgraded since you last saw her in action. I would be delighted to give you a tour once we are done."

Sunshine was one of the Cluster's two "carriers," former food transports refitted to carry a few dozen unshielded starfighters. They'd been handy in the relief effort, but Henry was surprised they'd kept them on as warships.

He couldn't *say* that, however.

"It will depend on how much time we have," he said stiffly. "My understanding is that the Arbiter would like this situation resolved as quickly as possible."

"So would we all," Zast agreed. "A Kozun observation post one skip away from La-Tar is concerning, even if we do not think they have been scouting us directly."

"Without subspace coms, they are limited," Henry noted. "Though that is why they would be sending ships to pick up the data dumps."

"Exactly what we think," Zast confirmed. "Come, Captain. I will show you what I can of our flagship on the way."

It was *flagship* now, apparently. Henry held his tongue as they walked through the still-very-clearly-civilian boat bay toward the rest of the ship. *Sunshine* was a ten-megaton food freighter at her bones. He wasn't sure what they could have done to her to make using her as a *flagship* worthwhile.

The moment the doors to the rest of the ship slid shut behind them, he started to understand. The corridor led to a row of brand-new in-ship transit pods. A directory hung next to the pods—internal networks like those used in the UPSF were rare in former Kenmiri space—listing ship location after location after location.

"How much did you add?" he asked.

"We had a lot of space," Zast said drily. "And, as it turned out, Tano had a lot of spare parts. A prefabricated conference center intended to be part of a space station here, a set of lasers intended as mining gear there..."

She grinned.

"You will see the conference and fleet-control facilities yourself," she promised him. "I will have my people send yours the current specifications."

"Current, huh?" Henry asked. He supposed the advantage to a merchant hull was that they could clearly open it up and install just about any prefabricated segment they wanted. "Still a lot of empty space?"

"The only real defense most of the modules have, yes," Zast conceded. "We have some armor around key components like reactors and heat radiators, but the emptiness of the ship is part of her protection."

A transit pod was already waiting for the Admiral, an armed soldier in face-concealing armor standing next to it. The guardian traded a calm nod with the GroundDiv trooper trying to be inconspicuous behind Henry and stepped aside.

"Come on, Captain," Zast told him. "We will have work to do."

"OUR ATTEMPTS TO locate the stealth scout have so far proven a complete waste," Casto Ran told the people in the meeting room a few minutes later. "We know there is *something* in the Satra System. It may be a concealed facility. It may be a ship equipped with technology we are unfamiliar with.

"Whatever it is, we need to identify it, locate it and either capture or destroy it," the Arbiter concluded. "Our UPA allies have agreed to provide us some assistance, but the key component is *Sunshine* herself. Admiral Zast?"

Zast nodded to her boss and joined him at the front of the room. Rows of semicircular chair arrangements focused on the stage, though the room was sized for ten times as many people as joined Henry there today.

From what he'd seen, most of *Sunshine*'s command facilities were structured like that. She was a command ship without a fleet, but she'd been future-proofed against a vast expansion of the Cluster's forces.

Hopefully, that would prove unnecessary, but he couldn't blame the Cluster for it. The UPA couldn't always be there. With five star systems to protect, a fleet of a hundred ships started to sound quite reasonable.

"Whatever stealth systems the ghost commands, they are more than sufficient to prevent our current generation of sensors from detecting the target with any certainty," she said calmly. "Our solution to this has two edges to the blade.

"Firstly, Captain Wong has agreed to bring *Raven* with us." She gestured to Henry. "*Raven*'s sensors are superior to any in our current possession."

The UPSF's current generation of sensor suites were superior to *any* sensors in the Kenmiri Empire, Henry knew. That meant they were almost certainly better than anything available to the Vesheron with their ex-Kenmiri systems.

The other El-Vesheron powers, the outsiders like the UPA who'd helped fight the Kenmiri, were more in question...but they were all a *long* way away now.

"The second part of the plan is to swamp Satra with sensor platforms," she continued. "We have rigged up a high-intensity detection array that can replace a missile on one of our starfighters, and Tano has helped the LCDF assemble a stockpile of these arrays.

"Mounting them on all of *Sunshine*'s fighters will provide us with over one hundred and twenty different sensor arrays. Combined with *Sunshine*, *Raven*, and the escorts we are bringing with us, I do not believe our mystery visitor will remain hidden for long!"

It was a good plan, partly relying on *Sunshine*'s having vastly expanded her fighter strength from the last time Henry had seen her. He hadn't thought there were a hundred and twenty starfighters in the Cluster.

The spacecraft were still what UPSF pilots referred to as "TIEs"

—fast and potentially decently armed starfighters completely lacking in shields of any kind. It was theoretically possible to fit energy shields on a starfighter-sized vessel, but Henry had only seen it a handful of times.

Without gravity shields, the Cluster's fighters were far more vulnerable than his own wing. For this mission, it wouldn't matter.

"What are we bringing with us for escorts?" he asked. "The plan seems solid to me, but we are assuming that this mystery scout is minimally dangerous."

"There are two escorts in the system, and we will be bringing two more with *Sunshine*," Zast told him. "We would welcome the presence of one of your destroyers, though we do not believe it will be necessary.

"I suspect we are looking at a small specialty vessel or potentially a minimally armed facility," she continued. "The worst case I can see is one of the Kozun's new cruisers, which would suggest dangerous abilities for those vessels."

"I cannot see them having a cruiser to spare," Henry admitted. The ships weren't dreadnoughts, but they were the largest ships he'd seen built by a Vesheron power since the war had ended.

Of course, the handful of Vesheron powers that had built their own capital ships during the war were a long way away. Kenmiri dreadnoughts and Drifter Guardians were all they knew of in the Ra Sector.

"Four escorts should suffice to level the field between *Raven* and *Sunshine* and any likely enemy," he conceded. "*Raven* is ready to move as soon as you are, Admiral Zast. I see no reason to delay, not without more information on this ghost than we have."

And if the Kozun had some kind of stealth-ship technology, he needed to know that *before* he took an ambassador to a prearranged meeting with their representatives.

Mal Dakis might be pragmatically ruthless, but he'd also always had a taste for recruiting assassins and agents who were...both more ruthless and less pragmatic than their boss. And one Henry Wong had made enemies of more than a few of those agents.

If anyone would use a peace negotiation as an opportunity to attack with a stealth ship, it would be the Kozun!

CHAPTER THIRTEEN

The Satra System didn't look particularly unusual to Henry once *Raven* arrived. A red giant star, it looked very similar to the dozens of similar systems used as stopover points for travel throughout the Kenmiri Empire.

Skipping between larger stars was faster than skipping between smaller ones, so most journeys would consist of skipping to a giant of some kind, and then skipping to several others before making the final skip to a regular-sized star.

Red giants tended not to have much in terms of planets. Satra had a midsized gas giant orbiting at several dozen light-minutes, but only asteroids and meteors otherwise.

"Ihejirika, show us the skip line to Kozun space," Henry ordered. "And then flag every ghost the locals have seen on the display for me."

The Cluster task force was still emerging from skip behind him. *Glorious* had come through in perfect formation with the battle-cruiser, but the La-Tar ships were being more cautious. *Sunshine* was the last ship through, arriving in a space already covered by the two escorts.

A green line on the displays around Henry already marked the skip line back to La-Tar. They could, at least theoretically, skip back to the agriworld's system anywhere along that line. It would require more careful calculations the closer they got to the star, but it was possible.

Two new lines appeared in response to his order, both colored dark orange. Henry's internal network filled in the names for him, marking them as the skips toward Kozun space.

One was a twenty-hour skip to another red giant that would be the first of several skips to get all the way to Kozun itself in about ten days. The other was a twenty-three-hour skip, almost the longest anyone would risk, to the nearest industrial planet under Kozun control.

"Any contacts yet?" he asked.

"Negative," Ihejirika reported. "Scatterplot of ghost contacts going up now. None of them are solid, so the whole map is probabilistic at best."

"Understood."

On the scale of a display showing most of a star system, even the largest probable zone for a single contact was a mere dot. The data provided by the Cluster ships speckled the star system with more tiny dots. There were at least two hundred of them, Henry estimated, which explained why Ran had decided there was definitely something out there.

"*Sunshine* reports that they are launching fighters," Moon reported. New blue icons spilled out from the marker for the carrier behind *Raven*. "Admiral Zast is requesting an update on your intentions, ser."

Henry nodded, studying the pattern of the dots. There wasn't a neat single concentration of them. They covered a broad zone, stretching from the moonless gas giant out toward all three skip lines.

"Get me Captain Orosz," he ordered. "I'll update Zast once we have a plan."

It only took a moment for the destroyer CO to appear on the

screens attached to his seat. He brought Iyotake in from CIC with a mental order and gazed levelly at the two Lieutenant Colonels.

"I assume you're both looking at the contact pattern," he said.

"Yes, ser," Iyotake confirmed. "No real solid answers here."

"No," Henry agreed. "I suspect we're looking at something near the gas giant, though. Orosz?"

"I guess the same," the woman said. "Your orders?"

"I want *Glorious* to go sweep the gas giant area," he told her. "There's less in terms of debris over there than in a lot of the system, so there shouldn't be anything to hide behind. You're authorized to use sensor drones at your discretion."

"Understood, ser," Orosz said. "What do you think we're looking for?"

"The contacts are too diffuse to be a facility," Henry said. "We're looking for a ship, potentially more than one. Make sure your scanners are calibrated for Terzan starfangs. If we know *anyone* with any kind of stealth tech, it's them."

The Terzan were El-Vesheron like the UPA, but they were most definitely *not* Ashall. They were ten-legged insectoids who communicated via organic radio. Unlike the rest of the Vesheron and El-Vesheron, though, the UPA knew the Terzan had gravity shields.

Better ones than the UPA, plus a generally more sophisticated tech base. Henry would back *Raven* against almost anything in the galaxy one on one. The *Corvid*-class battlecruisers had been designed to engage two Kenmiri dreadnoughts at once, after all.

Faced with a Terzan starfang, a ship the size of one of his destroyers, though, he'd hesitate. He was all too aware that the weapons and abilities the Terzan had shown in the war had been intentionally understated.

"The Terzan aren't anywhere near here," Orosz objected. "They're from near Londu space, over by the Set Sector, aren't they?"

"I don't expect you to find Terzan, Captain," Henry told her. "But they're the people most likely to have a stealth system of some kind that we have sensor data on. So, if someone is sneaking around, calibrating for a starfang is the most likely way to find them.

"Understood?"

"Yes, ser," she confirmed. "We'll set our course."

"And us, ser?" Iyotake asked.

"We set our course for the route to Kozun, the Vodo skip line," Henry replied. "If they're Kozun and they're looking to send any information home, they'll have something there.

"We have the best sensors in the system, so we'll take a look there."

"Understood, ser."

Henry closed the channels and turned to his bridge crew.

"Bazzoli, course for the Vodo skip line, if you please," he ordered. "Moon, inform Zast that we're sending *Glorious* to the gas giant and *Raven* is investigating the route to Kozun. We'll coordinate with units she's sending to either place, but the best use of her starfighters is a VLA."

A Very Large Array was made up of multiple ships spread out at precalculated distances with synchronized sensors. It would let them act as a telescope tens of thousands of kilometers across, providing a resolution no single ship's sensors could match.

"I'll pass that on, ser," Moon confirmed.

"Course set," Bazzoli reported.

"Engage."

EVEN AT HALF A KILOMETER PER second squared, crossing the distance across star systems took time. With the exception of *Sunshine*, the La-Tar ships were faster. The escorts and fighters were able to maneuver at one KPS^2, though the carrier was limited to the same half KPS^2 as *Raven*—and didn't have the engine power and acceleration tanks to push past that like the battlecruiser.

One of the escorts stayed with the carrier as the fighters spilled farther and farther out, their scanner data presumably feeding back to *Sunshine* to provide a detailed view of the star system.

Another escort, one of the ones already positioned in the system, was sticking close to *Glorious*. The destroyer was almost twice the escort's size but technically more lightly armed. She had three lasers to the escort's four—though hers were estimated at around twice the power level—and twelve missile launchers to the escort's twenty. Of course, the escort lacked even Kenmiri energy shields, where *Glorious*, one of the UPSF's new *Significance*-class destroyers, had a full gravity shield.

Another escort was accompanying *Raven* as she headed for the Kozun skip route, and the last escort was heading for the remaining skip line.

"*Sunshine* is feeding us the data from the VLA," Moon reported. "Not seeing much. So far, all that this mission is doing is proving the system is empty."

Henry nodded, pulling some of the data directly to his own screens. The La-Tar fighters had the worst sensors of any of the ships in the system, but with over a hundred of them synchronized, they had the best overall resolution.

The data he was seeing from the VLA was old by the time it reached him. Lightspeed delays meant that the minimum age was almost ten minutes, and it got older as he looked farther away from the fighters.

"We're counter-analyzing the VLA data," Iyotake told him. "We're not finding anything either. Zast is moving the array slowly and sweeping the system."

"Ihejirika, flag the zones that we've marked as clear on the display," Henry ordered.

A pale green haze lit up a large chunk of the system on his screens. It was slowly arcing across the inner system's asteroids and meteors as Henry watched, the different angles making even the largest chunks of debris useless as hiding spots.

"Looking like our friends were jumping at ghosts so far," Ihejirika said. "Except I've met too many of Ran and Zast's people to buy that."

"Agreed," Henry said. He studied the orange line they were drawing closer to. It wasn't in the green haze yet, but a good chunk of the space he'd actually expected to find trouble in was. There were no dense clusters of debris near the skip line, but there were asteroids and meteors, and he'd presumed their ghost would be hiding behind one of them.

"Moon, send Orosz a warning," he said calmly. "If we're not picking up anyone in the debris fields, then the most likely hiding spot left is that gas giant."

"Do we divert back, ser?" Bazzoli asked.

Henry hesitated. He was still certain that the Kozun would have something close to the skip route back to the Hierarchy's capital, but they weren't *seeing* anything.

"Do we have a telemetry link for *Bushel of Hope*?" he asked, looking at the escort keeping pace with his cruiser. "We might be able to see what's closest to us if we sync our sensors."

He didn't overly *like* sharing telemetry at that level of detail, otherwise he'd have asked for it already. He was fine getting their data, but the VLA data had been freely offered and he couldn't quite bring himself to *ask* for data without offering his in return.

"Upright-Hope wants a direct line, ser," Moon told him after a moment, the translated Enteni name sounding awkward to her.

"Put them through," Henry ordered.

The image that appeared in front of him looked like nothing so much as a mobile, smooth-exteriored Venus flytrap. The massive black-skinned mouth was facing the camera and wide open to allow Upright-Hope's eyes—mounted on stalks *inside* the mouth as a protective measure—to look Henry in the face.

"We is-are seeing nothing here," the Enteni officer told him. Even their Kem was an artificial translation; few Ashall had the hearing and visual acuity to register Enteni communication. "We feel this fate-time is-were clear of threats."

"If the Kozun are here, then there is a good chance of a relay station close to the skip line," Henry replied, speaking in Kem himself instead of relying on translators. "If there is nothing else, that will be concealed here and could give us clues. I suggest we synchronize our scanners and increase the distance between our vessels to see what we can find."

Upright-Hope hesitated, then fluttered a tendril in agreement.

"This will-can cost little," they conceded. "And the Kozun skip line is-will-be the greatest potential threat."

"Thank you, Captain."

The channel dropped and *Bushel of Hope*'s acceleration shifted as she moved away from *Raven*. Her acceleration shifted up to almost half again *Raven*'s, and Henry swallowed a moment of jealousy.

Someday soon, the UPSF would crack the interference problems and install Kenmiri-grade compensators in their ships. On that day, Henry would be rid of the last lingering sense of inferiority versus his allies and old enemies.

"Ser, CIC has picked out four objects large enough to conceal a small automated relay despite the VLA," Iyotake told him. "I'm flagging them on the display. If *Bushel* takes the right course, we should be able to clear all four within a few minutes."

"Moon? Pass on the details CIC is providing to our La-Tar friends," Henry ordered as the new icons appeared on the display. His understanding was that only about ten percent of *Bushel*'s crew was Enteni, with the rest being members of the several Ashall species living in the La-Tar Cluster.

Given that the Kenmiri had actively avoided letting an agriworld or industrial world have a population of one race, some of the warship's crew would even be Kozun.

More of the star system was being marked in green. Their ghost, whoever it was, was doing a disturbingly good job of hiding itself. As Henry looked over the displays, he received a notification that *Glorious* was deploying sensor drones above the gas giant.

There didn't appear to be anything in orbit, which was the last place he'd really expected to see anything.

"Contact!" Ihejirika suddenly snapped. "Spectrography on target four is wrong. She has ice facing *Bushel*, but *we* just pinged metal. That's not a meteor, ser!"

"Well done," Henry murmured. "Range, Commander?"

"Two hundred thousand kilometers," the tactical officer reported grimly. "They're *in* weapons range, ser. It's not a relay station. That's a ship."

"Charge the grav-driver and fire a warning shot from the lasers, Commander," Henry ordered. "Moon, summon them to surrender."

Icons across his displays lit up as *Raven*'s weapons activated. His two heavy lasers were probably the most powerful lasers in the star system, but he only had two of them. The spinal gravity driver that ran the full length of the battlecruiser took more power to fire, but her capacitors flashed green as the first laser flashed in the darkness.

"Unknown vessel, this is UPSV *Raven*," Moon barked into her microphone in Kem. "You are in violation of the security zone of the La-Tar Cluster. Stand down or be destroyed."

"They're rabbiting!" Ihejirika snapped. "Multiple explosions, damn."

The ship was smaller than the meteor it had embedded itself in, and had prepared for a situation where it might have to escape unexpectedly. Instead of bringing up their engines, they detonated a sequence of carefully planted explosives that hurtled them away from *Raven* at a full kilometer a second squared for several seconds—a crude but effective evolution of an Orion drive.

"Debris everywhere; I can't get a lock for a shot," the tactical officer reported. "Moon, is *Bushel* on them?"

Lasers flashed in the night as the unknown opened fire on the La-Tar escort. The same debris cloud that protected her from *Raven* prevented her from shooting the battlecruiser. It did *not* stop the ship firing on *Bushel of Hope*.

The escort had started to maneuver, but not quickly enough. Two heavy lasers smashed into her and sent the ship reeling off, her engines flickering to silence.

"Tell me she's still with us," Henry barked.

"Engines are disabled but scans show she's still intact," Ihejirika reported. "Orders, ser?"

"That's a Kozun corvette," Henry noted, identifying the ship as it blazed away from them at over a kilometer and a half a second squared. "Can we bring her down before she skips?"

"Debris field is still interfering with targeting; I think they must have seeded it with chaff to screw with our sensors," the big Black officer said grimly. "And she's only a million klicks from the line. We might catch her, ser, but...it's fifty-fifty at best."

And *Bushel of Hope* was leaking oxygen and fuel alike, a dangerous combination even in deep space.

"Fuck," Henry swore. "Bazzoli: intercept course for *Bushel of Hope*. Thompson, O'Flannagain: stand by for rescue operations.

"Ihejirika: if you get a shot, take it. But our priority is rescuing our allies, not chasing that prick."

At least they'd found the ghost. Or *a* ghost, anyway. Henry watched the no-longer-concealed corvette run for the skip line and shook his head.

That was definitely who the Kozun had been communicating with, but that disguise wouldn't have held up to any kind of maneuvering. He didn't *quite* buy that the La-Tar sentries would have missed the ship accelerating around the star system.

They'd found what they'd been looking for. But he had to wonder if they'd found everything that was there.

CHAPTER FOURTEEN

Trust in Fortune was exactly what Third-White-Fifth-Gold had named her: a casino ship.

Sylvia had let Chavez make the call over whether his people needed a relief enough for them to risk a vessel specifically designed to separate its customers from their valuables, and then waited until almost all of the crew had cycled through the ship before visiting herself.

She was touring the ship with the destroyer's XO, Commander Lilia Vasilev, a hawk-faced young woman from her own home system of Epsilon Eridani. Once the beating heart of the Novaya Imperiya prior to the Unity War, Eridani had become independent as part of the peace treaty.

In many ways, Eridanans like Sylvia were more-Russian-than-Russians now. She and Vasilev both regarded the glittering gaudiness of the public portions of *Trust in Fortune* with cold cynicism.

"I believe they are specifically stocking drugs tailored for humans," Vasilev noted. "I expect to find actual poker tables here somewhere."

"Kosa is close enough," Sylvia replied, naming the Kenmiri game of chance that mirrored much of Terran poker. It had twenty suits of five cards apiece instead of a Terran deck with its four suits of thirteen, but kosa and poker played surprisingly similarly, in her experience.

"I will need to check in with the MPs," Vasilev said. "We have been making sure people didn't gamble anything they weren't supposed to, but now I wonder if we were careful enough."

"I'd be more concerned with the spacers trying to smuggle people back aboard *Shaka* for assorted reasons," Sylvia said. "The Drifters *really* want our gravity tech, and they are willing to trade sex for far smaller favors than that."

None of the crew she could see were outside of the usual robe-and-mask assemblage of working Drifters, but they were Duty Masks, not Face Masks. No one aboard this ship was meant to be identified by guests later.

"I presume there are sections of the ship where they are wearing, ah, tighter robes?" Vasilev asked.

"That would be my assumption, yes," Sylvia murmured. "There always seemed to be when we were arranging resupply for the UPSF during the war."

The younger woman glanced at a cloth-shrouded booth that appeared to be selling personal energy weapons.

"I forget that you probably saw more of the Kenmiri Empire and Vesheron than I did," she admitted. "I was a gunnery officer on one of the carriers for Golden Lancelot."

Vasilev shivered.

"That was enough."

"I visited a lot of places and negotiated a lot of things," Sylvia agreed. "Food, missiles, allies, soldiers, ships—I've traded all of that for all of that at one point or another."

"Should we be being more careful about what we say aboard their ship?" Vasilev asked. "Even in English?"

"They know exactly how far we trust them—and vice versa," the ambassador said with a chuckle. "Yes, they are recording us, and yes, they can translate English by computer. We're far from topics I'd be concerned about."

The Commander chuckled and stepped over to the booth, studying the handheld energy weapons through their sealed display cases.

"I feel like we should be sending a quartermaster over here to stock up on these things," she muttered to Sylvia.

"That's part of what we were buying here," the ambassador admitted. "We picked up ten thousand beam rifles and five thousand pulse pistols. That's what's in the crates we loaded into *Shaka*'s cargo compartment."

That was what Felix Leitz had organized with the Convoy Quartermasters. The UPA was producing energy weapons of their own, but production wasn't where anyone would like—and their tech wasn't up to reliably producing pistol-sized weapons yet.

The Drifter shopkeeper emerged from behind a curtain, wearing the plain light blue Duty Mask everyone aboard *Trust in Fortune* was wearing.

"These are the finest examples of Convoy craft!" they insisted in Kem. "The Commander will not be disappointed. Protect yourself, your lover, your family!"

Vasilev managed to avoid looking trapped, but Sylvia suspected it was a challenge.

"I have a service sidearm for if I ever need one," she told the Drifter. "They are elegant-looking weapons, though."

Sylvia had to agree. Energy weapons were generally blocky things, to control heat dissipation and recoil. These had those edges smoothed into curves and filigreed with precious metals. They rivaled the pistol Henry Wong had lent her on one occasion—and *his* weapon had been a Kenmorad Consort's gun reengineered by a loyal crew.

"And you, Ambassador?" the shopkeeper asked. "An elegant weapon for an elegant diplomat, to show you speak with more than words?"

The Drifter was certainly well informed, though that wasn't entirely surprising. Sylvia figured the casino ship's crew had been briefed on all of the senior officers of *Shuku*'s crew.

"No, thank you," she told the Drifter. "My words are more effective than any weapon I could carry."

"Shame, shame. Well, look if you wish; I am here if you change your thoughts."

Sylvia was about to thank the Drifter when her internal network chimed.

The Drifter vessel they'd sent to Kozun had returned to the system. They were a day earlier than Sylvia had expected, which was either a very good sign...or a very bad one.

"Vasilev, I need to get back to *Shaka*," she told the other woman. "It looks like it might be time to get to work again!"

✦

SYLVIA ENDED up almost alone aboard the shuttle, the spacecraft heading back toward *Shaka* only carrying her and her GroundDiv security detail.

They'd crossed barely a third of the distance between the two ships when Leitz contacted her from the destroyer.

"Em Todorovich, we have a coms request from the Protector-Commander," he told her. "I can ask them to wait until you return aboard?"

"They're going to see it anyway, Felix," Sylvia replied with a chuckle. "Who are we hiding from? Relay it to the shuttle and I'll take it in my internals. Shouldn't add too much time delay."

"Understood," her chief of staff said. "We'll have them connected momentarily."

It was a bit longer than *momentarily* before the relay and connection were set up, but it was still only a couple of minutes before a two-dimensional projection of Third-White-Fifth-Gold appeared in front of Sylvia.

Since she was using her internal network, which had obvious issues with having an image of her, they were speaking to an avatar image of her. It wouldn't make much of a difference, but they would be able to tell.

"Ambassador, it appears my timing is less than optimal," the Protector-Commander noted.

"Teta," she agreed. The word meant *touch* and had the same connotations as *touché* in English. "But my mission here is important and I understand the courier ship you sent to Kozun has returned."

"It has," Third-White-Fifth-Gold replied. "We now have an official response from the Kozun Hierarchy to your request."

"And?" she prodded.

"They have agreed to the meeting but have conditions and terms that will need to be met," the Protector-Commander told her. "Some of those conditions involve the resources of Convoy Blue Stripe Green Stripe Orange Stripe.

"Would it be possible for you to meet with the Council of Ancients once more, Ambassador Todorovich? We believe this would be more readily negotiated in person."

That was ominous. More than anything, it probably meant that the Drifters were going to try and *negotiate* gravity-shield technology out of her again.

Swindle was probably too harsh a word, after all.

"I see no inherent issue with that," she conceded. "But I would like to review the terms the Kozun have requested prior to that meeting."

"If you wish to redirect your shuttle toward the garden ships, I will make certain a summary is forwarded to you," the Protector-Commander promised. "I think all will benefit from a speedier resolution to this situation."

That was a new sense of urgency that Sylvia hadn't managed to get out of them before. Though...it was also possible that urgency was merely at the realization they could get paid twice now.

It was easy to stereotype the Drifters as greedy, but the scale of the Convoy outside Sylvia's shuttle told her the truth: repairing and running those ships, feeding and caring for their crews...just keeping the millions of people living aboard the ships of Blue Stripe Green Stripe Orange Stripe was an immense and expensive task.

The Council was responsible for all of those lives. Every resource they could acquire was one more shield against a cold and horrific death for millions of people.

She could understand where they were coming from...even if she wasn't going to give them what they truly wanted.

Sylvia Todorovich was *also* responsible for millions of lives, after all.

CHAPTER FIFTEEN

By the time her escorts peeled off at the top of the
Council of Ancients' auditorium, Sylvia had gone over the Kozun's
requests three times and she was truly optimistic for the first time
since she'd started on her mission.

The Kozun had specified a location: a blue hypergiant three skips
from La-Tar. They were sending one of the Voices of the Kozun, the
religious and secular heads of the Hierarchy. They wanted both sides
to send three ships—specifying that at least one "Cluster" ship should
be UPSF—and they wanted a three-ship neutral detachment. They
weren't even setting any preconditions to the negotiations; everything
appeared to be on the table.

Of course, the *neutral detachment* was going to be a headache.
The rumors UPSF intelligence had heard suggested that the Kozun
were actively at war with at least two other nations—neither of which
the UPA was in contact with yet.

In fact, the only shared contact the UPA and the Hierarchy had
was the La-Tar Cluster, and since the negotiation was officially
between the Hierarchy and the Cluster, they definitely didn't count.
The only option on the table, of course, was the Drifters.

And that was why Sylvia made her way down the steps to face the robed and masked figure at the center of the auditorium. It was the same Ancient with the blue-whorl-marked silver mask as the last time, and they bowed slightly as she approached.

"Ambassador Todorovich, it seems the Kozun have listed several conditions for your negotiations," they told her. "We of Blue Stripe Green Stripe Orange Stripe are prepared to help you meet those conditions, if you so desire."

"It seems to me that the Convoy will ask for payment for such assistance," Sylvia pointed out. "And that such payment shouldn't be borne by merely one side of the negotiation."

"We could not send three Guardians away from the Convoy without significant compensation, no," blue-whorls agreed. "This Council could not do so, in fact, without guaranteed compensation."

"You did not answer my question," Sylvia pointed out. "Did the Kozun offer you any payment for this service?"

Blue-whorls chuckled and made a conceding gesture with his left hand.

"They did," he allowed. "Their payment would suffice for *half* of the rental of three Guardians. We will require payment for the Cluster's side as well, to guarantee our neutrality."

If one side was shouldering all of the mercenaries' bill, after all, the mercenaries weren't neutral.

Sylvia kept her face calm as she studied the Face Mask of the Councilor, then glanced around the tree-shrouded meeting space. They were right, both in that she didn't want the Kozun to be paying for their entire bill, and that in sending three Guardians away from the fleet was a major ask.

They probably didn't *need* three Guardians. But that was clearly what Blue Stripe Green Stripe Orange Stripe were going to send, which meant that the Cluster had to pay for it—and Sylvia was speaking for the Cluster there.

Which meant the UPA was going to pay for it.

"Well, then," she said. "Let us begin, then, with my rejecting the suggestion you are about to make. We will under no circumstances trade the gravity-shield technology for *anything*. I am prepared to pay in refined metals and willing to consider other potential agreements, but that is specifically off the table."

From the shuffling around her, that had been exactly what blue-whorls had been about to suggest—and no one there was particularly surprised by her shutting it down.

"It would certainly be our preference to trade in technology and change your thoughts on that point," blue-whorls admitted. "If that is not possible, for a task of this magnitude, refined metals will not be enough. They will be required as an initial payment, but future value must also be agreed upon."

"And what did you have in mind?" Sylvia asked carefully. She still had five tons of refined palladium and ten of refined iridium to work with, but she wasn't sure if that would be enough for even half of three Guardians.

"We require exclusive trading rights with the La-Tar Cluster for a period of no less than four thousand Kenmiri days," the Councilor told her. "Plus either eleven tons of refined palladium or twenty-two tons of refined iridium.

"The UPA will not give up our own trading rights to the La-Tar Cluster," she replied. "With that codicil, I am prepared to discuss *shared* exclusive rights with the government of the Cluster. I cannot fully commit them to that without discussions that are impossible from here.

"I can offer ten tons of refined iridium and, say, three tons of refined palladium, as well."

The councilors exchanged looks and she could hear whispered conversations behind the masks. The Drifters didn't have internal networks, but they *definitely* had radios built into their Face Masks.

"This is acceptable *if* the Convoy is permitted to establish a trading post in a UPA system with a population of at least four hundred million," blue-whorls finally told her.

Only decades of practice kept Sylvia's face calm. The United

Planets Alliance didn't have an *official* isolationist policy, but the general tone of her government's actions since the war had been to keep the former Kenmiri Empire in their own stars.

She had the authority to agree to said trading post, but she wasn't sure how well it would go down. On the other hand, it would probably be *good* for the UPA to have an alien presence in their own worlds.

"Done," she said sharply. "Details will need to be established later, but I can commit the United Planets Alliance to permit a trading enclave in the Procyon System."

Procyon had two billion people and was the closest of the major eight UPA systems to the former Empire. Sylvia wasn't entirely sure what a Drifter trading enclave would even *look* like, but it would probably be valuable to both sides.

"Then we have a deal," the Councilor told her. "We will send a trio of our Guardians to the Lon System for the agreed upon time. Is there anything else you would desire of us, Ambassador?"

"I believe our business is done," she allowed. "It has been a pleasure to trade with you, Councilors. I will have the final installment of cargo delivered while we retrieve our crew from *Trust in Fortune*, and then *Shaka* will leave for La-Tar."

She'd be sending a skip drone as soon as she was back aboard the destroyer, though. That way, everyone would know what was coming.

Soon enough, *Shaka* would be back in unquestionably friendly skies—and Sylvia Todorovich would be transferring back to *Raven*. Entirely to be aboard the more impressive and better-defended vessel.

Entirely.

Nothing to do with spending time with *Raven*'s captain.

CHAPTER SIXTEEN

"She did it." Iyotake sounded stunned as the briefing video from Todorovich ended. *Raven*'s senior officers were gathered around the table in their conference room, all of them looking at the spot where the hologram had just disappeared, with various levels of surprise.

"I had faith in Em Todorovich," Henry told his XO. "But yes. I'm more than a little surprised by the level of willingness to talk the Kozun are showing. There are only seven Voices of the Kozun, after all."

"What does that mean for the negotiations?" Ihejirika asked, the tactical officer looking thoughtful.

"It means that Mal Dakis is sending someone who absolutely speaks for him, who can commit the Hierarchy and who likely has no limits on what they're permitted to offer," Henry concluded. "The Voices are theoretically equal. No one is going to pretend the other six don't answer to Dakis, but he can't gainsay anything they say in public, either."

"Not without shooting another round of prophets, anyway," Alex Thompson said grimly. *Raven*'s GroundDiv commander was a solidly built blue-eyed and blond-haired man who could have stepped off a recruiting poster. "If he disavows a Voice's actions, I'm guessing he has to disavow the Voice entirely."

"And that's a threat to his power base he can't risk," Iyotake guessed. "So, if he's sending a Voice, he trusts them?"

"Completely," Henry said. "I'm as surprised by the escort rules as anything else," he continued. "I was half-expecting them to try to prevent us bringing *Raven*, but the requirement to bring a UPSF ship...they're practically inviting us. Specifically."

"Trap?" O'Flannagain suggested, the fighter officer looking tense. "They could be setting us up."

"They definitely could be," Henry conceded. "We're expecting some kind of trouble."

Only Iyotake and Moon were cleared to know about Yellow Bicycle. *Scorpius* and her battle group were two days away from their jump-off point, one skip away from La-Tar. That, if Henry was reading the timing right, would be perfect.

If the Kozun wanted to start a fight, they were going to have an ugly surprise coming.

"We'll probably bring *Glorious* with us, unless the La-Tar want to bring two ships of their own," he continued, letting that comment sink without notice. He'd brief his people on Yellow Bicycle once they were on their way—they'd need to know then and there'd be less chance of a leak.

"Who do you think they'll send to negotiate for them?" Iyotake asked. "I'm guessing we're not running that negotiation?"

"No, from what Todorovich said, we only took the lead with the Drifters because we had existing structures there and the Cluster didn't really," Henry said. "The Cluster will lead at Lon. I'm guessing they'll send Rising Principle. They spoke well to put together the alliance and their parent trusts them."

"And Adamant Will, whether they like it or not, is now First Standard of the Council of Supply," Iyotake agreed.

Adamant Will was an Enteni, the former head of the emergency council that had functioned as an underground government during the Kozun occupation. Their sole child was Rising Principle, the Enteni diplomat *Raven* had hauled around to every world in the Cluster to assemble an army.

"Well, I look forward to meeting the flytrap again," O'Flannagain observed, her tone jokingly disrespectful. "They had a surprisingly good sense of humor for a walking plant."

"Perhaps you think that because you have a terrible sense of humor for a human," Iyotake said repressively. "Behave, Commander. We have work to do."

"Your fighters are going to be one of our aces in the hole," Henry reminded the CAG. "There's a reason we kept you under wraps in Satra. The GMS birds are going to be an ugly shock to anyone who tries to jump this conference."

"That's what we're here for, boss," O'Flannagain agreed with a casual salute. "FighterDiv keeps everyone else breathing."

Henry forced his incipient grimace into a smile and a nod. Like O'Flannagain, he knew the corollary to that joke: FighterDiv *died* to keep everyone else breathing.

He'd lost too many friends and subordinates over the war to have forgotten that.

TO HENRY'S SURPRISE, O'Flannagain waited while everyone else left. A few moments after he'd dismissed the meeting, he was alone in the briefing room with his CAG and arched a questioning eyebrow at the younger woman.

"What trouble are you in this time, Samira?" he asked.

"No trouble," she told him. "Why do you assume I'm in trouble?"

"Because even though you've improved dramatically, you were sent to me as a discipline case," Henry observed. She'd had one *epic* drunken disaster before they'd hashed out some of her issues—mostly that crashing after a dogfight left her looking for alcohol or sex, neither of which was safely available to a senior officer on a battle-cruiser.

"And I think we both know that Old Man Barrie sent me to you because he figured you'd get what was going on," O'Flannagain told him. "*He* certainly did, though the CAG on *Scorpius* wasn't as, ah, patient."

Henry winced.

"Please...do not refer to my ex-husband as 'old man' to my face," he noted stiffly. "I accept that neither of us are spring chickens anymore, but Commodore Barrie is only a year older than I am."

O'Flannagain snorted.

"Maybe it's his gold oak leaf, ser, but...you're a stiff with a stick up your ass, but he's *old*."

Henry raised a warning finger. He'd tolerate quite a bit from O'Flannagain—she was a spectacular pilot and growing into a more-than-competent officer—but there *were* lines.

"I assume you did not stay behind to remind me about my ex," he told her. He was *reasonably* sure that his CAG didn't know about Yellow Bicycle, either, so she wouldn't know why Peter Barrie was currently on Henry's mind.

"What's up?"

"Todorovich is on her way back?" she asked.

"Yeah. *Shaka* would have left about six hours after the skip drone." He shrugged. "They'll be here in two days."

"La-Tar might be focused on food production, but they've *got* gardens," O'Flannagain pointed out. "I'm pretty sure you could find a florist in two days."

Henry stared at the redheaded woman blankly for a moment.

"And *why* would I need a florist?" he asked.

O'Flannagain chuckled and took a seat on the briefing room's table, one leg tucked under her in an awkward-looking fashion.

"I know your type, boss," she told him. "Takes you a long time to fall, but when you do, you fall *hard*. And you've been falling for the Ambassador at *least* since Tano."

"That's quite the assumption to make," Henry replied automatically. "The Ambassador isn't my type."

His oft-repeated joke sounded false even to *him*, though. The joke was that *no one* was his type—he'd been attracted to three people in his entire life. Except...O'Flannagain was correct. *Four* people.

"*She's* been making eyes at you since before that," the fighter pilot told him. "And she's not in your chain of command."

This time, Henry held up a warning hand, and O'Flannagain, thankfully, stopped.

"Might I suggest that matchmaking your captain is generally considered poor form?" he said drily. "I'm twenty years older than you, Commander, I can handle my own relationships."

O'Flannagain gave him a completely undiscouraged grin.

"But like most men, you can use the occasional brick to the head," she replied. "To realize what *you're* thinking, let alone what she's thinking."

"Even coming from FighterDiv, there are days I swear we give you rocket-jocks too long of a leash," Henry said with a chuckle. "Consider your brick thrown, Commander, and butt out."

"Wilco," she said, then paused with a thoughtful look on her face.

"What is it?" Henry asked.

"*Rocket-jock*," she echoed back at him. "There's no rockets on a One-Thirty, Skipper. Some maneuvering jets, but they're so secondary as to be irrelevant. We're going to have to come up with a new slang for fighter pilot."

He shook his head at her and latched on to the change of subject.

"I've tried your simulators for the Lancer," he reminded her. "There's definitely some *rocketing* going on, even if we aren't leaving burnt hydrogen anywhere anymore. If we can reliably get the damn things into space, they're going to be useful."

"We're working on that," O'Flannagain said. "We've got the first squadron in actual service; problems were going to happen."

"Let's hope they don't happen when we have a Kozun battle group charging at us with blood in their eyes," Henry told her.

BACK IN HIS OFFICE, Henry caught himself looking to see if there was a florist on the space stations above La-Tar without fully realizing what he was doing.

He had to laugh. He wasn't entirely sure he bought in to O'Flannagain's "brick," but he definitely missed Todorovich. The sharp-edged diplomat had been a valuable partner ever since he'd been tasked with transporting her to the Great Gathering of the Vesheron.

Most of his work since then had been ferrying her around as they tried to hold together the worlds the Kenmiri had abandoned. They'd been in each other's back pockets the whole time, and he'd grown used to having her to lean on for advice and counsel.

He was pretty sure *that* feeling was mutual. They had different points of view and skillsets, which meant that she had useful opinions on his missions, and he hoped he had useful insights on hers.

There was a large gap between *that* and the type of romantic and physical interest that O'Flannagain was suggesting. She'd made jokes about Todorovich being interested in Henry before, but he'd written those off as jokes.

Except.

Except that he was self-aware enough to realize that she was right. It would have taken him longer to realize it on his own, but now he was facing up to it, she was right. At some point, Sylvia Todorovich had slipped over that invisible line in his head from *person* to *attractive person*.

That was something that happened rarely enough for Henry that he wasn't sure how to deal with it even when it *wasn't* potentially a giant complication. Sylvia Todorovich might be a civilian and outside his chain of command, but she'd also been his civilian counterpart and his partner for a year now.

He couldn't risk disrupting the well-oiled machine they'd become. Working together, they'd saved the La-Tar Cluster. Working together, he was certain they could negotiate the peace the Cluster needed to rebuild safely.

So long as they had to work together, trying to make something more of their professional relationship was not only stupid—it was *dangerous*. Friction between them could end up risking other people's lives.

And *that* was unacceptable to Henry Wong. *Personal* was not the same as *important*.

Thanks to O'Flannagain, he was aware of the trap his emotions had laid for him now. He could prevent it from causing problems when Todorovich returned aboard *Raven*...but he wasn't going to need flowers anytime soon.

CHAPTER SEVENTEEN

Shaka emerged into the La-Tar System exactly on schedule, leaving Sylvia clenching the arms of the chair in her quarters tightly. Skipping was never pleasant, but for whatever reason, the skip back to La-Tar this time had been even harder than normal.

"Ambassador Todorovich?" Captain Chavez's voice echoed in her implants. "We have arrived in La-Tar and are on course for the planet. I make our estimated time of arrival eighteen hundred hours GMT.

"Do you know where we'll be dropping you off yet?"

Six hours to travel six light-minutes was reasonable, even if it left Sylvia feeling impatient.

"Let's plan for First City," she replied. "I can relay from there to *Raven* or one of the Cluster ships if needed, but I need to speak with the First Standard and the Arbiter before we do anything else."

"Understood, Ambassador. I'll have a shuttle standing by for you and your staff when we reach orbit," Chavez promised. "Is there anything else you need from us before you arrive?"

"No, thank you, Captain," she said. "You and your crew have done everything I could desire. I appreciate all you've done and hope your crew get a chance to take some R&R in a more normal circumstance soon."

"If nothing else, Em Ambassador, we're back in a space where I can run my crew through exercises," he told her. "I couldn't justify those while we were with the Convoy."

"Good to hear, on both counts," Sylvia replied. "Thank you, Captain."

"*Shaka*'s pleasure, Em Ambassador."

The channel closed and Sylvia regarded the virtual screen her internal network was projecting on her eyes. The screen showed what little data the UPA had on the Lon System, but she wasn't seeing the blue giant.

She was seeing a mixed-race face, with Chinese angles softened by American chubbiness. She'd missed Henry Wong and not, if she were being honest, just because she could use his advice.

But Sylvia Todorovich was not much of a believer in the "friend zone." Her attachment to Henry might not be merely platonic, but the man was a worthy friend and that was far more than a consolation prize.

She was looking forward to going through her experiences with the Drifters with him. His insights would be useful, especially since she suspected the Drifters were trying to play more than one game.

There were a lot of layers going on at the peace conference she'd just spent most of a month arranging. The UPA didn't want to keep a battlecruiser group in the La-Tar Cluster for extended periods, so they wanted to reduce the threat to their ally.

The Cluster wanted peace—but also justice for wrecked ships and murdered innocents. The Kozun had agreed to peace talks more quickly than Sylvia had expected, which suggested that they had their own agenda there. And then there were the Drifters, theoretical neutrals who inevitably had an agenda of their own.

It was going to be a *fascinating* meeting.

✯✯✯

"WELCOME TO FIRST CITY, AMBASSADOR TODOROVICH," the armed Eerdish soldier greeted Sylvia in Kem. The Eerdish were an Ashall race that looked almost identical to humanity, though their skin tones started at Earth-African black and ranged up to pale green.

The man giving Sylvia a fist-to-chest salute had dark green skin and familiar features as he smiled.

"Trosh," she greeted him. "How are you doing?"

Trosh had been the noncommissioned officer–equivalent in charge of Rising Principle's personal security during their extended tour of the La-Tar Cluster.

"I am doing well," he replied carefully, gesturing to the small squad of soldiers with him. "The Arbiter asked that I meet you at the shuttle pad and see you safely to the meeting."

The brilliant sunlight at First City was almost painful to Sylvia's eyes, but she could see several low-slung cars behind Trosh. Like almost every piece of hardware on La-Tar, the cars would have been manufactured off-world.

"My staff and escorts will need to accompany me," she warned Trosh.

"Of course; we brought enough vehicles for an extra twenty."

Sylvia laughed.

"That is a few more than needed," she conceded. "Lead the way, Trosh."

She was sure the Ashall officer had a rank of some kind, but no one had ever given it to her. The Cluster's military was still in the process of taking shape as a unified entity, with five different planets' worth of personnel from seven different species.

It was a chaotic mess she was glad she wasn't responsible for, but it seemed Trosh had his own team well in hand. The cars moved up and opened in smooth order, allowing Sylvia and her people to board with mixed local and GroundDiv escorts.

"Are there any threats I should be worried about?" she asked Trosh, looking at the scale of the escort.

"We do not know of any, but we cannot risk the Ambassador from the United Planets Alliance," the noncom told her. "We value both our alliance and you highly."

"I appreciate that, I think," Sylvia replied with a chuckle.

LA-TAR HAD minimal local industry and a *lot* of agriculture, but the administration of a planetwide agriculture system required vast numbers of clerks and bureaucrats and logistics managers and...

First City was one of several metropolises on the planet that existed to support that infrastructure. When the Kenmiri had left, that bureaucracy had turned itself from managing the planet on behalf of their overlords to trying to make sure five worlds stayed fed.

Despite the interruption due to the Kozun, they'd managed it. The estimates Sylvia had seen suggested that the Cluster had lost several million people to hunger—but they *could* have lost up to ninety percent of the population of the industrial worlds.

There had been a Kenmiri governor, and there was the traditional Kenmiri governor's palace, which was where Sylvia was expecting to be taken. They drove past that site, however, and she saw that a work crew was busily dismantling the luxurious residence.

Presumably, the underground command bunker would remain intact, but she saw the propaganda virtues of destroying that symbol rather than using it.

Instead, their convoy drove into the central administration district, where a cluster of hundred-story towers held the tens of thousands of workers who had turned their skills from extracting the largest quantity of food from their planet to trying to run a balanced economy across five star systems.

They stopped at a seemingly random tower, and Trosh's people formed a perimeter to allow Sylvia and her people to access the office building. While there was nothing aggressive or forceful about the perimeter, there were definitely crowds gathering outside it.

Sylvia was halfway into the building when she realized the crowds had gathered to see *her*, the human diplomat who had helped save their world. She'd spent so long fighting the Kenmiri that she barely registered what she'd done for La-Tar as unusual.

To the crowds carefully gathering to try to get a glimpse of her, she was one of a handful of people responsible for saving their entire planet.

She took a moment to look over the crowd and wave back to them. It was a small gesture, but it seemed to mean something to the La-Tars—and it helped remind her what she was working toward.

THE ARBITER'S office was completely barren. A corner office two-thirds of the way up the building, it had probably belonged to a senior Artisan-caste Kenmiri, but the decorations had been stripped down to a desk, a table, and the chairs around each.

The view of the city was enough. First City was small to Sylvia's eyes—and likely to Casto Ran's, given the industrial factory-cities he was used to—but it had been built on hills that couldn't be readily farmed.

Those hills gave it an enviable elevation, and from the tower on the edge of the central cluster, the view stretched out for untold miles of glittering golden fields.

Casto Ran stood next to the glass, looking out at those fields. Two familiar-looking Enteni were perched on stools near the table, and those three were the only occupants of the room.

"Arbiter Casto Ran," Sylvia greeted the semi-elected leader of the La-Tar Cluster in their shared Kem. "Standard Adamant Will. Rising Principle."

She wasn't sure what title Adamant Will's child would currently command, though their presence suggested they'd be the Cluster's representative at the peace conference.

"Thank you for coming, Ambassador," Ran told her, still looking out at the fields. "We received the update from your skip drone. The Kozun have agreed to meet with us."

It wasn't a question, but Sylvia nodded anyway.

"They have. More quickly than I expected," she said. "They may need peace themselves, more than we anticipated."

"If they have-will aggravate all the worlds around them, then they must-will make peace or fate-time will see their ending," Adamant Will replied. "The news we receive is-was of war all around them."

"The Kozun made no friends in their expansion," Ran agreed. "They may well see us as the one conflict they have an opportunity to end before they lose too much while they are challenged on other fronts. We may be able to exert more pressure than we hoped."

"The opportunity to make alliances and push them back exists," Sylvia said. "The UPA has no interest in a war of that magnitude, and our commitments to the Cluster are entirely defensive, but I would be remiss as an ally to not point that opportunity out."

"We can-will not be the agents of fate-time death on that scale," Adamant Will told her. "Our children must-will cry for peace."

"Almost as importantly, dragging the Cluster into an extended war would be an obstacle to establishing proper long-term governance," Ran said, finally turning around and joining the two Enteni at the table.

"The mandate I wield is one I was given by the various leaderships of our worlds, but none of those leaderships are the unquestioned voices of their people," he noted. "I am designated to arbitrate conflicts between worlds, not decide the fates of all of our worlds at once.

"If the Cluster is to wage war, that decision should belong to a government that is truly chosen by and speaks for the entire population. *I* lack the moral authority to commit our worlds to a conflict that is not solely in our defense."

"The United Planets Alliance is fully committed to assist in the security of the La-Tar Cluster," Sylvia reiterated. "We acted as your agent to arrange this conference, but this is a conference between you and the Hierarchy. The UPA is…more than an observer, but we are not at war with the Kozun."

"I am not certain the Kozun must-will see these fate-times the same," Rising Principle noted, the younger Enteni sounding amused even through the translator.

"As I reminded the Drifters when they suggested the same thing, the Hierarchy knows how the UPA makes war," Sylvia said. "They still exist, which means they are not at war with us."

It would take roughly two-thirds of the active UPSF units to guarantee victory over the Hierarchy, but Sylvia knew that the UPA could have sent those ships and soldiers if they'd actually felt threatened by the Kozun.

The Peacekeeper Initiative was out there to try and fix the problems the Kenmiri had left behind, but it would forever be the poor sibling among the UPSF. The United Planets Security Council did not think anything in the Ra Sector could threaten the UPA—and that the forces that could were a long way away.

"Like the Kozun, I have seen the UPSF make war," Ran said quietly. "I would rather not see that ruthlessness again."

"Neither would we," Sylvia agreed. "At this point, Arbiter Ran, the next steps are up to you. We know that a Voice of the Kozun will be in the Lon System in ten days. We are prepared to provide the one UPSF unit the Hierarchy requested, and I will, of course, accompany the delegation.

"But the delegation must be the Cluster's and the choices must be yours."

The room was silent for a full minute.

"Ambassador Rising Principle will speak for the Cluster," Ran finally told her, gesturing to the Enteni diplomat. "They have served all of our people well before and I have faith in them."

"Your assistance is-was of immense value before and can-will be of immense value again," Rising Principle told Sylvia. "We would-will be ecstatic if you joined us."

"I intend to," she replied. "My intention, that I will confirm with

Colonel Wong, is to travel aboard *Raven* to the Lon System. The Kozun requested that each side bring three ships."

"We will send *Carpenter* with Rising Principle aboard," Ran said instantly.

Carpenter was one of the escorts he'd commanded as a Vesheron leader. As Sylvia understood it, those ships had the most experienced and long-standing crews available to the Cluster.

"Given the need for security over firepower, I would ask that the UPSF provide a second ship," Ran continued. "One of your destroyers would add more survivability to the delegation than another of our escorts."

"*Carpenter* has-will be updated to act as a meeting site," Rising Principle told Sylvia.

Sylvia didn't know what that might entail from the Cluster's perspective, but it would probably be useful.

"Again, I will need to confer with Captain Wong," she admitted. "But I see no problem with us committing both *Raven* and one of our destroyers to the delegation.

"I did also commit to the Drifters to present their price for providing the neutral security detail to you," she continued. "Blue Stripe Green Stripe Orange Stripe required exclusive trading rights with the La-Tar Cluster—shared with the UPA—for ten Kenmiri years in exchange for this service."

Ran's head tendrils twitched.

"You did not, I note, commit us to this without our permission," he said. "That is appreciated, though I see little choice on our part unless we want to abandon the entire conference."

"It is possible that you could negotiate a different deal if you reached out to them yourselves," Sylvia said. "I did not have the authority or the desire to commit you myself."

"Which is, again, appreciated," Ran told her. "But the reality is what the reality is. We will agree to these trading rights." His tendrils shivered again. "It is not as if we are trading with anyone other than ourselves and the UPA so far. I do not surrender much."

"They have committed three Guardian warships to secure the conference," she said. "I do not believe the Kozun even *have* a force that could defeat three Guardians in battle."

"Even with the UPSF's support, I am certain that *we* do not," Casto Ran agreed. "We will want to get our ships in motion sooner, Ambassador. If we are agreed on the plan, I ask that you speak with Captain Wong and we will prepare our expedition."

"Of course, Arbiter," Sylvia said with a small bow. "The UPA is here to support your people in any way we can."

CHAPTER EIGHTEEN

If O'Flannagain hadn't already smashed a brick into Henry's emotional state, his reaction to waiting for Sylvia Todorovich to arrive aboard *Raven* would have been enough of a hint on its own. Years of practice kept his face impassive as he stood with a formal welcome contingent, but he was *nervous* to see her again.

He found that realization more than a little amusing, using it as a shield against the emotional somersault his heart turned when the Ambassador stepped out of the shuttle in *Raven*'s bay.

He was fifty-one years old, for crying out loud. He had no business reacting like a lovestruck schoolboy at the sight of a conservatively dressed forty-year-old woman.

"Company, attention!"

The GroundDiv honor guard snapped to obey the barked order, creating a clear path from the shuttle ramp to where Henry and Iyotake were waiting.

Todorovich gave the guards a firm nod of acknowledgement and crossed the shuttlebay, her own staff trailing behind her like a flock of goslings.

"Welcome back aboard *Raven*, Ambassador Todorovich," Henry

greeted her, taking her hand and bowing over it. "We are delighted to once again play host to your delegation."

"*Delighted*, is it?" she replied with a smile. "That might be the most pleased a UPSF crew has ever been to have us aboard."

"Most UPSF crews didn't watch you save five star systems, Ambassador," he said. "*Raven* knows your worth."

"And I know *Raven*'s," she agreed. "I have detailed updates that weren't in the skip drone, and I presume you have updates for me. Can we schedule a meeting for once I have my staff settled?"

"I have several slots clear this afternoon, Ambassador," Henry confirmed. "And you and Em Leitz are invited to dine with myself and the senior officers this evening, of course."

"We'd be *delighted*," she said, with a sharp sparkle of amusement in her eyes. She turned back to her chief of staff. "Felix, check over our schedule versus the captain's and schedule a meeting for myself at the best time you see fit."

Henry coughed delicately.

"Bring Em Leitz, please," he told her quietly. "I'll have Iyotake as well. Our...understudies need to be briefed on some things as well."

"I see," she said. "Felix, include yourself in that meeting."

"Yes, ser," the chief of staff confirmed. "Anyone else I should include, Captain?"

"No," Henry said. "Just the four of us."

He needed to brief the two senior diplomats on Yellow Bicycle, but the fewer people who knew about their covert backup, the more likely they were to be able to keep it secret.

"Understood. Well, the sooner we get ourselves settled and unpacked, the better off we are," Todorovich told him. "Shall we get to it?"

"Chief Headley, please show the Ambassador and her staff to their quarters," Iyotake said from beside Henry. The Chief Steward had managed to be almost invisibly unobtrusive up to that point, materializing from behind Henry with three large muscular subordinates to take the diplomats' luggage.

V

MOST OF THE TIME, Henry was willing to trust his crew one hundred percent. Despite his orders to keep Yellow Bicycle secret, he wasn't overly worried about it leaking to his officers and spacers—he trusted their discretion and their competence. Equally, he had faith in the obstacles that would prevent Kozun intelligence agents getting any reports back to the Hierarchy. With the Kenmiri subspace network permanently offline, interstellar communications were slow and obvious.

But his orders said Yellow Bicycle remained need-to-know, kept from even his senior officers until they were on their way. His XO and his communications officer knew, but that was it.

That meant he needed a secure briefing room to talk to Todorovich and Leitz in. Fortunately, *Raven*'s designers had lavished every security measure imaginable on the captain's office. The small breakout meeting room attached to his working space was just as secure as the battlecruiser's three official secure briefing rooms.

That room was more than large enough for this meeting, and he gave his steward a grateful nod as she laid a tray of prepared coffees on the table and added a carafe of black coffee.

"The ambassador is on her way," the noncom told him. "Do you need anything else, ser? I have a tray of donuts about to come out of the oven as well. They should beat the Ambassador here."

"That sounds perfect, Em Guarneri," Henry replied. "Thank you."

The donuts arrived at the same time as Todorovich in the end, allowing the ambassador to carefully snag what appeared to be a glazed carrot donut in careful fingers as she passed the tray.

Iyotake and Leitz at least waited for the tray to be placed on the table before grabbing snacks of their own. Henry was well aware of the quality of treats the officers' mess put out and was perfectly willing to grab a donut last.

None of the pastries would have been unacceptable, after all.

"We've sorted out a plan for meeting the Kozun?" he asked Todorovich as she finished her donut and wiped her fingers on a napkin.

"We have," she said. "You saw most of the details we sent, yes?"

"Went over the entire package with my officers, yes," he confirmed. "Three ships from each side, three Guardians from the Drifters. It sounds balanced but has the potential to be messy."

"It does," Todorovich agreed. "The Cluster has asked us to send *Raven* and one of the destroyers to escort their ship. They seem to think that our warships are more protected than theirs."

"They're not wrong," Henry said. "I'd been planning on something like that. We'll bring *Glorious* with us—she's one of the *Significance*-class ships, with almost half again the firepower of the *Tyrannosaurs* that make up the rest of the battle group."

"That's your area of expertise, not mine," she said. "I promised I would discuss it with you and make sure we were bringing the right ships."

"They're sending an escort, I presume?" Henry asked. "I imagine they wouldn't want to risk *Sunshine* with just UPSF protectors."

"*Carpenter*," she confirmed. "Apparently, she's been refitted to handle this kind of mission. I have no idea what that looks like, but I'll take their comments at face value for now."

"Did the Kozun give any sign of what kind of ships they'll be sending?" he said.

As he spoke, he was giving his internal network commands. Six holographic models appeared above his desk. *Raven*, *Glorious* and *Carpenter* were all true-to-life, current images from *Raven*'s sensors. The three Guardians were placeholders, standardized versions of a type of ship that was never standard.

"Only that they were sending three ships. My understanding is they don't even *have* three ships that could stand up to a Guardian one-on-one?"

"They have *one*," Henry confirmed. A new model appeared above the table, hovering away from the other two groups. "The

Kenmiri-built dreadnought *Mal Toranis*, named for Mal Dakis's grandfather.

"They lost their other dreadnought at the Gathering." Under the command of an assassin-turned-diplomat, the ship had tried to ambush *Raven*. It hadn't ended well for the Kozun warship.

"Are they likely to send *Toranis*?" Leitz asked, the chief of staff looking askance at the model of the dreadnought. It was smaller than the Guardians but it was also more clearly built for this exact purpose. The eight-hundred-meter-long dreadnought was sleek and intimidating in a way the crudely assembled Guardians weren't.

"No," Henry guessed, waving the ship away. "From what I understand, *Toranis* hasn't left the Kozun System since Mal Dakis took control of his homeworld. She is the last line of defense for the Kozun Hierarchy, and they won't risk sending her out."

"My guess would be that we'll be looking at one of their new cruisers with a pair of escorts," he continued. Holograms of those ships appeared where *Toranis* had vanished. The escorts were rough ovoids, a familiar shape to them all. The Kenmiri had built the half-megaton warships in their thousands to maintain order across the Empire.

The broad flying-wing shape of the cruiser was new, and there were still a lot of questions around the vessel's capabilities. *Raven* had fought and defeated one at La-Tar, but that only meant that the remaining units had probably been upgraded.

"Can we handle that force?" Todorovich asked.

"The Kozun force? Yes," Henry replied. "*Raven* was designed to engage and destroy dreadnoughts. I'm *concerned* by Kozun cruisers, especially since the Kozun clearly have sufficient resonance disruptor warheads to pose a real threat to our gravity shields, but I'm confident in our ability to handle a single cruiser."

All nine vessels hung above the table, and Henry pointed an accusatory finger at the Drifters.

"I'm worried about the Drifters," he admitted. "Blue Stripe Green Stripe Orange Stripe was in what is now Remnant space during Golden Lancelot and didn't leave for some time afterward. They weren't in the right place to supply the pirates who ambushed *Raven* on our way to the Gathering, but they have definitely followed a course that would have allowed them to supply the Kozun with disruptor warheads."

The breakout room was quiet.

"That was the Diplomatic Corps's assessment as well," Todorovich said. "It's possible that the Hierarchy developed the disruptor warheads themselves and provided them to those pirates, but the Drifters had far more exposure to our ships in action than any other single Vesheron group."

"If anyone had the data to develop a weapon against our gravity shields, it was them," Henry agreed. "While *this* Convoy wasn't in position to supply those pirates, IntelDiv was keeping tabs on several at the time that could have managed it.

"And since the subspace network was still online at that point, the Drifters could have been acting as a single group then. They lost that with the rest of us, but they may still be following a plan they set into motion before the Gathering."

All four of them looked at the three Guardians in the floating display for a few seconds. They were ramshackle ships, assembled from whatever was to hand, but they all shared extremely powerful energy screens and large numbers of the same superheavy plasma turrets that made the Kenmiri dreadnoughts so dangerous.

"So, what do we do?" Leitz asked. "Are you expecting them to betray us?"

"I think the Kozun betraying us is more likely," Henry admitted. "If the Drifters betray us, though, *Raven* and our Cluster friends can't win that fight. Potentially, given sufficient warning, I can cover *Carpenter*'s retreat, but I can't fight three Guardians.

"However, UPSF command has even less trust for either of these groups than I do," he told them. "Lieutenant Colonel Iyotake is already briefed on this, but I'm tasked to update our senior diplomats on Operation Yellow Bicycle."

"*Yellow Bicycle?*" Leitz asked.

"All operation names are randomly generated," Todorovich explained before Henry could say anything. "You've piqued my curiosity, Captain. What is this operation?"

"If everything goes according to plan, you have a peaceful and calm discussion with the Kozun and we resolve the conflict between them and the Cluster," he said. "If that happens, there will never be any sign that Yellow Bicycle existed. It is a backup plan for if one or both of our counterparts in the Lon System betray us.

"If we are betrayed, however, Yellow Bicycle has been put in place to make certain that we have heavy reinforcements one skip away. Timing will be a problem, given minimum skip times, but having an entire carrier group one skip away is much more helpful than having them in UPA space."

"An entire carrier group?" Todorovich said.

"Battle Group *Scorpius* will have received the update on the peace conference by now and will have adjusted their course," Henry said. "I don't have a name or a designation for the system they will be waiting in, but it is on my maps. We will make certain that our skip drones back to La-Tar and the UPA pass through that system, allowing Commodore Barrie and Admiral Cheung to remain fully updated on the situation."

"That is reassuring," the ambassador noted drily. "I'm surprised the UPSF was willing to even lend the Initiative a fleet carrier, let alone her entire battle group."

"Yellow Bicycle is not an Initiative operation," Henry admitted. "Battle Group *Scorpius* remains part of Fifth Fleet and answerable to the regular chain of command. This operation is intended to minimize a threat to the actual Alliance as opposed to our Ra Sector allies and protectorates."

"I see." She brought a holographic map up above the table, shifting the images of the ships to one side. "I take it our route to the Lon System will bypass the carrier group?"

"Yes. The shortest route for our drones back to Zion, however, passes through the system they will be waiting in," Henry told her. The ship models vanished with a thought, allowing the map to be more clearly seen.

"Do we have an allowance for what happens if we *stop* communicating?" Todorovich asked. "That seems almost more likely, unfortunately, than our calling for help."

"There's nothing official in the orders I've seen," Henry admitted. "I imagine that Cheung would deploy forward if he didn't hear from us, but I don't think there is an exact time frame specified."

"We'll want to fix that. Am I able to communicate with the Admiral?" she asked.

"I see no reason not to," he said. "Talk to Moon; she's fully in the loop on this and has been including small detours on several of her drones. You should be able to exchange messages with the Admiral with...well, about the delays we'd expect. We do want to make sure we don't do anything too obvious with the drones."

"So, we're not even telling the Cluster?" Leitz asked. "That seems...rude."

"*Scorpius* isn't entering anyone's claimed space," Henry noted. "The Lon System is enough away from everyone that no one regards it as strategically important; that's why the Kozun picked it.

"That works to our desires, as it means Admiral Cheung will bypass everyone getting into position...and returning to the UPA, if everything goes smoothly.

"We don't want to admit we ever had a carrier group outside the UPA," he told them. "My understanding is that the reason for that is twofold: one, that the Security Council doesn't want to be seen spending that much money outside Terran space right now; and two, that we don't want our allies thinking that we are willing to send carrier groups out to fix their problems.

"A potential betrayal by the Drifters represents the first thing I've seen Command and the Council regard as a serious strategic threat since the war ended," Henry said flatly. "And I think they're right.

There are no other players as geographically widespread or as technologically advanced.

"Even the Kozun are operating with what is fundamentally the Kenmiri base-level tech. The Drifters aren't. They've been working on that tech for years, and they've been skimming off the best and brightest of the Kenmiri slave worlds for generations."

"They've been hugely valuable allies," Leitz reminded him. "It seems strange to regard them as such a threat."

"That's why Yellow Bicycle is as quiet and low-key as it is," Henry said. "We'd very much like to be wrong. If the Kozun are honestly coming to talk peace and the Drifters have made honest deals to be neutrals at the peace talks, then *Scorpius* and her escorts get an extensive exercise in long-distance logistics.

"But if our fears are realized, there will be multiple capital ships a day's flight away, ready to come haul us out of the fire."

Henry might not like the idea of being rescued by his ex-husband, but he'd take that over fighting a squadron of multiple Guardians without any kind of support or backup.

"That's reassuring, at least," Todorovich agreed. "I'm going to suggest a twenty-four-hour dead-man order to Admiral Cheung to make that even more reliable. If we don't send a message for twenty-four hours, he brings the carrier group through."

"We'll need to make sure we have the skip drones to send a message at least every twenty-four hours—preferably every twelve, really—but that limits the worst-case scenario."

"It does," Henry agreed. "I'll back you on that, Ambassador."

He looked at everyone in the room as he snagged a second donut.

"Iyotake, Em Leitz. Questions? This is only a high-level summary, though it's not like there's much in terms of detail to share."

"Do we know the skip time to the system they'll be waiting in?" Iyotake asked. "That could become critical."

"It's a red giant eleven light-years from Lon," Henry said. "We don't have exact masses for either star, but they're big. My calculations say nine hours, plus or minus forty minutes if the mass data is off significantly."

"So, we need a plan to survive against three Guardians for eighteen hours," Iyotake noted. "Even that is a hell of a call, ser."

"I know," Henry agreed. "But barring stealth tech the UPSF definitely doesn't have, we can't hide a fleet in the Lon System. We work with what we've got, Colonel."

"And we hope that I can keep everyone talking," Todorovich concluded. "No pressure, I take it?"

"Between the Cluster and the Hierarchy, these talks will decide the fate of twenty-one inhabited worlds and about fifty billion people," Henry said quietly. "I don't think worrying about betrayal should be adding much to the pressure."

CHAPTER NINETEEN

Home.

It was strange to Sylvia, but that was very much the feeling that being back aboard *Raven* was giving her. The crew wasn't entirely the same as it had been before, but the losses in the La-Tar Campaign hadn't been that large.

She hadn't known many of the dead well enough to grieve them, but she knew the people who remained well enough to trade greetings and courtesies with many of the battlecruiser's crew. *Shaka's* crew had been respectful enough and had grown more accepting of her over the time she'd spent aboard, but they hadn't made it to the level of warmth she shared with *Raven's* crew.

The stewarding crew had put her in the same quarters as her last stay aboard. If anything had changed while she'd been away, they'd made certain to put it back exactly the way she'd left it. By the time she got back from her meeting with Henry Wong, much of her gear had been unpacked for her and the room looked *exactly* as it had before.

It felt like home and she smiled to herself as she took a seat at *her* desk. If her experience with the UPSF suggested anything, this would be the last tour of *Raven*'s current complement. They'd all achieved too much for the next round of promotions not to tear huge holes in the battlecruiser's hierarchy.

If the UPSF were *smart*, they'd move people up inside *Raven*'s hierarchy and shift as few people off the ship as they could. That would keep the battlecruiser at nearly the same superb level of competence and function.

On the other hand, she could see why the UPSF would want to take the officers who'd been blooded at the Gathering and in the La-Tar Campaign and move them over to other ships. The Peacekeeper Initiative, especially, was in need of officers who'd fought alongside nonhumans and could both speak Kem and respect strangers.

Those three criteria were true of more of *Raven*'s officers than most ships, and that would only make it worse. The promotions would be well deserved, but they'd leave Henry Wong with gaping holes in his crew.

Assuming, of course, that Wong went unpromoted himself. Sylvia knew her own reports had been positive enough to contribute to his making the jump to a Commodore's gold oak leaf, and who knew what would happen to *Raven* when the man became the Peace-keeper Initiative's second flag officer.

She checked through her messages. They were much what she expected. Rising Principle and their escorts and staff would be aboard *Carpenter* by morning First City time. Once the Cluster representative was ready to go, the entire delegation would get underway in a few hours.

It would be five days to the Lon System. The scheduled date was a week away, though Sylvia expected the Kozun and Drifters to beat them there. Both the Kozun and the Drifters had slightly farther to go, but they'd known sooner than the Cluster had.

That didn't help her fear of a trap, but the UPSF seemed to have that well in hand.

She smiled as she remembered the meeting. It was good to be

back on *Raven* and it was good to see Henry Wong again. Hopefully, she'd have a chance to bend his ear in private after dinner.

Having spent time among the Drifters again, she was curious what his impression of them was. She'd always been in Convoys negotiating with them, but he'd actually fought alongside Drifter officers and been in forces that had relied on the Drifters for logistics.

The Drifter Convoys had been a critical component of Golden Lancelot, after all. The UPSF hadn't had the logistics infrastructure to launch their assassination attacks on the Kenmorad across the entire space of the Kenmiri Empire—only the Convoys had made that possible.

And now that she thought about it, she wondered if the UPA had warned the Drifters just what that operation entailed. It would have been...typical of how Golden Lancelot was conducted for the UPSF not to have told them.

They hadn't even told most of the officers involved what the full scope of the operation was, after all!

DINNER ONLY DOUBLED down the feeling of coming home. By the time dessert was being cleared away, Sylvia was the closest to fully relaxed she would let herself become outside of her home in the Eridani System.

"Officers and diplomats." Henry Wong rose from the table, holding the only glass of wine she'd seen in his hand all evening. "I give you the United Planets Alliance and peace among humanity!"

"The UPA!"

Sylvia took a sip of her own wine, concealing a smile behind her glass. The UPA hadn't necessarily delivered on that promise as thoroughly as its founders had hoped, what with the war against the Kenmiri, but they'd come closer than many feared.

It had been born out of the bloody three-way Unity War between the United States Colonial Administration, the Novaya Imperiya, and the hastily assembled United Nations Allied Fleets.

Like Henry Wong, her ancestors had fought on one of the losing sides of that war. She'd dedicated her life to the organization born out of the defeat of the Novaya Imperiya, recognizing that only standing together made humanity strong.

"I've received final confirmation," Wong announced as the toast died down. "Rising Principle and their delegation will be aboard *Carpenter* in just over four hours. *Glorious*, *Raven* and *Carpenter* are all fully stocked and supplied.

"We ship out in ten hours exactly. I suggest you all get what rest you can and double-check everything in your departments before we leave. There will be limited opportunities for repair or resupply once we're underway.

"The last thing we can afford is to appear weak in front of the Kozun," he reminded everyone. "It is our promise to protect the La-Tar Cluster that has brought the Kozun to the negotiating table. While the negotiations will be in the capable hands of Ambassador Todorovich and Rising Principle"—he raised his glass toward Sylvia—"*our* part in this requires us to look capable and intimidating.

"We will not give the Kozun a moment's hesitation. From the moment we arrive until the moment they sign the peace treaty, we stand guard. We're going there to end a war, people, but we will show no weakness. Understood?"

There was a rumble of agreement, followed by a few minutes of companionable quiet before the first person—O'Flannagain, Sylvia noted—slipped out.

Once the dam had been broken, the rest of the officers followed over the course of about five minutes. Leitz arched a questioning eyebrow at Sylvia as Iyotake left, leaving the two of them alone with Wong.

"Go check over our people," she told him. "I'm sure we have everything, but, as Captain Wong said, let's be certain."

"Yes, Em Ambassador."

Leitz rose and bowed himself out of the dining room, leaving Sylvia alone with Captain Wong...and two barely touched glasses of wine.

"Being careful, I see?" she asked, gesturing toward the wine.

"I find that my nightmares are worse when I have too much alcohol," he noted. "I'll trade my fondness for wine and brandy for better sleep and more control."

She raised her own glass in silent salute.

"Anything fascinating happen while I was gone?" she asked.

"Beyond the Bicycle?" He shrugged. "The Kozun have been clever about keeping an eye on the Satra System, and it's making the Cluster's defenders twitchy. I can't blame them."

"I didn't think hiding a ship was something you could do."

"It apparently depends on how much ice you're prepared to embed a small starship in," Wong said. "They stuck a corvette in an ice meteor. It worked better than I would have expected, though..."

He stared silently into his wine glass for a moment before sighing and swapping it for a glass of water.

"Though?" Sylvia prodded.

"That ice-coated corvette wasn't in the right spot to account for all of the ghosts the La-Tar sentries saw," he admitted. "She did enough damage to one of the La-Tar ships that we pulled back anyway and called it a win, but I have to wonder. We might have missed something."

"It sounds like that's about all the Kozun could have done, though, isn't it?" she asked. "I presume the sentries are looking for similar ships now?"

"They are," he confirmed. "I just have an itch on the back of my neck that says we missed something."

Sylvia chuckled.

"I know that feeling," she confessed. "The Drifters kept trying to say that we needed to give them grav-shield tech for whatever we wanted them to do. It was almost a joke by the end, but...I have to wonder how desperate they're going to get. They'll do a lot to keep their people safe."

"They will," Henry agreed. "That's why we're worried about them. I don't think I've ever met a Drifter who I didn't like and respect, but..."

He shook his head and drank more water.

As he was thinking, Sylvia followed his example and swapped her wine for water.

"I can't blame the Drifters for being focused on their own people," he finally said. "We did the same thing when the war ended. Everything the UPSF ever did was to protect our worlds. It took a lot of effort for us to get the Security Council to sign off on trying to do *anything* outside our borders.

"But they were always more willing to embrace...expediency, let's say, than I liked." Henry was staring off into space, and Sylvia shivered. She couldn't see what he was seeing, but she doubted it was pleasant.

"Hey," she said sharply. "Here and now, please, Captain Wong."

He shook himself and smiled wanly at her.

"Apologies, Ambassador," he said. "The war was not...pleasant. The Drifters enabled some of the less-pleasant aspects, even putting aside our own endeavors in Golden Lancelot.

"They survived under the Kenmiri by providing enough value and being dangerous enough that they weren't worth the effort to destroy," he continued. "They were working with the Kenmiri to the very end—probably still are, in the Remnant. They didn't help us for moral reasons, Ambassador.

"They helped us because they thought they would be richer and safer without the Empire. I'm not certain what that looks like to them, but I can say this: if the Drifters think the UPA is a threat to that safety, especially, they *will* betray us."

"So, I need to convince them we aren't a threat," Sylvia concluded. "I wish that felt easier. They were very specific which ships they let us on and even where on those ships we went."

"That's my experience as well," he agreed. "Even when we were renting lab space from them and had a destroyer division helping the Protectors guard the Convoy, we were very limited in where we were allowed on the Convoy."

"You don't trust them?" she asked.

"I don't trust many people at this point, Em Ambassador," he admitted. "There are Drifters I would trust, officers I have fought alongside and who I think I can predict. But the Drifters as a society?"

He shook his head.

"Their goals are their own and they don't talk about them," he warned. "I can't argue with what I know of their goals, but it could easily put them in conflict with us."

Sylvia nodded and sighed.

"That's fair." She took a sip of her water and raised her glass in a faux toast to Henry. "But I believe you've forgotten something, Henry."

"Oh?" he asked.

"I seem to recall telling you to call me Sylvia."

CHAPTER TWENTY

Any interstellar journey was made of alternating periods of boredom and minor discomfort, interrupted on a semi-regular basis by extreme discomfort as icosaspatial impulse generators kicked the human brain in sensitive parts.

The flight between skip lines was generally the boring part. *Glorious* and *Raven* could both fully compensate half a KPS^2, which made that the standard acceleration of the journey. At that acceleration, no one on any of the three ships felt any thrust at all.

Skip drones accelerated faster enough that there was no problem with the robotic couriers catching up to the ships, allowing Henry to maintain a loose communication with La-Tar and Zion.

He was keeping enough attention on that cycle to recognize when a drone appeared that was listed as from Zion and was completely off-schedule.

"Commander Moon, I'll review the feed from that drone in my office," he told the coms officer. "I expect an eyes-only message."

"Understood, ser."

"You have the con," he concluded, rising from his chair and

passing command authority to Moon. She knew the likely source of the drone as well as he did.

On his way to his office, he pinged Todorovich through his internal network, letting her know to meet him there.

The data download from the drone was locked behind the security seals he expected. It took him long enough to work through them that the ambassador was stepping into his office as he finished inputting the last security code.

"We're keeping things under lockdown," he told her. "I need to brief Orosz and my senior staff on Yellow Bicycle sooner rather than later, but this is what I was waiting for."

A skip drone was capable of carrying dozens of petabytes of data. The ones Henry was sending back to Zion contained twelve hours of full telemetry from *Raven*'s scanners, for example. This one contained a single video file.

"This was sent my-eyes-only," he continued. "But there was a codicil including you once I was halfway through the security codes."

"I appreciate that someone thought to include me in the messages," the Ambassador said.

"Honestly, I was planning on including you anyway," he admitted. "This is your mission as much or more than mine."

"I appreciate that as well," Todorovich repeated with a small smile. "Shall we see what we've been sent?"

Henry swallowed a breath that he hoped Todorovich didn't notice and started the message. A holographic image of two men in UPSF uniform appeared above his desk, and Henry was glad for the breath.

He hadn't seen very many images of Commodore Peter Barrie in the four years since their divorce. It was still hard.

Barrie looked...good. He was a tall man with pale blond hair, still muscular into his fifties, with warm brown eyes. The uniform fit him like he'd been born in it, and the gold oak leaf of his rank glittered in the lights of his own captain's office.

"Captain Wong, Ambassador Todorovich, this is Rear Admiral

Cheung Jian Chin," the other man in the hologram greeted him. Henry's attention was yanked away from his ex-husband and he focused on the squat Chinese Admiral.

"We have received various direct and indirect updates on your positions and plans, and I wanted to make certain that you were aware of Battle Group *Scorpius*'s progress," Cheung told them. "The effort you have made to keep us fully informed without revealing our presence has been of immense value, Captain.

"We are en route, as I hope you presumed, to the system we are designating Ra-One-Seventy-Five. Our navigators' assessment is that Ra-One-Seventy-Five is the most logical system for your skip drones to pass through on their way to Zion, which will allow you to keep us informed on the progress of negotiations."

The Admiral smiled.

"We should also be able to load messages onto Zion's drones as they pass us, which will allow us to communicate more readily than we have so far. We estimate that we will be in position sixteen hours after you arrive in the Lon System."

Henry was relieved. His only real concern about heading out as early as they had was the fear that they'd be in position well before their reinforcements were. If everything went as promised, that would be fine...but he was *expecting* a trap.

"We did receive Ambassador Todorovich's suggestion of a dead-man order," Cheung noted. "We considered it in the planning stages of this operation, but doing so depended on us being able to set up a communication chain that wouldn't draw attention. Since we will be able to watch your drones to Zion, we *have* that chain and her suggestion makes sense.

"If we don't hear from you for twenty-four hours once you have reached the Lon System, I will bring Battle Group *Scorpius* into the system ASAP. We will be positioning ourselves on the skip line to minimize the response time, but keeping everyone alive until we can arrive will fall on you, Captain Wong.

"Your record gives me faith that this will not be an insurmountable challenge, but I urge you to remember that the survival of your crew and the people under your protection will be the highest priority in that circumstance." Cheung smiled drily. "In other words, when the shit hits the fan, *run*, Captain. Don't fight unless you're certain you can win."

Henry figured *that* part came from Barrie. They'd both been headstrong fighter pilots once, after all.

"If everything goes as we hope, we will meet up in Zion and I will buy you a beer," the Admiral promised. "If it doesn't...well, you'll be seeing us sooner than that.

"Good luck, Captain Wong, Ambassador Todorovich. *Scorpius* out."

THE HOLOGRAM FROZE and Henry leaned back in his chair. He looked at the still image of the two officers for a moment and then closed it.

"That was your ex?" Todorovich asked.

"Commodore Peter Barrie, captain of *Scorpius*," Henry agreed. "One of our, what, five fleet carriers? At least I know the quality of my backup."

His companion was silent for several seconds.

"Is that good or bad?" she finally asked.

"Good," he said with a chuckle. "Don't get me wrong, Sylvia. Peter and I didn't part on good terms—we hadn't seen each other in over two years when we divorced, and I found out later he'd been having an affair with his Admiral's intelligence officer—but I *know* him. He's one of the best in the UPSF for starfighter tactics.

"If *Scorpius* has to come for us, we have some of the best people out here coming to our rescue. And he won't hesitate. Our former personal relationship is more likely to motivate him to jump too quickly than too slowly."

Henry sighed, remembering the conversation with the apologetic IntelDiv officer. He'd thought Henry and Peter had the kind of *arrangement* common with fleet officers—and Peter hadn't disabused the man of the belief.

"Good to know, I guess," she said. "And Cheung? Do you know the Admiral?"

"By reputation only," Henry said. "I've probably been in the same star system as him on a few occasions, but I've never served with or under him."

The UPSF was a small world in many ways, but it wasn't *that* small. Henry had only personally met a quarter or so of the UPSF's flag officers, and that was probably high even for a capital-ship commander.

He met Todorovich's gaze and ground a momentary inner spark under a mental heel. If there ever *was* going to be an appropriate time to mention his feelings, it wasn't going to be while they were preparing for a negotiation that could set the fate of tens of billions of lives.

"Is there anything we need to send back to *Scorpius*?" she finally asked.

"I don't think so," he said. "They'll start getting the regular updates we send Zion pretty quickly now, and that's all they need until and unless we actually call for help."

"I still think I'd be more comfortable if they were less than twenty-four hours away," she admitted.

"Me too," he said. "But it is what it is."

He shook his head and pulled up an astrogation chart.

"I need to brief the senior officers on Yellow Bicycle," he told her. "Do you want to sit in?"

"I think that's best left between you and your officers, Henry," she said. "No reason to drag the civilian into the middle of it."

"All right. Let me know if your team needs anything," Henry said. "We're two days out."

"I think we have everything we need until we see just what everyone has brought to the party," Todorovich replied. "I'm planning for the actual talks to take place on *Carpenter*. The Cluster are the people this is all about, after all."

CHAPTER TWENTY-ONE

"All right, everyone," Henry told his officers. They'd taken over the secure briefing room again and he'd even dragged Lieutenant Colonel Anna Song out of Engineering for this. Two people, Lieutenant Colonel Heléna Orosz and *Glorious*'s executive officer, Commander Agnethe Van Andel, were linked in from the destroyer via encrypted hologram and laser tightbeam.

"All of you know our mission," he said. "We're the primary escort for the La-Tar Cluster side of this negotiation. You also all know that the Drifters are providing a neutral security force that is probably as powerful as our escorts and the Kozun force combined."

He smiled thinly. From the reactions, not everyone had thought through what "three Guardians" meant as a potential threat.

"I, frankly, do not trust the Kozun as far as I can throw this battle-cruiser," he told them. "And while I trust the Drifters in many circumstances, I also trust them to follow their objectives over mine... and I don't necessarily know their objectives here.

"Command agrees with me, which resulted in what we're calling Operation Yellow Bicycle."

He waited a moment to see if anyone said anything. Moon and

Iyotake were already briefed, but this was news to everyone else. He had the attention of the ten officers physically and virtually present.

"If the Kozun or the Drifters betray us, our objective becomes the survival of our delegation at all costs," he told them. "We will use our fighters and gravity shields to protect *Carpenter* while all three ships run for whatever cover we can find as fast as we can go.

"As we're running for the hills, we're going to fire a salvo of skip drones at one of the skip lines," he continued. "On the other side of that skip line, unknown to anyone outside this room except Ambassador Todorovich, will be a UPSF carrier group."

"Wait, *what?*" Orosz demanded. "What's a carrier group doing this far out?"

"Being very quiet and hoping to not be needed," Henry told her. "UPSF Command suspects a trap. I agree with them, though no one is certain *which* of the potential ambushers will pull the trigger.

"In either case, our job will be to keep everyone alive for twenty-four hours until our backup can arrive. Unless the Kozun have shaken up three dreadnoughts that we don't know about, our carrier group will be easily able to handle the combined Kozun and Drifter forces we expect in the Lon System."

Henry looked around at the officers.

"Questions, people?" he asked.

"Which carrier?" O'Flannagain asked. "No offense to the rocket-jocks I serve with, but there are carrier groups I'd rather take care of myself than rely on help from."

"Your old base," Henry replied. "Assuming you're willing to take help from them?"

"Yeah," the pilot grunted. "They're good peeps with good birds and solid escorts. I'll take *Scorpius* over dying alone; that's for sure. Some of the others would just result in us dying with extras."

"The hope is to avoid anyone dying at all," he reminded everyone. "The existence of Operation Yellow Bicycle is not to be distributed further, understood? This remains need-to-know. While no one is actually *expecting* the battle group to go unactivated, that would definitely be our preference."

"Hope for peace but prepare for war," Iyotake murmured.

"We can go into all of the various pithy sayings on that one for days and days," Henry told his executive officer. "I want you all to put your heads together on how best to protect *Carpenter*. Worst-case scenario, even *Glorious* has a better-than-even chance of surviving the full firepower of the Guardians long enough to get clear.

"*Carpenter* doesn't and will likely be carrying the delegation."

"Question, ser," Ihejirika said slowly. "If we're expecting the Drifters to betray us...what do we do about the Kozun in that circumstance?"

Henry paused. He hadn't thought about that, but his tactical officer had a point.

"If they betray us, they also might be betraying the Kozun, I suppose," Henry conceded. "It's possible the two will be working together against us, though, which I think has been everyone's default assumption."

"If the Kozun really want peace and the Drifters blow this up because they want us at each other's throats, don't we have a responsibility to protect them as well?" Ihejirika asked.

Henry exhaled sharply...and then nodded.

"It will depend heavily on the circumstances," he admitted. "Most likely, if the Drifters betray us both, the Kozun delegation will be aboard *Carpenter* and we'll protect both delegations at once. They're as capable of outrunning the Guardians as we are, and depending on the situation, we may even tell them that help is coming.

"I don't think that we can decide our response to the Kozun in advance," he told his people. "Ihejirika is right, though. We need to consider the possibility that the Drifters are setting *everybody* up, with the intent of keeping the war going."

"Why would they want to keep the war going?" Bazzoli asked.

"Because it doesn't include them," Thompson said grimly, the

GroundDiv commander looking ill at the thought. "We and the Kozun represent the largest potential competitors to the Drifters as trade partners or even just cargo shippers. Our merchants are already beginning to penetrate the Ra Sector.

"A Hierarchy that's made peace with its neighbors could be a significant commercial power as well. But if we're busy fighting each other..."

"The Drifters are the only people available to haul cargo long distances and to buy tech from," Kuroda, the battlecruiser's logistics officer, concluded. "They wanted exclusive trading rights with the La-Tar Cluster as part of their price for protecting the peace conference.

"If we and the Kozun get stuck fighting each other instead of expanding our trade networks, the Drifters benefit."

"And two threats to the Convoys are neutralized," Henry added. "That's high on their list of priorities; remember that. They want the people they're responsible for to be safe. Any threat they can remove is a benefit to them."

"No matter what it costs," Iyotake concluded softly.

CHAPTER TWENTY-TWO

THE MOMENT OF DISORIENTATION ON RETURNING TO NORMAL space was an old friend for Henry. It made him grateful that there was no way to predict where a ship would emerge from a skip along the line. There were more likely areas, but nothing that would allow a ship to be ambushed on arrival.

It was easier to predict where someone would enter skip, though that was as often a matter of knowing where they were and how fast they could accelerate. Maneuver cones were useful prediction tools.

"Report, Ihejirika," he ordered. His internal network and the displays around him were focused on *Raven*, informing him that the battlecruiser was at battle stations. He hadn't sent everyone to the acceleration tanks, but in every other way, his ship was ready for battle.

Expanding his view showed him that *Glorious* and *Carpenter* had arrived around him, maintaining the formation they'd entered skip with.

"Well, nothing has changed about the star compared to the Drifters' survey data," the tactical officer said drily. "One very large

OB-type blue star. An asteroid belt. Looks pretty much exactly like what we were expecting."

"Are we alone?" Henry asked.

"Still resolving...no," Ihejirika concluded. "I have three Kozun cruisers in open space near the skip line back to the Hierarchy. They're half a light-hour away, so I'd say they've been here for at least two hours. They didn't beat us by much."

"No sign of the Drifters?"

"We're all here early," his subordinate pointed out. "They're not due for a couple more days."

"Well, that's going to be entertaining, isn't it?" Henry said. "Moon, record for transmission to the Kozun ships."

He closed his eyes for a moment, mentally recalibrating to the Kenmiri trade language before he began speaking in Kem.

"Kozun ships, this is Captain Henry Wong aboard *Raven*," he introduced himself politely. "I am acting as escort for the delegation from the La-Tar Cluster as well as the UPA ambassador intended to assist in negotiations.

"In the interests of avoiding any potential problems before our neutral guarantors arrive, I suggest we both remain at our current positions until the Drifters are here. That way, we are well outside each other's weapons range and can be certain of the safety of our respective delegations."

He paused, considering the recorder.

"I assume we are all here in good faith, but this seems a reasonable precaution to keep us all safe."

He ended the recording and nodded to Moon.

"Send that over, Commander," he told her. "Bazzoli, coordinate with *Carpenter* and *Glorious*. We'll maintain position for the moment; it's going to be at least an hour until we hear from our friends."

"Assuming the spikeheads *are* actually friendly."

Henry very carefully did *not* identify the voice that had said that.

"We are here to negotiate the end of war," he pointed out. "Let's not risk that with childish insults, shall we?"

He gave that a moment to sink in across the bridge. He figured the silence meant he'd made his point, and he turned his attention on Ihejirika.

"Focus all of our passive scanners on those ships," he told his tactical officer. "Iyotake, I want you to link up with *Carpenter* and *Glorious* and pull their sensor data for collaboration.

"I need you to confirm that count on ship types. IntelDiv thinks the Hierarchy only *has* four cruisers, but if they sent three of them here, that suggests we've underestimated them," Henry warned.

"We'll confirm the IDs, ser," Ihejirika promised.

"Already on synchronizing the sensor telemetry," Iyotake said in his ear. "Should we be standing down from battle stations? They are thirty light-minutes away."

In theory, they could still hit each other with their heavy lasers. In practice, at thirty light-minutes, the beams would be so diffuse, they'd be lucky to cause sunburns. There was no real threat at this distance.

"Stand down to Status Two," Henry ordered. "But get me that confirmed ID."

Three cruisers meant that Henry was actually concerned. Each of the ships outmassed *Raven* by fifty percent and they were built as pocket dreadnoughts, with the same heavy plasma guns as the larger Kenmiri ships.

He was reasonably confident he could *take* all three, especially with *Glorious* in support. He was concerned that he wouldn't take out all three before they destroyed *Carpenter*. That was the concern here and now...but the strategic message was a big one too.

If the Hierarchy even had six cruisers instead of the four IntelDiv calculated, the balance of power at the negotiations wasn't what they'd expected. That could cause Todorovich all kinds of problems.

Henry leaned back in his chair, carefully projecting relaxed calm as he looked at the displays around him.

They'd been in the system for less than ten minutes, and the carefully built forecasts and assumptions they'd built their plans on were already crumbling.

"SER, INCOMING TRANSMISSION FROM THE KOZUN," Moon told Henry an hour later.

The downside to keeping everyone at this distance was that communications were going to take *forever*. It was hard to carry on a conversation with a full-hour time lag.

"Put it on, Commander," he ordered. He closed the analysis he was going through with a mental command and a concealed sigh.

Everyone aboard *Raven*'s little flotilla was agreed: there were *definitely* three of the Kozun's homebuilt cruisers in the Lon System. Unless the Kozun were playing games at a technical level the UPA couldn't match, they'd sent three capital ships to the negotiations.

There were a lot of possibilities behind that, though one point was clear to Henry: regardless of whether the Kozun had sent all of their capital ships or a tenth of them, they'd sent that many to be impressive.

"Sending the message directly to your internal network, ser," Moon informed him.

Henry was about to question why the Lieutenant Commander was sending him the message in a private format when it began—and he found himself facing the familiar eyes and forehead plates of a woman he'd thought was dead.

"Captain Wong, this is Star Voice Kalad of the Kozun Hierarchy," his old friend told him in Kem. She was speaking slowly, as if she knew he'd be taking the time to study her face and be certain it was her.

Like any Kozun, Kalad looked human enough up to about the level of her eyes. Instead of eyebrows, however, the Kozun had plates of bony armor that rose up from what would be eyebrows on another Ashall and angled back across the front half of their skull.

Kalad herself had close-cropped auburn hair on the back half of her head and burning crimson eyes that were leveled calmly on the camera. Despite her apparent calm, though, Henry Wong had long since learned to read the microexpressions shared by all Ashall.

They couldn't necessarily be attached to specific emotions, but he could identify if an Ashall was feeling positive or negative—and the longer he'd known someone, the better he could read them.

Kalad was as relieved to be speaking to him as he was to see her. When they'd last spoken, she had inherited command of a Kozun battle group after he'd destroyed their flagship and sent them running. She had taken responsibility for ordering the retreat and had clearly expected to be punished for it.

Instead, she appeared to have been promoted. She'd been a Star Lance—equivalent to his own Colonel—then. Now she was a Star Voice, equivalent to a UPSF Commodore.

Mal Dakis, it appeared, was perhaps not as lost to reason as even his own people feared.

He realized he'd completely lost track of Kalad's message and reset it to the end of her introduction.

"I am in command of the escort of the Third Voice of the Kozun, Oran Aval," she told him. "In the interest of preserving Her Holiness's safety as well as the security of my command, I agree with your suggestion.

"We will maintain position at the Sodulis skip line until the Drifter contingent arrives. In the absence of treachery on the part of the La-Tar Cluster, I can assure you of the safety of your ships.

"By the word of the Voices of our Gods, we are here to make peace. Not wage war."

She bowed her head and the message ended.

Receiving the message in his internal network meant that his moment of shock had been almost entirely inside his head. Moon had clearly realized that was a possibility as soon as she'd IDed the Kozun officer, and made sure to give him the chance to internalize it before the crew saw it.

If his reviews hadn't already been glowing enough to guarantee Moon's next promotion, he'd have had to edit them after that!

"Thank you, Commander Moon," he said quietly, then straightened. "All right, everyone," he continued sharply. "Our old friend Star Voice Kalad is in command of the escort over there and has agreed to hold positions until the Drifters arrive.

"Now, I trust Kalad, but we still can't assume that she's not under orders to lie to us," he continued. "We'll keep a *very* close eye on our Kozun friends the whole time we're here.

"For now, though, we wait. The Drifters should be here soon enough."

CHAPTER TWENTY-THREE

"Captain Wong to the bridge, Captain Wong to the bridge."

Years of practice made waking up instantly an old habit for Henry. There was a moment's more delay than usual this time, as he had been having surprisingly pleasant dreams. Given his normal range of nightmares, even somewhat-awkward dreams about his civilian counterpart were a welcome change.

"What is it?" he asked over his network as he grabbed his uniform and began dressing.

"New contacts," Iyotake told him. The XO was on the bridge, holding down the night watch. "We have three very large contacts on the line we're expecting the Drifters along. It looks like things might finally be getting underway."

"Understood." Henry replied. "I'll be there in two minutes."

Practice meant he was overstating that by thirty seconds, but it still gave him plenty of time to straighten the uniform—it was self-pressing and almost impossible to wrinkle, which helped—and quickly run a comb through his hair and a depilator over his face.

He emerged onto the bridge perfectly turned out and looking entirely calm. Iyotake rose from the central seat as Henry approached, gesturing his captain over.

"Report," Henry ordered.

"Three contacts, as I said," the XO told him. "Engine signatures suggest eight to ten million tons apiece."

Henry nodded his understanding—and ignored the choked whistle of one of the junior tactical officers as they confirmed that number.

"I see we got Blue Stripe Green Stripe Orange Stripe's best," he observed. Kenmiri dreadnoughts ran up to ten million tons, but he'd never seen anything except the smaller six- to seven-megaton units in Vesheron hands.

The Drifters assembled Guardians at both scales, but he doubted Blue Stripe Green Stripe Orange Stripe had more than a handful of ten-million-ton warships.

On the other hand, the Kenmiri wouldn't send three unescorted dreadnoughts anywhere. If a Kenmiri Remnant force had decided to crash this party, those three dreadnoughts would have brought at least thirty smaller ships with them.

"Do we have any communication from them yet?" he asked.

"Not even identity beacons," Iyotake said. "They've been in-system for ten minutes plus lightspeed delay. They have to know we and the Kozun are here."

"And that we're both a dozen light-minutes or more away from them," Henry said. "They've got the time to sort out what they want to do."

"True enough. What do we do?" his XO asked.

"We wait for them to hail us—and then we turn the whole situation over to Todorovich and Rising Principle. This is only our show for a few more hours, XO."

IT TOOK over an hour for the Drifters to finally contact Henry's flotilla. He had to suspect they'd talked to the Kozun first, but he had no way of proving that and he wasn't sure it would matter.

The figure that appeared on Henry's screens was shrouded in the same robes as every Drifter he'd ever encountered. They wore a Face Mask in reds and blue, and a doubled length of silver chain hung around their shoulders and held a steel shield in the center of their chest.

"Captain Wong, Ambassador Todorovich, Ambassador Rising Principle," they greeted everyone in Kem. "I am Protector-Legate Half-Blue-Third-Red. I am tasked to act as the neutral guarantor of the peace negotiations between the La-Tar Cluster and the Kozun Hierarchy.

"My ships are en route to a specific set of coordinates well away from the skip lines and local debris, to make certain of our security from unexpected surprises," Half-Blue-Third-Red told them. "Those coordinates will be attached to this message.

"I expect all of your vessels and the Kozun vessels to rendezvous there in twenty-four hours, at the exact time agreed to in the prior arrangements. Where things proceed from there, I leave to your delegations, but I will maintain security of that zone and neutralize any force that threatens the peaceful completion of these negotiations—whether that force is external or internal to those negotiations."

The mask twitched slightly.

"I do not guarantee *success*; that is up to you. I merely guarantee that no outside force will prevent you and the Kozun completing your discussions, however they end."

The message ended and Henry silently studied the image.

"Did we get those coordinates, Moon?" he asked the coms officer.

"Yes, ser," she confirmed.

"Forward them to Bazzoli and the other ships," he ordered. "Let's get this show on the road."

He pinged Todorovich via his internal network as *Raven*'s engines came online.

"The Drifters are here," he told her. "They've set the coordinates for the meeting, and everyone is headed there. We're all expected to be there in twenty-four hours, so that's how long we have to sort out the plan."

"Anything of concern yet?" she asked.

"Everybody showed up with a heavier force than I was expecting," he admitted. "I expected one Kozun cruiser and three smaller Guardians, not three cruisers and three of the larger Guardians I've seen.

"There's a lot more firepower in this system than I was expecting, and it's making the back of my neck itch."

"Is it enough to risk the backup plan?"

"No," he conceded. "Everyone is saying and doing the right things so far. Do you think you'll get everyone on board with meeting on *Carpenter*?"

"That everyone has brought capital ships might actually make that easier," Todorovich told him. "*Carpenter* might be the least threatening starship here!"

"There's no 'might' to that," Henry admitted. "Everything else here has shields of some kind, if nothing else. That makes her look quite fragile right now."

"We'll be fine, Henry," she said. "*Fragile* is to our advantage, especially once we've got the Third Voice of the Kozun aboard."

He could feel the surprise in her tone through the network.

"You're surprised they actually sent a Voice?" he asked.

"I'm not entirely sure how the ranking of the Voices breaks down, but yes," she admitted. "Is the Third the third-most powerful? That's what I would guess, but from what we know, any of them would be a commitment here.

"They've sent someone who can actually bind the Hierarchy. That's as positive a sign as I can get for them actually wanting peace."

Henry nodded, biting back his follow-up. He *really* didn't want to put Sylvia Todorovich on the most fragile starship in the system...but he had no real reason he could give for that other than not wanting to risk her.

And *that* wasn't something the commander of her escort could permit to get in the way of her job.

CHAPTER TWENTY-FOUR

SYLVIA MADE ONE LAST CHECK AROUND HER OFFICE ON *RAVEN*. To her eyes, it was horrendously overdone, but every single piece of decoration served a specific purpose. The commissioning seal of the battlecruiser, a side view of a bird in flight with a quill pen, was inlaid on the wall behind her in gold.

Flanking that seal on either side was the eight-star half-circle-on-blue flag of the United Planets Alliance. The flags were stiffened with wire, just enough to keep the symbol fully visible.

The big faux-wooden desk with its built-in screens, holographic projectors and haptic interfaces was actually Henry Wong's spare, currently using those screens to show another copy of the raven-with-quill symbol.

"We're ready, Em Ambassador," Leitz told her from the door. "Are you?"

"Everything is in place," she confirmed, checking her own stiff suit carefully in a holographic mirror. "I'm good."

She took her seat behind the desk and leveled her best sharp look on the recorder.

"Voice Oran Aval, I am Ambassador Sylvia Todorovich," she

introduced herself in Kem. "I am here in the Lon System to assist Ambassador Rising Principle in the negotiation of a peace treaty between the La-Tar Cluster and the Kozun Hierarchy."

The time delay was down to about five minutes, but she was still sending this as a prerecorded message. Five-minute gaps in the conversation did not lend themselves well to remaining professional.

"While I understand that you do not regard the United Planets Alliance as entirely neutral in this matter, I stand sufficiently outside the involved parties to act as somewhat of a third party," she continued. "As such, I feel I am best suited to establish the fundamental final details of our negotiations.

"The primary piece still outstanding, I believe, is the physical location of the talks. The Drifters are only acting as guarantors of our physical security. Their own rules and regulations will prevent them from hosting the discussions that we need to have.

"Equally, I hesitate to put myself or Ambassador Rising Principle in your hands aboard a Kozun capital ship," she continued. "While I, of course, would prefer to carry on these discussions aboard *Raven*, I recognize that would be unacceptable to you.

"Given the vessels available to everyone present, I would like to suggest that we meet aboard *Carpenter*, for two reasons: firstly, *Carpenter* is the least heavily armed and defended vessel here. She is a former Kenmiri escort, lacking energy shields or heavy plasma cannons. We all know the type, and despite being a formidable vessel, she is the most vulnerable of our options.

"That creates a shared vulnerability that I believe is the best option available to us," she told the Voice.

"Secondly, however, all of this began with the Kozun invasion of the La-Tar Cluster," Sylvia noted coldly. "It seems appropriate to me that this conflict end on a vessel belonging to the people of the La-Tar Cluster.

"While we are certainly prepared to consider other suggestions, I believe that meeting aboard *Carpenter* is our best choice.

"I await your response, Voice Oran Aval."

She cut off the recording and relaxed slightly in the chair.

"Felix?" she asked.

"Said everything we need to say," he confirmed. "You look intimidating as hell."

"That's not hard when aboard *Raven*," Sylvia said. "And the Voice isn't going to have much difficulty feeling intimidating when she's sitting on Star Voice Kalad's flagship. That's part of why I want to have the talks on *Carpenter*. That gives Rising Principle an advantage, one they can use."

"And we don't necessarily need that advantage, Em Ambassador?"

"The Kozun know damn well that if they actually push the UPA too far, we have the power to *end* them," Sylvia said quietly. "I think that's more than enough weight in my corner, don't you?"

"Fair," Felix conceded. He stared vaguely off into space for a few moments, the sign of someone accessing their internal network. "I'm no Forces officer, but those look like big ships to me. Is that what we were expecting?"

"No," she said. "That's sixty percent of what we thought their capital-ship strength was." She brought up the image of the three cruisers in her own internal network.

"IntelDiv estimated they would have been able to build five of those ships, and Wong blew one of them apart at La-Tar," she continued. "So, they believe that the Hierarchy has one dreadnought and four cruisers. If there's three cruisers *here*, then..."

She shook her head.

"I don't know enough to judge the validity of IntelDiv's estimates," she admitted. "Nor do I know the Kozun as well as Captain Wong. I could see them sending *half* of their cruisers here, to make an impression, but even that would mean IntelDiv was badly off on their estimates."

And if they were off on the estimate of how many heavy warships the Hierarchy had, even the assumption that the UPA could take the Kozun out began to be suspect.

"That's...concerning," her chief of staff murmured, clearly following her line of thought.

Any further discussion was interrupted by a ping from Lieutenant Commander Moon. The Kozun had replied. With a mental command, Sylvia wiped away her view of the tactical situation and put the Voice of the Kozun's message on the holoprojectors.

Like Sylvia's own office, Voice Oran Aval's surroundings were very clearly carefully constructed. While Kozun warships almost always had chapels of some kind aboard, she doubted they carried thrones delicately carved with religious iconography.

The white-stone seat was probably eight feet tall, with an immense back rising well above the slim figure of the Third Voice of the Kozun. Sylvia wasn't familiar with the script or the imagery of the artwork carved into the seat, but she suspected the throne predated the Kenmiri occupation of the Kozun homeworld.

It was probably designed for this exact purpose, but it still represented a religious and cultural artifact of unquestionable value. The tapestries hung to either side of the throne were easier for Sylvia to read, with scenes of what would have been saints and miracles for a Catholic Christian on Earth.

Combined, the Third Voice had clearly assembled a miniature religious throne room aboard the ship carrying her, a temple as much to her power and authority as to the Kozun gods.

"I am Oran Aval, Third Voice of the Kozun," the Kozun woman introduced herself, her voice surprisingly soft and delicate. She was a frail-looking woman, though some of that could have been the background, with pale blond hair pinned up into a hairstyle that partially covered her forehead armor plating. What was visible of the armor plates was covered in a mesh net of gold chain set with sapphires that matched the Voice's eyes.

"We speak for the gods," Aval continued. "And after them, we speak for the people of the Kozun Hierarchy. We reject, Ambassador Todorovich, your description of our actions in the La-Tar Cluster.

You misunderstand the holy duty of the warriors sent to the Cluster. We did not invade anywhere...but that is a discussion for a later time.

"Your suggestion of holding those discussions aboard the escort *Carpenter* is acceptable to us," she finished. "We will be accompanied by an escort of sixteen sacred guardians, Paladins of the Seven.

"They will be permitted their arms and armor. If we are to step aboard one of your vessels, this is nonnegotiable." A hand waved delicately through the air and Sylvia focused on the fingers for a moment.

Delicate Oran Aval might appear, but her hands were callused and scarred. She had not only worked with her hands in the past, but some of those scars were familiar to Sylvia: they were a distinct pattern that resulted from repeated use of portable energy weapons.

Even the best shielding, after all, didn't entirely keep the heat from the hands of the wielder.

"I and my Paladins will arrive aboard *Carpenter* thirty-seven minutes after we reach the rendezvous," Aval concluded. "We will speak further then, Ambassador Sylvia Todorovich."

The message ended and Sylvia snorted.

"I see that we aren't going to be given a choice in how Her Holiness comes to us," she said aloud. "Fortunately, her *assumptions* are well within what Rising Principle and I discussed. We're fine."

"Should we push back, just to make the point?" Leitz asked.

"No," Sylvia said. "Let her pretend she has an upper hand for the moment. All of us know the reality, I suspect."

"Or she's fucking delusional," her chief of staff observed.

"Then these negotiations are going to be *very* interesting," Sylvia replied.

Given that she wasn't expecting to make it through the peace conference without *somebody* betraying her, *interesting* was a default assumption.

CHAPTER TWENTY-FIVE

Raven's shuttlebay was a buzzing hive of activity when Sylvia reached it. She had sent a full suitcase of personal effects on ahead, but she'd thought only one shuttle was heading over to *Carpenter.*

Instead, it looked like at least *three* were being prepped—the three she recognized as having gravity shields.

"That seems excessive," she noted aloud.

"Sixteen GroundDiv troopers, full armor for the same, supplies for twenty-some humans for a week, and making sure the ambassador has an escape route if everything goes wrong," Henry Wong said from behind her.

She turned to find the captain standing by the door, watching the activity with a small smile. He was in his working uniform—black slacks and the white-necked black turtleneck of his rank—and he raised a sardonic eyebrow at her.

"You didn't expect us to leave your security in the hands of the La-Tar Cluster, did you?" he asked. "Thompson's been coordinating with Em Leitz for a bit. If the Voice is bringing sixteen guards, we're sending you with sixteen guards."

"And Rising Principle?" she asked drily.

"Rising Principle has eighty of La-Tar's elite commandos aboard *Carpenter*," Wong pointed out. "The same terrifyingly dangerous people who *captured* surface-to-orbit weapon installations and turned them on the Kozun for us.

"I'm not concerned about or responsible for the La-Tar ambassador's security," he concluded. "I *am* concerned about *and* responsible for *your* security, Em Ambassador."

Sylvia chuckled. Something about his concern warmed her heart, though she suspected she was reading far too much into his professional façade.

"The concern and the escort are appreciated, Henry," she told him. "Anything I should be watching for?"

"Thompson is in direct command of your escort," he said, his voice suddenly coldly serious. "He's carrying a high-powered encrypted transmitter with frequency-shifting codes and everything we could think of. It *should* penetrate any jamming or security to at least send an SOS. We've coordinated hourly check-ins with *Carpenter*'s command crew, but I want you to check in as often as you can as well.

"We'll have at least a company of GroundDiv on standby at all times, and both *Glorious* and *Raven* will be remaining at Status Two at all times." He shrugged. "*Everybody* has their shields up, so no one is complaining about mine."

"Skip drones?" she asked.

"Standard twelve-hour update sequence for Zion is already programmed in," he told her. "Full telemetry downloads under our best encryption. Every update we get from you will be automatically downloaded to the drones, and everything is fired off back to the Alliance twice a day."

"Everything so far looks aboveboard," she said. "We might actually manage to negotiate a peace treaty here."

"I hope so," he agreed. "I'm concerned for your safety, Sylvia," he admitted. "I don't like you being on the most vulnerable ship here."

"I suspect that Star Voice Kalad is even *less* happy about having one of her religious leaders on that ship," Sylvia pointed out. "It's an equality of dissatisfaction, Henry. That was the point."

"I know. I don't like it," he repeated.

"My dear Captain, be careful," she warned him with a chuckle. "I might start to think you care under that professional façade."

He arched that damned eyebrow again.

"Be careful," he told her. "We're here if something goes wrong, but there are distinct limits in how much we can physically do."

"This isn't my first dangerous negotiation, Henry," Sylvia reminded him. "I'll be fine."

THE GROUNDDIV PILOTS managing the shuttles didn't even let Sylvia's shuttle land on *Carpenter* first. A GroundDiv security team touched down first, eight of the armored soldiers spreading out and coordinating with the La-Tar commandos before letting the Ambassador aboard the ship.

Two figures waited patiently for her once she was finally aboard. Sylvia couldn't read the body language of the Venus flytrap–like Enteni ambassador, but the Sana man standing next to Rising Principle was *very* readable.

Like most Ashall, the Sana could have passed for human at a distance, though his chlorophyll-colored green hair and gold-tipped tusks would cause problems close up. His grin didn't take much cross-species experience to interpret, either.

"Ambassador Todorovich, you is-are welcome aboard *Carpenter*," Rising Principle greeted her in their stilted Kem. "Be known-knowing Captain Atchi."

Atchi bowed, his ponytail flopping across the shoulder of his stark white uniform tunic as he did.

"Welcome to my ship," he said simply. "We have places for your shuttles if they are staying?"

"That is my understanding, yes," Sylvia agreed. "Thompson!"

Her bellow brought the GroundDiv officer over instantly. The massive blond man gave the two La-Tar representatives a crisp salute.

"Em Ambassador?" he asked—in Kem, to be polite.

"How many of the shuttles are we keeping aboard *Carpenter*?" she replied.

"As many as Captain Atchi has space for," he said. "Captain?"

"You brought three? They can stay," Atchi confirmed. "We will regrettably have to limit the Kozun to just one shuttle."

"That is-was no concern of ours," Rising Principle murmured. "Are-were you ready for the fate-times of this meeting, Ambassador?"

"This is mostly your show, Ambassador," Sylvia reminded them. "The UPA has limited desires here, and they are not critical to the treaty. I am here to support you."

The United Planets Alliance would *like* commitments to sentient rights and better treatment for the worlds they had to leave under Kozun rule. Sylvia was quite certain that a few of the corporations back in Terran space would be *delighted* to have trading rights in Hierarchy space, too.

She didn't want to leave planets under Kozun rule without some promise that they would be treated as member worlds instead of slaves, but peace for La-Tar was more important.

"It is-will-be appreciated," Rising Principle told her. "*I* am-will-be ready."

Atchi shook his head, lowering his hand from a concealed earpiece—none of the people in the former Kenmiri Empire had internal networks, something to do with the Kenmiri controlling the technology they'd use for neural implants—and coughed to interrupt them.

"The Voice is almost here," he told them. "We need to get your things moved to your temporary quarters and the shuttles cleared. It will go faster if the three of us leave the shuttlebay for a few minutes."

SYLVIA WAS HALF-EXPECTING the Voice's shuttle to be gold-plated or chromed or something similar. Instead, it was a standard Kenmiri heavy assault shuttle. Significantly larger than the UPA-built craft she'd arrived in, it was the largest parasite craft the Kenmiri had built, capable of landing an entire company of the Warriors' elite.

It was overkill for sixteen troops and a diplomat, but that was in line with what Sylvia had seen of the Third Voice.

Even as the big shuttle settled onto the deck, several weapons systems were visibly tracking the occupants of the bay. In response, anti-intrusion turrets lowered from the bay's ceiling to return the favor.

No one was shooting yet, but a lot of guns were pointing each way. Several seconds of pointed silence followed as Sylvia tried not to hold her breath.

Then the ramp finally lowered and four armored soldiers advanced. Their armor was modern enough, clearly adapted from Kenmiri Warriors' power armor, but *this* had been chromed. In the artificial light of the shuttlebay, the lead escorts gleamed.

"Well, that will be headache-inducing," Thompson murmured in English next to Sylvia.

From Atchi's body language, the Sana Captain might not understand the GroundDiv officer...but he agreed with the sentiment.

After a moment, the four Paladins split, stepping to either side of the ramp as four more armored bodyguards followed them down the ramp. They advanced to meet the honor guard of La-Tar commandos.

The two collections of soldiers glared at each other for a moment, the La-Tar commandos gleaming significantly less but still looking just as deadly as the Paladins, before the Kozun troops turned and effectively joined the honor guard.

The Third Voice came down the ramp, flanked by two more Paladins. She didn't even seem to be paying attention to the soldiers—or anything else, for that matter. The blonde Kozun priestess-leader walked calmly down the ramp in a lavender-blue robe that set off her eyes and the sapphires in the gold nets over her armor plates.

She paused at the La-Tar honor guard, taking a moment to visually review the commandos before giving them a nod of quiet acknowledgement and continuing on. That was more respect than Sylvia had expected from the Kozun, surprising her enough to let Oran Aval reach where she and Rising Principle stood.

"Ambassador Todorovich, Ambassador Rising Principle," she greeted them.

"Voice Aval," Sylvia replied. "I believe Captain Atchi has prepared quarters for you."

"That will not be necessary," Aval said. "If it is necessary, I will sleep aboard my shuttle for everyone's safety. For now, we believe that all are best served by commencing the discussions immediately.

"Shall we proceed, Ambassadors?"

CHAPTER TWENTY-SIX

Sylvia didn't know what else had been included in the refit *Carpenter* had undergone to serve as a diplomatic ship, but it had included a conference room large enough for all three of the negotiators to have staff and bodyguards.

The space was clearly a new addition, lacking any of the decoration Kenmiri Artisans insisted on installing on any warship they designed. Simple rugs had been laid down over bare metal in an attempt to conceal the utilitarian nature of the chamber, but there was only so much the escort's crew could do.

The part that impressed Sylvia was that the crew *had* managed to come up with banners to hang behind each representative's seat. The half-circle of stars of the UPA hung behind her seat, where a stylized sheaf of grain surrounded by five swords hung behind Rising Principle's stool.

She hadn't actually seen the Kozun flag before and was intrigued by the imagery. It was a white-cup-on-black flag, with seven differently colored "gems" on the cup, one for each of the Kozun's gods and their Voices.

Aval didn't slow on entering the room, taking the seat in front of the Hierarchy flag and waving her guards and staff to the seats behind her. Sylvia gave a nod to Leitz and Thompson to do the same as she took her own seat.

Rising Principle's staff were already waiting, but three commandos took the rear seats intended for the security detail.

Three representatives, a dozen bodyguards and half a dozen staff. The room was big enough to still feel half-empty, like this was far too few people to decide the fate of entire star systems.

Sylvia remained standing as the other two took their seats, a formal leather folio held in her hands.

"I think the simplest place for us to begin is a clarification of the source of our respective authorities to negotiate for our countries," she told them in Kem. She opened the folio and laid it on the table between them. "This is my commission of plenipotentiary authority from the Security Council of the United Planets Alliance. I am authorized to commit the UPA to any treaty that I negotiate."

That wasn't *entirely* true—the Security Council and Assembly could refuse to endorse the treaty she negotiated. That would end her career and have serious consequences for the long-term interstellar relations of the UPA, so it was highly unlikely.

But it *was* possible.

"I am-was charged by the planetary governors and the Arbiter of the La-Tar Cluster to speak on their behalf," Rising Principle stated without standing. "I am-was tasked to bring the fate-time of war to ending."

Oran Aval eyed them both as Sylvia took her seat, then nodded carefully. Her hairstyle bobbed sufficiently with the nod to suggest that care was needed.

"I am the Third Voice of the Kozun," she said simply. She waited for a moment, then sighed. "I speak for the gods, the people and the Hierarchy of the Kozun. I am one of the Seven who guide our people, a leader of our planet and our Hierarchy. My words bind the Kozun."

That was about what Sylvia had expected. The UPA had a formal structure for diplomats and had sent a senior diplomat—her.

The La-Tar Cluster barely had a formal *government* and had specifically designated someone they all trusted to speak for them.

The Kozun had sent a member of their governing council, one of the most powerful sentient beings in the Hierarchy.

"If that is insufficient for you," Aval continued after another moment's pause, "know that my mate is Mal Dakis and I am here with his complete trust."

That was not what Sylvia had expected. Sending the Third Voice, which she figured to be the third-ranked member of their government, was a sign of good faith and intentions. Sending the wife of the unquestioned dictator of the Kozun?

The Hierarchy might be even more serious about these negotiations than she'd hoped.

"I am prepared to accept that as a basis for these negotiations," Sylvia said. "Rising Principle?"

"The word-intent of this fate-time suffice," they agreed.

"Good," Aval told them. "Then I will begin. La-Tar was peacefully annexed by the Hierarchy's forces as we attempted to bring stability and prosperity to this region. Our goal is and always has been to provide a shared path forward.

"In response to our peaceful efforts in this region, first the United Planets Alliance and then the terrorist forces now styling themselves the La-Tar Cluster attacked our ships and people without provocation, killings thousands of brave Kozun who were attempting to help the people of La-Tar and destroying multiple starships.

"Despite these provocations and atrocities, the Hierarchy is prepared to make peace," she continued. "To do so, we will require compensation for the lives, equipment and ships lost in the vicious and unjustified campaign of violence waged against our interests in the Cluster.

"We are prepared to negotiate on the nature and quantity of the reparations required, but the Hierarchy will require amends to be made for the damage to our assets in the region."

Sylvia was impressed at the sheer audacity of the Voice's position.

The Kozun had invaded the Cluster, obliterated an allied fleet—mostly belonging to the Tano—above La-Tar and conquered the only source of food for five worlds.

"I do-will not understand what fate-time you think has-was passed among these stars," Rising Principle said calmly as Sylvia tried to muster her own thoughts. "We can-will not negotiate based on lies-false-fates."

They laid a tablet on the table and a tendril tapped a command. Two holograms appeared above the table. One was a three-dimensional visual of the First Battle of La-Tar, showing a Kozun cruiser and her escorts tearing their way through the allied fleet desperately defending the agriworld.

The other was a list of names. It was scrolling automatically and *kept going.*

"The Hierarchy invaded La-Tar," Rising Principle said flatly. "This is-was the true-fate-time of what passed. You destroyed our allies. Destroyed our defenses. Invaded our cities. Murdered our Standards."

As they spoke, the holograms shifted. First the space battle. Then orbital bombardment. Then Kozun landers exchanging fire with the defenders on the surface.

"You withheld our crops from the worlds we feed," they continued. "Five worlds could-were threatened with death if they defied you. The UPA helped us save-rescue ourselves. And you say-speak these lies-false-fates?"

Whoever had edited Rising Principle's display tablet had done a phenomenal job, Sylvia saw. Even having seen most of the footage before, it sent shivers down her spine. The Kozun occupation of La-Tar had *not* been gentle—and the invasion had been worse.

"You could-would have left the worlds-we-feed to die," the Enteni told Oran Aval. "I will-can not listen to your lies-false-fates."

They rose from the stool, a somewhat awkward process for the trilaterally symmetrical being.

"Speak true-fates or we will-have wasted fate-time in gathering here," they told Aval. Gesturing with a tendril for their people to follow them, Rising Principle began to head for the door.

"Sit down, Ambassador," Oran Aval said quietly. "We have both demonstrated our *extreme* positions, I think. But neither of us will cling to those over peace. We are here to talk."

She gestured toward the Enteni-style stool.

"I have stated where the Voices begin. Now let us hear where the Cluster begins...and perhaps we can find a space somewhere in between where no more blood needs to be shed."

Sylvia saw Aval's purpose now. By setting an impossible expectation, she gave the Kozun ground to give that she could demand concessions for—like trying to reduce the reparations the Cluster was going to, quite justifiably, demand.

"I think we must state, first, that the UPA will not accept any treaty that does not admit the Kozun's responsibility for the invasion of the Cluster," she told Aval. "I will not permit you to use a false claim of damages to reduce the depths of the Hierarchy's crimes.

"The Hierarchy brought blood and fire to these stars. They have conquered worlds and made slaves of peoples freed by the Kenmiri's fall. The United Planets Alliance will not stand aside while you rewrite history to erase these actions."

She smiled thinly.

The Kozun weren't going to get a starting point of "you pay *us*" to negotiate down from. Not while Sylvia Todorovich was part of the negotiations, anyway!

CHAPTER TWENTY-SEVEN

Raven's bridge was a quiet place. It was far from empty—
the battlecruiser was on Status Two, which meant there was a shift
and a half on duty—but what conversation was happening was doing
so quietly and thoughtfully.

It was Okafor Ihejirika's watch and Henry wasn't needed on the
bridge at all. He had every faith in his tactical officer to handle
matters unless things went very wrong, and yet he found himself
drawn to the big command center and its detailed displays of the
space surrounding them.

"Ser!" Ihejirika greeted him, beginning to rise from the command
seat before Henry waved him back down.

"As you were, Commander," Henry ordered. "It's your watch;
I'm just observing."

Suiting actions to words, he settled into the observer seat next to
Ihejirika.

"I haven't seen any alerts," he said quietly. "Anything going on?"

"We're all just sitting here, glaring at each other while the diplomats talk," Ihejirika told him. "I'm guessing no one knows how long
that's going to go on for?"

Henry chuckled.

"Ask me later, once Todorovich has sent an update over," he said. "Right now, I know as much about the negotiations as anyone else. I'd *guess* that we're looking at a week or so, at the minimum.

"No matter how cut-and-dried the situation seems to us, there's always complications when nations sit down at the negotiating table. The distances mean a ceasefire isn't even needed, so long as both sides are waiting to hear what happens here."

"It's going to be a twitchy week," Ihejirika admitted. "Everybody's shields are up, but energy shields are more transparent to scanners than gravity shields."

From the inside, Henry's people knew the exact magnitude of the gravity shear impacting the incoming light and radiation. They could reconstruct what happened outside easily enough. Those on the outside couldn't see through the shear with any detail at all.

"Are you poking at our neutrals and peace-bonded enemies, Commander?" Henry asked.

"Not...yet," Ihejirika replied. "Just watching energy signatures. But."

"But what, Commander?"

"If we synchronize scanners with *Glorious* and adjust her position slightly, we can get clearer images of everyone else," the tactical officer told him. "We won't get perfect data right away, but a few hours of recorded sensor information should be enough for us to tell you anything you want to know."

"I'm listening," Henry allowed.

"We can also probably sneak some drones out, get more detailed closeups."

"*Probably* is overestimating our odds there," Henry said calmly. "At least your odds of closeups." He shrugged. "You could sneak drones out through the missile launchers, I suppose. Low-impulse magnetic launches; keep the drives turned off until they're well away...you could hide them but you wouldn't get any use out of them at a valuable range.

"We wouldn't be able to bring up drives or sensors until they were at least ten million klicks away, at which point they're not adding much to your sensor take." He shook his head. "There's no point, Commander."

Ihejirika paused, considering his arguments, then sighed and nodded.

"Fair. I'm just not used to having this kind of opportunity to get a close-up look at enemies and friends anymore," he admitted. "I don't think we've had this close a look at even a Guardian in a while—and these cruisers are post-war construction."

"I didn't say don't take a look," Henry said. "Get that coordination with *Glorious*. See what we can do with our positions without drawing too much attention, and dig out every passive sensor we've got or can fabricate.

"Point everything we can at the cruisers and the Guardians alike, and learn *whatever* you can. I want to know what Protector-Legate Half-Blue-Third-Red drinks in the morning. Do whatever you think can get us more data on what we're looking at."

"Yes, ser," Ihejirika said.

"Just don't get caught," Henry finished. "We can do a lot with passive sensors, so let's do that. But we don't want to do anything that's going to make Ambassador Todorovich's job harder. Understood?"

"Yes, ser," the tactical officer repeated. "I've got a maneuver pattern already drawn up. Do you want to take a look?"

"Are you confident in it?" Henry asked. "Because you're the tactical officer, Em Ihejirika. I trust your judgment, but I'll take a look if you want."

"I'm confident, ser," Ihejirika told him. "But since you're here, I won't turn down a second set of eyes."

Henry smiled.

"Good answer, Commander, good answer," he said. "All right, show me your plan."

EVENTUALLY, Henry left his bridge crew in the process of setting up the maneuvers and analyses necessary for Ihejirika's plan. He hadn't had much to change on the maneuver pattern—and what he'd changed had only been optimizing.

His crew were a well-oiled machine. Ihejirika, like many of his officers, was ready for the next step. Technically, however, the United Planets Space Force was at peace. That meant its officers were operating under peacetime promotion patterns—in the UPSF, a twice-yearly review.

That review of his people's files would be taking place on Earth in the next few weeks. That review could have three main results: deferred, promoted, held for formal board.

There were other results, but the most common would be deferred or held for a formal board. The reports and files submitted had to mark spectacular actions and improvements for a promotion to be passed entirely on the recommendation of an officer's immediate superiors.

It happened, though, and unless simply being part of the Initiative was a black mark, Henry expected to see a *lot* of his officers and spacers getting well-deserved promotion notices in the near future.

Ihejirika deserved his own XO slot or even his own destroyer. Iyotake deserved the XO slot on a carrier or his own battlecruiser. Everyone would ripple upward through the crew, and it was going to be a giant *pain* for Henry to deal with.

And if he had to write those reports and recommendations again, they'd probably be even more glowing.

He was allowing himself a rare grin when his internal network chimed to let him know he was receiving a communications request. He checked his schedule. He was *supposed* to be reviewing heat radiator reports at the moment, in preparation for meeting with Lieutenant Colonel Song to go over their usage rate of the thousands of the feather-like devices that covered *Raven*'s hull.

Then Henry realized the request had the tags for an external contact and was being relayed directly to him by Moon's senior deputy. It was a direct tightbeam radio from one of the Kozun cruisers...and that meant Henry knew *exactly* who was calling him.

A mental command opened the channel, routing it to the holo-projectors over the desk in his office. He adjusted his own position so the recorder was picking him up clearly—and the commissioning seal and UPA flag behind him.

That precaution proved unnecessary as Star Voice Kalad's image appeared above his desk. She was clearly in her own office aboard her cruiser flagship, but she appeared to be alone.

"Hi, Henry," she said in slow English. "It's good to see you."

"It's good to see you," he agreed. "You didn't seem to think it would happen when we last spoke."

"'The falcon cannot hear the falconer,'" Kalad quoted at him. She'd acquired a taste for Yeats when he'd been teaching her English a long time ago. Back when he'd been the XO of the UPSF battle-cruiser supporting the Kozun Vesheron.

"You misestimated Mal Dakis?" Henry asked.

"So it seems," she said. "Star Commander Kan bore the burden of his failures alone. I met with the First Voice."

Kan had been the officer in charge of the fleet that had tried to hold La-Tar against the Cluster and the UPSF. He'd died with his flagship, leaving Kalad in command of the fleet and stuck ordering a retreat she'd expected to cost her life.

Now, the Kozun officer was silent for a moment. She was probably not only deciding what to say but *how* to say it in English.

"The First Voice agreed with the decision to withdraw. I was commended for my wisdom and promoted, as you see."

"He is wiser than I had dared hope," Henry admitted. A wise enemy was also a dangerous one, which wasn't *great* for the UPA, but he'd live with that since it had saved his friend.

"He fears you," Kalad said. Those three words alone told him that she was confident in the security of their communication. That was *not* a phrase an officer of the Kozun Hierarchy should be using about the First Voice. "Not the UPA, Henry. *You.*"

"I have no ill will for Mal Dakis," Henry told her. "He knows that."

"Perhaps."

The channel was silent. It was an awkward silence, of friends who'd become enemies and weren't quite sure what to say.

"Your mate and child?" Henry finally asked. "They are well?"

"They are," she confirmed. "My mate...feared the First Voice's wrath as well. But I am here...and Star Commander Kan's name is...shit."

"Mud," Henry corrected with an unforced laugh. "*His name is mud* is the metaphor you're aiming for, I think."

"*Shit* fits better for Kozun culture," she told him, her tone playfully prim for a few seconds before she turned serious again.

"Tell me, Henry Wong. Is the Cluster truly prepared to accept peace?"

"They never wanted a war, Kalad. Your people brought it to them, not the other way around," he reminded her.

"We..." She closed her eyes, struggling for a moment before continuing in Kem. "We would hunt vengeance across a thousand stars, as we did against the Kenmiri."

Henry took a moment to process that before shaking his head gently.

"Then perhaps it is best for everyone that the La-Tar Cluster's leaders are more forgiving than the Kozun," he suggested, staying in English. He knew Kalad could follow it even better than she could speak it.

"You have faith in them, then?"

"If Oran Aval has come for peace, she will find it here," Henry told his old friend. "If there is anyone here I doubt, my old friend, it is your people."

And the Drifters, but he wasn't going to say that. Not yet.

"We are here for peace," Kalad insisted.

Henry wished he could believe her...but he knew all too well that Kalad, friend as she was, was entirely capable of lying to him.

CHAPTER TWENTY-EIGHT

Rising Principle might have been using an electronic translator because their native communication involved color and scent changes too subtle for most Ashall species to even register, but their opening statement was brutally precise.

Even Oran Aval remained silent as the Enteni laid out the impacts of the Kozun invasion. The war dead were one thing, but they continued on with the actions of the Kozun occupation. Retaliatory executions. Random home invasions.

A long catalog of actions that Sylvia could only classify as war crimes—though she had to admit that neither the Kozun Hierarchy nor the La-Tar Cluster were signatories to Earth's Geneva Convention.

The room was silent after Rising Principle concluded their estimate of the costs of the Kozun invasion to the Cluster. It wasn't an explicit demand for compensation, but the intent was clear.

Aval finally leaned forward after a minute or so of silence and leveled her gem-blue gaze on Sylvia.

"Neither accepting nor denying the Cluster's clear demand for compensation, I want to understand what *everyone*'s starting position is," she said in her calm Kem. "So, Ambassador Todorovich. What does the United Planets Alliance want here?"

"We want the war to end," Sylvia replied. "We want the Kozun to acknowledge that they invaded without provocation. We want to avoid being dragged back into conflict in this region by our promises to defend the various planets we have signed treaties with.

"We *will* defend those worlds, but we would far rather see the Ra Sector flourish in peaceful trade." She smiled thinly.

"In a perfect universe, we would see the Kozun Hierarchy change," she told Aval. "We do not acknowledge the transfer of authority by military conquest. By that standard, the vast majority of the territory the Hierarchy claims is illegitimate in our eyes."

She raised a hand before Aval could object.

"*That*, Voice Aval, is not part of these negotiations," she warned. "There are ways, perhaps, that the Hierarchy could come to an agreement with the UPA that would allow future treaties and trade, but the *minimum* starting point for that is peace with the La-Tar Cluster."

Sylvia would be delighted but surprised to be able to have that conversation with Oran Aval. The UPA's government and the mega-corporations now beginning to grow their trade networks in the Ra Sector would love to have treaties allowing trade into the Kozun worlds—so long as those worlds weren't enslaved.

"I see," Aval allowed. "It is healthy, I think, for all three of us to know where the others stand as we begin these discussions. We all have our objectives and missions here, but we are all here to discuss peace.

"In the interests of a good-faith demonstration of our intent, the Voices of the Kozun have ordered a unilateral cease-fire on our side. No Hierarchy warships will enter Cluster space until and unless I confirm these discussions have ended in failure."

"And what about the scout ships in the Satra System and else-where?" Sylvia asked.

"The Satra System is a skip nexus outside the stars of the La-Tar

Cluster," the Kozun told her swiftly. "Whether it belongs to the Cluster should, perhaps, be negotiated instead of assumed, yes?"

Sylvia held Aval's gaze, neither of them so much as blinking.

"But yes," Aval finally confirmed. "All of our ships have been withdrawn a minimum of two skips away from the systems of the La-Tar cluster. We wish to avoid any potential misunderstandings that could undermine these discussions."

Sylvia took a moment to consider what Oran Aval had said—or more exactly, *how* she'd said it. She'd replied instantly, but she'd spoken about the *system*, not the ships. *Raven* and their Cluster allies had chased a corvette out of Satra, but was it possible Aval didn't know about that?

If she didn't know, that suggested that Aval wasn't being briefed on everything. That was a dangerous possibility. It meant that the Third Voice's mission could be entirely aboveboard so far as *Aval* knew—and *still* a trap.

"I can-will assure you that the La-Tar will-can-not launch an offensive of our own until these discussions are-can be completed," Rising Principle told the Kozun. "This cease fire fate-time is-was mutual."

"That will help us all, I think," Aval replied. "If we can keep our respective fleets at harbor, that gives us time to sort through the complexities of this situation and find a mutually acceptable agreement."

Rising Principle glared at her, a gesture that was even more intimidating from an Enteni as it required their mouth to be wide open.

"I must admit, Voice Aval, that the situation is not particularly complex from my point of view," Sylvia observed. "The question is not what happened but what the Hierarchy is prepared to do to guarantee that it won't happen again."

"Our word is insufficient, then?" Aval asked.

"Your word is drenched in blood."

The room was silent again and Oran Aval bowed her head slightly.

"I believe we have all postured sufficiently for the opening events," she told the other two diplomats. "I would like a chance to withdraw to my shuttle and review the information you have provided."

"None of this should-could be new to you," Rising Principle objected.

"Perhaps not. Perhaps you have provided more detail than I had before. Perhaps I merely need to consider the opening positions you have presented," Aval said calmly. "In any case, I suggest we adjourn for twelve hours and meet again then.

"That will give us all time to consume the positions we face."

Sylvia glanced over at Principle. The Enteni probably needed the time to chill out. They were gifted at this and had acquired hard-earned experience assembling the alliance that had liberated their world, but they were still young.

"I agree," she said firmly. "We will all take some time to consider our positions and meet again in twelve hours. Rising Principle?"

The Enteni finally closed their mouth and bowed their head in concession.

"Good." Oran Aval shot up to her feet. "I will return to my shuttle and rest there. We will speak again soon."

The Kozun contingent was halfway out of the room before Sylvia could say a word. She let them leave before exhaling a muted sigh.

"That one has-owns no shame," Rising Principle said grimly.

"That is her job," Sylvia warned them. "Whatever her morals or opinions, she has to negotiate the best deal she can for the Kozun." She shook her head. "If I was in her position, you would say *I* have no shame."

They'd be *wrong*, just as Sylvia suspected the Enteni was wrong about the Third Voice. But that shame wouldn't change the positions that Sylvia would present at the negotiating table.

And if, as Sylvia suspected, the Third Voice was sickened by what had been done at La-Tar, Oran Aval wouldn't let it impact her stances. Her duty was to extricate the Hierarchy from the war at a minimum price.

Sylvia's duty, on the other hand, was to make sure the Hierarchy paid so heavily to extract itself from the La-Tar Cluster that they would hesitate to launch another campaign of conquest.

CHAPTER TWENTY-NINE

"Ser, do you have a moment?"

Henry looked up from the command seat to see Ihejirika standing just inside the central pit of *Raven*'s bridge. A wave of his hand closed the screens he'd been working on—though he didn't let himself actively sigh in relief.

As was entirely reasonable, Chief Engineer Song was still on his case about the heat radiator usage rates. Keeping the battlecruiser at Status Two with the gravity shield up required at least three of her four fusion reactors to be online, which produced a *lot* of heat.

Raven's hull was covered with featherlike heat-radiator vanes. Fully extended, as they currently were, they made the ship look even more like her bird namesake that she normally did. Unfortunately, any given radiator vane had a limited useful operating life. Most of the time, the ship was only running two reactors outside of combat or skip space, which meant Song could cycle through the radiators and stretch that life.

Right now, that was proving harder than usual and they were burning through the stock of spares almost twice as fast as expected. That meant they only had enough spares for two months instead of four, but it was Song's job to be concerned about that and find ways around it.

But Henry still found heat-radiation charts to be the single most boring part of his job.

"What do you need, Commander?" he asked Ihejirika.

"We found something odd, going over the Drifter and Kozun ships, ser," the tactical officer told him. "May I show you?"

"Is it dangerous?" Henry asked.

"Probably not," Ihejirika said. "Just...interesting."

"Go ahead," Henry told him. A mental command surrendered control of several of the large screens around the pit to the tactical officer.

Two images appeared on the screens, two-dimensional projections of a ship part that Henry instantly recognized. They were superheavy plasma-cannon turrets, the main weapon of every Kenmiri and most Vesheron capital ships.

"One of these is the forward turret from one of the Kozun cruisers," Ihejirika told him. "The other is a randomly selected turret from one of the Guardians. If you can pick out which is which, I'd be surprised, but that's not entirely relevant right now."

"What is relevant, then, Commander?" Henry asked.

The two images moved together, overlaying on top of each other. One was shaded in red, the other was shaded in green...and very little red was visible.

"I thought you said these were from two different ships," he asked. Even the Kenmiri only had so much consistency between turrets.

"I did," Ihejirika confirmed. "The red-shaded turret is from the Kozun cruiser. The green-shaded turret is from the Drifter Guardian. Their profiles are fundamentally identical. And to make the point very clear..."

A third turret projection, shaded in blue, appeared next to the overlaid pair. As Henry watched, it converged with the others to overlay again.

A lot more blue was visible than red now. The blue turret was distinctly different from the other two.

"The blue turret is the standard schematic projection of a Kenmiri dreadnought's heavy turret," Ihejirika noted. "It would have slight variations from the actual construction of any given turret, but it would be close. I would *expect*, in fact, to see about the variation between the Kozun and Drifter turret between any two Kenmiri turrets."

"You're suggesting the Kozun bought their turrets from the Drifters?" Henry asked.

"Not just from the Drifters," Ihejirika said. "From Blue Stripe Green Stripe Orange Stripe specifically. Not all of them, though."

A fourth turret, this one shaded yellow, appeared on the diagram. This one was clearly different from *all* of the other three.

"This one appears to be homebuilt, but it's from the same ship," Ihejirika explained. "Each of the cruisers carries four heavy plasma guns, but only *five* of the turrets across three ships are homebuilt.

"The rest were built by Blue Stripe Green Stripe Orange Stripe," he concluded. "Even their most powerful homebuilt warships relied on the Drifters for their armaments. I...I'm not sure what that means, ser, but I couldn't help but think it was important."

Henry nodded slowly, looking at the four overlaid turrets.

"If nothing else, it tells us that these particular Drifters have their fingers *deep* in that particular pie," he said. "Not as neutral as they'd have us believe."

"That's a problem, isn't it, ser?"

"Potentially," Henry stressed. "Not definitely. I assume we're watching the Drifters as much as the Kozun, yes?"

"Yes, ser," Ihejirika confirmed. "Everyone is sitting at much the same status as we are. Not full battle stations, but capacitors are charged and shields are up. We've got better eyes on them than they have on us, though. We'll have at least fifteen, maybe twenty seconds' warning before they can bring the plasma guns online—and we could bring the grav-driver up without anyone noticing."

"*We* are not blowing up the negotiations," Henry said drily. The image of the four overlaid turrets made him nervous, though. He couldn't put his finger on why, though.

"Of course not, ser," his tactical officer said quickly. "So far, everything actually looks completely honest. Everyone is doing exactly what they said."

"The negotiators have only had one meeting so far. Todorovich is due to update me on how that went in a couple of hours," Henry said. "But you're right. So far, everything I see suggests everyone is doing exactly what they said they'd do."

"That's good, right?" Ihejirika asked.

Henry chuckled.

"Yes," he agreed. "And yet I keep expecting the trap. I could be wrong. I could be paranoid. But there's *nobody* here I actually trust, Commander. So, we keep our eyes open."

"That's the job, ser. We'll warn you if anything changes."

"Thank you." Henry looked at the overlaid turrets again. "Good work on this, Okafor. I don't quite know what it means, but I think it's important."

"One of the junior petties noticed it, ser," Ihejirika told him. "Second Class Lau Yi. I flagged the comparison with the Kenmiri and helped ID the locally built turret, but PO Lau noticed the similarities between the Kozun and Drifter installations."

"Make a note of that, Commander," Henry said. "That goes in their file."

"Already done, ser."

"I'M REASONABLY certain I would have noticed everything exploding, so I presume the situation outside is progressing calmly?" Sylvia Todorovich's holographic image asked.

Henry snorted and poured himself a cup of black tea.

"That's a way to describe it," he told her. "I think everybody is just waiting for somebody else to pull a trigger. We're not going to, but we're expecting everyone else to. I have the vague feeling that everyone *else* is in the same boat."

"That sounds about right to me," she agreed. "I don't have a feel on the Drifters, though. They don't have anyone at the negotiations." She shrugged. "Not their part in this. They're here to make sure no one else does anything stupid."

"I'm wondering if we even needed them now," Henry admitted.

"We needed someone to play courier with the Kozun, if nothing else, and the Kozun wanted a neutral third party," Todorovich pointed out. "It wasn't our call."

Henry nodded, trying not to draw *too* much warmth from even her holographic presence. He was surprised by how *unconflicted* he was feeling with regard to Todorovich these days. The smarter part of him was convinced it was a trap, in more ways than one, but his emotions didn't seem to care.

"Well, we're here and everyone is watching each other like hawks," he told her. "You've met the Third Voice now. What do you think the chances are?"

"Of peace?" Todorovich asked. "High. I'm surprised to say it, but I think Aval is actually under orders not to leave here *without* a deal. I suspect there are probably prices she won't agree to, but I think she is honestly here to negotiate.

"I think she's going to drag it out as long as she can to cover for whatever *else* the Hierarchy is up to right now and to convince us to let them off as easily as she can, but she's honestly here for peace."

"Are you sure you can read her that well?" Henry asked. "Cross-species and cross-culture...it's hard to read someone *that* clearly."

The microexpressions that all Ashall shared could help, but they were limited in what they communicated. Enough, in his experience, to win a poker game. Not enough, he would guess, to carry high-stakes interstellar negotiation.

"It's not just that," she told him. "With a few exceptions, she's negotiating the way I would with those orders. Though she *did* start with the Cluster having to compensate them for everything they'd lost in the failed invasion."

Henry had to pause at that.

"Seriously?" he asked.

"She knew it was a nonstarter, but it was a place to start that gave her room to concede," Todorovich replied. "I shut it down, I think, but she's playing for ground she can give up without costing the Hierarchy anything."

"And here I thought the Hierarchy was rich and powerful," Henry murmured, considering the discussion he'd just had with Ihejirika. "Now I'm wondering..."

"Henry?" she asked.

"We ran an analysis on the cruisers' weapons," he told her. "Most of the heavy turrets are Drifter construction. They either bought or were *given* heavy weapons by Blue Stripe Green Stripe Orange Stripe.

"My general impression is that the Drifters *don't* sell heavy weapons without more than money on the table," he concluded. "There's more going on here than I know, and it's making me twitchy."

"The Council didn't make it sound like they were that close to the Hierarchy," Todorovich said. "But playing games is what they do. Their job is to protect the Convoy, after all."

"So long as we can make peace with the Kozun, I don't give a shit about the Convoy," Henry admitted. "They're far from harmless, but so long as they're heading in the opposite direction from us, they can do whatever they want."

"I'm not sure they are," Todorovich warned. "Part of the price they demanded for playing third-party security here was the right to set up a trading post in UPA space. I think they want to get out into our stars and see what trading they can do beyond the former Kenmiri Empire.

"Where else are they going to find truly new opportunities, after all?"

"That could work out well for all of us," Henry said. "Every time I add up the numbers, Sylvia, I come up with the fact that nobody wins if this conference goes sideways."

"But?" she asked.

"But I still feel like someone painted crosshairs on my back," he told her. "Be careful, Sylvia. There's a point where *our* paranoia becomes a threat to someone else...potentially one worth acting on."

"That's why nobody knows about Bicycle," she replied. "Everything is under control, Henry. I promise. Nothing is going to happen to *Carpenter*. Or me."

Henry wasn't sure why she'd added the last, but it helped. He gave her a wan smile and bowed his head slightly.

"I know," he conceded. "But it's my job to worry. And yours, I suppose, to bring this whole mess to a conclusion."

"And we are both *very* good at our jobs," Todorovich told him with an uncharacteristically bright grin.

CHAPTER THIRTY

THE CONFERENCE ROOM FILLED MORE QUICKLY THE SECOND time, with all three groups arriving simultaneously and being expertly guided into the room's three separate doors by *Carpenter*'s crew. Sylvia wasn't sure where the Cluster had found that many diplomatic junior officers and spacers, but it had probably been part of the refit to make *Carpenter* a diplomatic vessel as well as a warship.

She waited for Aval and Rising Principle to sit down with the rest of their staff, while remaining standing herself. She met each of their gazes in turn with a small smile before speaking.

"Good morning. Are we ready to get started on this?" she asked them. She didn't wait for a response before plowing on. "The way I see it, we have two fundamental choices here.

"Firstly, we can decide whether we are all here for peace," she said. "If we are, then everything after that is details, is it not? If we start from that point, we are more likely to end this in a deal for everyone.

"Secondly, we can either start with the easy parts or the hard parts. We all know reparations are going to be the hard part. So..." She spread her hands. "While the UPA has a role in this, the main discussion is between the Hierarchy and the Cluster. I leave those two decisions to you."

She took her seat, watching and waiting to see just what happened next.

For a few moments, what happened was nothing. Then Oran Aval gestured for Rising Principle to speak and leaned back in her chair.

"The Cluster wants peace," Principle said calmly. "But we must-will require that the Hierarchy pay for their crimes. We did-could not bring war to our own fate-time-place. The Hierarchy did-could that. All that followed is-was by their choice."

"War happens," Oran Aval countered. "Tens of thousands of our soldiers and spacers died as well, killed by your alliance and the UPSF. You deny us any claim for compensation for those deaths but demand that we pay compensation for the deaths of your soldiers and spacers?"

"We did-would not invade your worlds," Principle said. "We did-would not instigate the conflict. You did."

"I have to agree with Rising Principle here," Sylvia said. "You attacked the Cluster. To claim that a blood debt is owed to the Hierarchy for those who died in the Hierarchy's invasion is hypocritical at best."

"We are prepared to concede that point, *perhaps*, but we are not prepared to bear the weight of every loss the Cluster wishes to blame us for," Aval said. "Military campaigns cause losses on both sides. We are not responsible for every death while we were present in the Cluster."

"We could-will accept the surrender of the architects of the plan to face justice under Cluster law," Rising Principle suggested.

Sylvia swallowed an urge to applaud. *That* was no concession to offer, and Rising Principle knew it. If nothing else, she was reasonably sure the First Voice had been instrumental in that planning. Plus, the Hierarchy wasn't going to admit that their actions on La-Tar had been criminal.

But since it *sounded* like a concession, and such a reasonable one, Oran Aval was going to have to backpedal *hard*.

"We do not accept that our operations in the Cluster qualify as crimes requiring justice," Aval replied after a few moments of silence. "A nation, a people, must follow their own interests. This is no crime."

"So, the Kenmiri your people executed on Kozun were innocent of crimes?" Sylvia asked.

"They had invaded and enslaved our people!" Oran Aval snapped instinctively, only realizing that she'd walked into Sylvia's trap a moment too late.

"*Exactly* as the Kozun did in La-Tar," she told the Kozun Voice. "Your own people's actions suggest that invading and enslaving worlds for their resources, forcing entire nations to bend to another's will...you have called these grand crimes and executed both invaders and collaborators alike.

"Does that same standard not apply to the Kozun, Voice Aval?"

"We came to La-Tar and the cluster of surrounding worlds to bring stability and prosperity," Aval said. "Had we not been met with violence and agitation, everyone would have benefited."

"I have heard the same words in the mouths of Kenmiri, Voice Aval," Sylvia reminded the other woman. "They, too, claimed that all they did was for the benefit of everyone. So, tell me, Oran Aval, does puppeting the words of your slavemasters taste like ash in your mouth?"

The conference room was deathly silent for at least twenty seconds.

"What would you know of slavery, *Terran*?" Aval spat. "You from your glittering cities and untouched worlds beyond the reach of the Kenmiri?"

"It is-was not the Terrans you invaded," Rising Principle interrupted before Sylvia could speak. "It is-was La-Tar. La-Tar knows-knew slavery. The Kozun invasion is-was not the first fate-time soldiers marched our streets. It is-was not the first time innocents are-were murdered for the actions of others.

"We know-knew your kind. We know-knew the Kenmiri. Your words change-changed nothing. You wore-wear masks, but you are-were the same. Between Kenmiri and Kozun, both is-are *slavers*."

Aval visibly exhaled, laying her hands on the table with her thumbs and forefingers pressed together.

"While I will not offer reparations for losses incurred in open battle, I will accept that Kozun enforcers on La-Tar exceeded their orders and mandates," she said, her tone surprisingly level. "We are prepared to *consider* a demand for reparations based on civilian deaths and collateral damage to nonmilitary sites on La-Tar.

"What happens in battle is war. What was done after the annexation...while I will not call them crimes, I will call them *errors* for which we will consider making amends."

Rising Principle produced another tablet from inside their robes and slid it across the table.

No one needed to ask what it was. Oran Aval picked it up and read the text on it. She scrolled through the data with ease—La-Tar and Kozun were both still using fundamentally Kenmiri tech. It would be a long time before the software diverged enough to cause usability problems.

Aval's poker face was perfect. She kept scrolling through the data, not even microexpressions showing her emotions as she went through the information Rising Principle had provided.

"May I keep this, Envoy Rising Principle?" she asked. "I will need time to...consider this information."

"Yes."

The tablet disappeared into Aval's tunic and she leaned back in her chair.

"My staff and I will assess the data from La-Tar," she promised. "We will have an...offer by the time of our next meeting. As part of that, I believe we should consider a discussion of borders."

She laid a small holoprojector on the table, creating a three-dimensional map of the La-Tar Cluster and the surrounding stars and skip lines. The Cluster was highlighted in a pale orange color, while the visible portion of the Hierarchy—Aval wasn't kind enough to provide a full map of the Hierarchy's current territory—was teal.

The closest the two territories came to each other was at La-Tar itself, four skips from the industrial world of Sitros. Sitros was two skips, just under forty-eight hours' travel, from La-Sho, an agriworld definitively under Kozun control.

"Satra is-was not negotiable," Rising Principle said sharply, a tendril pointing at the large star one skip away from La-Tar. It wasn't the only giant on the map, but it was the one right between the Cluster and the Hierarchy.

"That is acceptable, though it is not a concession without value," Aval warned. "My suggestion, in fact, is that Satra, Ichnu, Relo and Kort all be formally recognized as belonging to the Cluster."

Sylvia took a moment to place all four of those star systems in the map. None were inhabited systems. All were closer to the Cluster than the Hierarchy, but close enough to Kozun space that they *could* project power to them.

All of them were red giants or blue hypergiants, easily skipped to from vast distances. They would be critical components of the trade networks that everyone was hoping to grow across the Ra Sector.

Right now, they were almost worthless and easy concessions for the Kozun to make—but everyone could see the *potential* value of the systems, which made them an argument for lesser reparations.

"We would, of course, consider the value of these systems and our recognition of the Cluster's ownership as we assess the rest of the treaty," Aval purred.

Sylvia had to respect the other woman. She'd managed to maneuver Aval into a position where she had no choice but to concede on reparations, and the Kozun had promptly produced a series of concessions that cost the Kozun nothing but could be counted against the value of the debts owed.

"We already control those stars," Rising Principle pointed out.

"Kozun recognition is meaningless without true effort. A commitment to help the Cluster *defend* that ownership, perhaps."

The UPA ambassador leaned back in her chair. The Enteni envoy also clearly recognized what Aval was doing and had their own tricks. A mutual-defense agreement with the Kozun, even if only for the skip nexuses, would definitely have its advantages.

Sylvia was opening her mouth to suggest they take a recess to consider the points raised when the world went mad.

CHAPTER THIRTY-ONE

If Henry hadn't been on *Raven's* bridge, he might never have known what happened. He was having a spirited discussion with Anna Song about the heat radiators, one that had been on and off since they'd arrived in the Lon System.

"The ship simply isn't designed to run the gravity shield twenty-four seven for weeks on end," Song told him, the engineer's image gesturing energetically in Henry's screen. "She *can*, yes, but it's going to wear on the heat radiators."

"All right, Colonel, and what's the solution?" Henry asked. "We're not turning the shield *off*, so…"

"If we reduce the shield's shear factor by fifty percent, our safety equipment should suffice for thirty-minute work shifts on the exterior hull," Song told him. "A team of ten can replace an average of two radiators a minute. If we do a careful analysis of which sectors of radiators are in the worst shape, we can replace them in batches of sixty. One thirty-minute work shift every day should keep us ahead of the degradation from running the shield nonstop."

"And if we don't risk reducing the shield power?" he said.

"We will start seeing radiator failures after five days," she replied. "Potentially before that."

"We can continue to operate at full capacity with up to ten percent of our radiators offline," Henry pointed out. "How long until that metric, Colonel Song?"

"Nine to eleven days, depending on our luck," she admitted.

"This hopefully won't last nine days," Henry said. "And if it's starting to look like it will, we can readjust. I don't want to weaken our defenses when we have enemies right here, Colonel."

"They won't even be able to see from the outside," the engineer argued. "Eight thousand gravities of shear versus sixteen thousand... it's still going to screw up anything they're seeing."

"We can reverse the shear effect from this side to get accurate sensor data," he reminded her. "I'd be very surprised if the Drifters, for example, can't tell the difference between *Raven*'s shields and *Glorious*'s. And that, Colonel Song, is only four thousand gravities of difference.

"Keep an eye on everything," he ordered. "I am reviewing the reports and I *do* see the problem, Colonel, but right now, we need that shield more than we nee—"

"VAMPIRE!"

The shouted alert shocked Henry to silence—it shocked the entire bridge to silence as Cornelia Ybarra, the assistant tactical officer on duty for his shift, bellowed the single word warning.

Missiles incoming.

"Evasive maneuvers," Henry barked as his attention snapped to the tactical displays. "Ybarra, weapons free. Point-defense lasers go!"

There'd been no warning. One moment, everything was continuing on as normal. The next, every single one of Kalad's cruisers had opened fire, spitting missiles at the La-Tar and UPA ships.

Twenty missiles were targeted on Carpenter, forty on *Glorious* and sixty on *Raven*—fired at point-blank range with a thousand kilometers per second of launch velocity.

Thirty seconds should have been enough, but everything had

been calm for days. Henry had talked to Kalad; she had seemed fully peaceful. Todorovich had told him that the Kozun ambassador even seemed aboveboard.

And all of that, it seemed, was a lie—and it seemed Mal Dakis had decided his Third Voice was expendable.

Carpenter was the first ship to get any of her missile defenses online, several seconds ahead of *Glorious* or *Raven*. The La-Tar ship didn't have any passive defenses that could save her, though, and the range was just too short.

She shot down six of the twenty missiles. The rest detonated, converting themselves into short-range plasma cannon that washed over the half-megaton escort in the blaze of stellar fusion.

Glorious and *Raven* weren't able to help. They shot down fewer missiles than the La-Tar ship, and Henry's world shrank as his ship's gravity generators *screamed*.

He knew the sound. He'd heard it twice before, but only once this badly. Resonance-disruptor warheads tore into his ship, sending feedback loops crashing back into her shield projectors.

And then silence. Devastating, damning, silence...for a fraction of a second before the entire battlecruiser rang like a bell.

The battle stations alert rang through the ship, but Henry would never remember hitting the button. A second alert added as he hit a second command.

"All hands to acceleration tanks," he barked. He took a moment to meet Song's gaze in the intercom screen. "Relay through Henriksson, Anna," he told her.

He rose from his seat, taking in the situation around his command even as the panel in front of him slid open. He didn't even look at the stand with its mask and hose as it rose up to meet him, his feet finding the right spots instinctively.

Carpenter was gone, obliterated by a dozen conversion warheads. Sylvia Todorovich was gone with her, and Henry *could not* let himself feel what that meant to him.

Glorious was no better. They'd estimated twenty-five resonance-disruptor warheads would take down a destroyer's shields—and he suspected these ones had been upgraded again. He'd have to go back through the sensor records to learn exactly how *Glorious* had died, but *Raven* was alone.

He closed the mask over his face, shutting his eyes as he switched his attention to his internal network. Even the automated reports were still updating. Less than a minute had passed since the Kozun ships had opened fire, except...

The Kozun weren't firing now. The cruisers were frozen in space, even their engines offline. They weren't maneuvering, they weren't firing—they hadn't even activated their heavy plasma cannon.

They weren't following up on their overwhelming alpha strike. If they were expecting him to surrender, Star Voice Kalad was going to learn a harsh lesson about his patience.

"We are maneuvering at point five KPS-squared," Bazzoli reported, her voice breathless as Henry finished sinking into his tank. He didn't even need to check to know that the navigator wasn't on the bridge. She'd been off-duty and would be in the tank in her quarters.

Once they were in the tanks, the true bridge was a virtual space now. Her avatar was present in that space, which made her physical location irrelevant.

They lost efficiency from using the virtual space—but less than they'd lose to being under the twenty gravities they'd face at full acceleration.

"Get us away from Kalad's people," Henry barked. "We're at eighty percent in the tanks. The *instant* we hit one hundred, you take us to everything the girl will handle."

"I don't have engineering reports on the damage; I don't know what that is," Bazzoli admitted. "Compensators are online now; we've definitely got half a KPS-squared, but I don't know if she'll take *any* uncompensated accel."

Ninety percent in the tanks.

"Ser, damage reports updating," Henriksson cut into Henry's

head. "Gravity shield is offline; we've got drones inspecting but no idea when we'll have a timeline."

"That's not the worst of it," Henry said grimly. He could hear that.

"No, ser. The…" She swallowed. "The keel is broken, ser. Gravity driver is offline. Lasers are offline. Structural integrity is…questionable at best. Colonel Song doesn't believe the heavy weapons are repairable, ser."

Henry said nothing as he processed. The keel was the central chamber that ran the length of the ship, the heavily armored core that contained both the lensing chambers for *Raven*'s heavy lasers and the gravity tube for her main gun.

If the damage had penetrated *that* deeply in the hull…

"How are we still *here*?" he asked.

"There weren't any conversion warheads in the salvo that hit us," Ihejirika told him, the tactical officer linking into the command net. "Just disruptor weapons. And ser?"

"What?"

"The Guardians."

Henry's situational awareness had been laser-focused on his ship and the threats to his ship. For whatever reason, the Kozun hadn't continued firing—no one was even following *Raven* as she accelerated away from the wrecks of her charges.

Presumably, the last several minutes had been filled with a desperate exchange of messages between the Drifters and the Kozun, but that was clearly over. The Guardians opened fire first, the three Drifter ships mustering thirty heavy plasma cannon between them.

They weren't even using missiles at this range. Massive blasts of plasma hammered into the shields of the Kozun cruisers, and Kalad's ships finally stirred from their shocked stillness—to fire back.

"You still have us in range," Henry murmured. "You didn't finish us off."

"Ser, the Kozun…not all of their cannon are firing," Ihejirika reported.

"I'm guessing the numbers line up with the weapons we know they built themselves," Henry said quietly.

There was a long pause.

"Yes, ser," Ihejirika agreed.

Henry checked. Only ninety-two percent of the crew listed as being in acceleration tanks. There were still dozens of people scattered through the ship, many of them likely trapped by debris and damage.

Others were dead. The system was giving him that estimate and he refused to let it do anything but define whether all of his people were in the tanks.

"Dr. Axelrod," he said grimly, linking himself to the medbay. "You have three minutes to get the wounded into acceleration tanks."

"That's not possible," she replied. "I only have twelve surgery tanks and they're already full. We still have people on their way to medba—"

"Get them into the nearest emergency tanks," Henry told her. "They're as safe there as they are in the tanks in sickbay if you don't have surgery tanks free for them."

"Ser, some of them will die."

"Lieutenant Commander Axelrod." He intentionally used Shani Axelrod's military rank instead of her medical title. "If we don't get clear of the battlespace, we're all going to die. You have three minutes."

He cut her off and turned his attention back to the virtual bridge.

"Moon, fire off the Yellow Bicycle skip drones," he told his coms officer. "Code is D, I repeat, the code is D."

His attention shifted to the engineering officer, the young woman responsible for collating damage reports from across the battlecruiser and telling him what he needed to know.

"Lieutenant Henriksson, you have three minutes to work out how much strain *Raven* can take," he told her. "Because in three minutes, Commander Bazzoli is going to take us to the maximum acceleration we can handle."

The battle had well and truly been joined behind them, but Henry knew the risks. His ship had only added ten thousand kilometers to the range. He needed to add *five hundred* thousand kilometers before he'd be safe.

At half a KPS^2, that would take over twenty minutes. He'd save seven minutes if *Raven* had her full acceleration.

"I'm sorry, old friend," he murmured to Kalad as her three cruisers flung their crippled weapons at the Guardians. "I can *suspect* but I can't *trust*."

And it wasn't like *Raven* was going to change the course of that battle in her current state.

CHAPTER THIRTY-TWO

Despite the handicaps the Drifters had inflicted on the Kozun, *Raven* was almost a quarter million kilometers distant when the first cruiser finally died. Everyone, including Henry, appeared to have underestimated the shield upgrades the Kozun had installed on their new warships.

"Remaining ships are breaking off," Ihejirika reported. "Guardians are pursuing."

"That's going to be painful to watch," Iyotake said from the CIC. "The cruisers have point four KPS-squared on the Guardians, but they're not going to make it."

Even as Henry's XO spoke, the Guardians finally started launching missiles. The range was short enough that they would be coming in slowly. Without surprise, they'd be vulnerable to Kalad's missile defenses. Some would get through anyway.

Raven continued to open the range at point seven KPS^2. It was all the battered starship could take, and Henry was praying for every second Kalad's ships could buy him. The Drifters might just be enforcing the peace as they'd promised...but *nobody* was talking to *Raven*.

"Ser, we have a problem," Moon told him. "The skip drone..."

"Commander?" Henry asked. "What happened?"

"I launched eleven skip drones at the Ra-Seventy-Oh-Five skip line," she reported. "We also had one prepositioned eighty percent of the way there. Paranoia, I thought...but they're all gone."

"Gone," Henry repeated, turning his attention to that section of the display. There were no skip-drone icons on the display...and there was a glittering array of new red hostile icons near the Ra-175 skip line.

"Data is limited," Moon said quickly. "But it appears that someone positioned laser satellites along the line to Ra-One-Seventy-Five. They were tracking our skip drones as they were sent home before, so when new drones went out..."

"They shot them down." The satellites were millions of kilometers away, well outside the range at which Henry could do anything about them. The presumably robotic craft would be no threat to *Raven* in her normal state, but right now...

"Launch a new spread," he ordered. "At least twenty drones; send them as far around as you can."

"Yes, ser," Moon confirmed. "Already programming the courses and messages."

"Include all the data we have on the mines," Henry told her. "They shouldn't be able to threaten Battle Group *Scorpius*, but let's make sure."

"The Kozun just lost another cruiser," Iyotake reported as Moon set to work. "It's almost over."

"What's their maneuver cone?" Henry asked. "Are we out of their range?"

"Their vector is away from us now. Combined with our own acceleration, we'll be clear of their laser and plasma range in two minutes," Ihejirika reported. "Maneuver cone is similar. We have a small thrust advantage, less than we'd have normally, but..."

The vector cones appeared in the virtual screens around Henry. He could keep the range open for a while. In the long run, the

Drifters would be able to spread out and cut off his escape routes... even ignoring their fighters.

"When was the last drone dispatched to *Scorpius*?" he asked Moon.

"The light from its skip arrived thirty seconds before the Kozun launched," she told him after a moment. "They were watching for that."

"Forty-eight hours," Henry concluded. "Twelve hours for that drone to arrive. Twenty-four for them to realize they're not getting more messages, and then twelve hours for *Scorpius* to skip here."

He shook his head.

"Let's hope the second wave of drones gets through," Iyotake reported. "Because I don't think we're going to get two days."

"New bogeys, ser," Ihejirika reported. "Multiple bogeys. I am detecting fighter wings deploying from all three Guardians. Estimate sixty, six-zero, starfighters...vectors hostile. I repeat, *vectors hostile.*"

That meant they were on an intercept course and weren't communicating. Sixty starfighters...

"Acceleration?" Henry asked.

"Two point..." Ihejirika swallowed. "Two point two KPS-squared, ser."

"Understood." *Raven*'s captain looked at the icons and wished he could change *something, anything*, about the situation unfolding around him. Two point two KPS^2 was ten percent higher acceleration than any Vesheron or El-Vesheron starfighter the UPA had on record.

It was less than the Lancers *Raven* carried and that was their only hope.

He closed his eyes. With the data coming via his internal network, it made no difference to what he was seeing but it made him feel better.

"Designate Drifter contacts hostile," he ordered. "Leave the Kozun hostile for now; there's not much we can do either way there."

"Understood," Iyotake said softly. New data codes flashed across the display and Henry took a moment to take status of the entire situation.

New red icons started to glitter out by the skip line as he watched, and he simply nodded as his expectations were confirmed. There were at least a hundred laser platforms blocking the route to Battle Group *Scorpius*. In her current state, those mines were a threat to *Raven* herself.

The skip drones didn't stand a chance.

The Drifter starfighters needed to shed their motherships' velocity before they came after him. They carried full-size missiles and could engage at long range, though. If they wanted to chase him down, they could do so—but everything he saw said *he* still had missile launchers.

The real weapon against them was his own starfighters, though, and he checked their status. The line of red icons that answered his mental query was *not* what he expected, and he swallowed a curse.

"O'Flannagain, report," he snapped.

"When we get back home, I am going to hunt down the *ratfucker* who designed the Lancer's storage protocols, and I am going to carve their genitalia out with a *rusty fucking spoon*," *Raven*'s CAG snarled into the radio.

"Report," Henry repeated, though he suspected he was going to agree with her assessment.

"The SF-One-Thirty does not run its internal compensators while in storage status," O'Flannagain ground out. "None of our starfighters do. Every *other fucking fighter* I've ever flown, however, could *take a fucking hit*.

"The Lancer is too fragile," she concluded. "The GMS system is carefully aligned. An unexpected impact throws everything *out* of alignment. So, I have eight multi-million-dollar starfighters that can't fly until we fully recalibrate their engines.

"Which we can't do under subjective thrust."

"There are sixty starfighters chasing us, O'Flannagain," Henry said mildly. "Slowing down isn't a great plan."

"No shit," she agreed. "My techs are throwing the manual out and attempting recalibrations via remote drone while under eleven pseudogravities of subjective thrust. The worst case is we write off a starfighter, and, unfortunately, I can spare one. Two of my people are in medbay. Gaunt is dead."

Henry could have seen that, but he couldn't look at casualty reports right now. He was keeping his grief compartmentalized, both for his crew and for Todorovich.

He couldn't look at the lists of the dead until this was over.

"Best-case scenario?" he asked.

"Twenty minutes and I'll have one bird," she snapped. "If it *works*, we'll have the rest ten minutes after that. At that point, ser, I'll be looking for pilots."

"We'll see what we can buy, CAG, but you might only have ten minutes," he warned her.

"It's supposed to be a two-hour process in one gravity," O'Flannagain replied. "Cross your fingers, ser."

Henry's attention turned back to tactical. The starfighters were now heading his way and he didn't even have *shields*.

"Ihejirika," he said calmly. "I read our missile launchers are online?"

"Yes, ser," the tactical officer confirmed. "We've also got about sixty percent of our antimissile lasers."

"Best news I've had all day," Henry admitted grimly. "Those starfighters don't have magazine capacity. We do. Open fire as you can range on them."

"Yes, ser."

He turned to Henriksson.

"Lieutenant?"

"Yes, ser?" the engineering officer replied, her voice strained.

"Tell me I have a gravity shield."

"We rebuilt with all of those new breakers," she said quietly. "If we flip them all and power back up, there's a sixty percent chance we have the shield back. We have drones inspecting them all as we speak."

"I'm guessing I wouldn't like the *other* forty percent in those odds?" Henry asked.

"Song says…twenty percent chance we pop a couple more breakers and nothing happens. Twenty percent chance one or more of the breakers is melted through and we permanently burn out the gravity generators."

Henry exhaled and nodded against the viscous gel surrounding him.

"And how long until we've checked all those breakers?" he asked softly.

"Fifteen minutes, ser."

He looked at the pursuing starfighters.

"You have five."

CHAPTER THIRTY-THREE

Sylvia woke up to darkness. It took her a solid several seconds to realize that there was a damp cloth wrapped around her head and reach up to touch it.

"How badly is she injured?" she heard Oran Aval ask in Kem.

"She will live," Alex Thompson replied. "And if she does not, *you* will not."

She had no idea what was going on, but it didn't sound good.

"I'm fine, Commander," she managed to get out, trying to sit up. She could understand Kem, but speaking it felt beyond her.

"You are no such thing," Thompson replied sharply. "You hit your head, Ambassador. You have a minor concussion and you were bleeding pretty badly."

"What happened? How long was I out?" Sylvia demanded. She reached up to try and remove the cloth, but a firm hand intercepted her.

"Leave it for now, Em Todorovich," the GroundDiv officer told her. "You're still bleeding. As for what happened..." He sighed. "The Kozun opened fire. *Carpenter* was destroyed; we don't know what happened to the rest of the task group."

Her head felt fuzzy but something in that didn't sound quite right.

"We're *aboard Carpenter*," she finally noted.

"We were," Thompson agreed. "Now we're in some kind of heavily armored safety capsule in the wreckage of a ship that had three hundred people aboard. People the Kozun killed."

"Right." Sylvia had to recalibrate her brain for Kem and *fast*. "I need to see, Commander. Can you move the bandage that much?"

"Give me a moment. Roi!"

Another set of hands touched her head a moment later, delicately adjusting the cloth so that it eventually lifted above her eyebrows. She still couldn't see and she could *feel* the crust of dried blood now.

"Close your eyes," the French noncom helping Thompson told her. "We need to clean them."

Sylvia obeyed and a new warm wet cloth passed over her face, clearing away the dried blood.

"Bien," Chief Bilal Roi said, stepping back to survey their handiwork. "It's not perfect," they warned her. "The wound has mostly stopped bleeding, but your internal network is working overtime to keep the concussion under control. The more you can rest, the better."

"You're a GroundDiv field medic, Chief," Sylvia pointed out with what she knew was a wan smile. "When was the last time your patients actually rested?"

Roi snorted and stepped back, allowing Sylvia to look over the rest of the room. Everyone who'd been in the room when she'd blacked out was still there, but the Kozun group was now pressed back against a wall, under the guns of her third GroundDiv trooper and the La-Tar bodyguards.

"Felix?" Sylvia said quietly.

"I'm here, Ambassador," her chief of staff replied, stepping into her field of view.

"Thanks. Turning my head hurts," she admitted. "Where are we at?"

"Voice Aval ordered her people to lay down their weapons as soon as we realized what had happened," Felix Leitz told her. "They've been under guard since; you were only out for twenty minutes. Long enough to scare us."

"The security pod contains the conference room and not much more," Thompson explained. "If anyone other than the diplomatic contingents survived, we don't know. We have life support and heat control for a little while, but I don't know how long."

The big GroundDiv officer shook his head.

"I don't know fucking anything, ser," he admitted. "We have *Carpenter*'s sensor data up to the last moment, but there wasn't enough warning for anything. The Kozun opened fire and *Carpenter* was closest.

"If it wasn't for this armored safety pod, we'd all be dead with the ship."

"And everyone else probably thinks we are," Sylvia murmured. "All right. I need to talk to Rising Principle."

"Are you up to that?" Leitz asked.

"No choice," she told him. She leaned on Roi to get up to her feet, nodding to the noncom before carefully crossing the conference room to where the Enteni was standing.

They still had artificial gravity. Of all the things they could be wasting power on, that seemed ridiculous to her—but very few people in the concealed escape pod had zero-gee experience.

"Ambassador Rising Principle," she greeted them in careful Kem. She was certain she was speaking noticeably slower, but she didn't have much of a choice.

"Ambassador Todorovich. I am-was grateful you survived," the Enteni told her. She couldn't read them well, but she had a sudden overwhelming sense of youth from the La-Tar diplomat. Rising Principle was young for their job, and *this* was outside their experience.

"The Voice?"

"Is-was detained after her people attacked," Rising Principle said.

"She surrendered. If you had-was died, she would-should have-were joined you."

That wasn't diplomatic at all, though Sylvia could understand it.

"This module," she said. "How much power and life support do we have?"

Principle gestured a familiar Ashall officer over to them.

"Trosh, how much fate-time do we have-has?"

The dark-green-skinned officer grimaced.

"Life support, eight La-Tar days," he told them. "Power, about the same. The problem is that we did not expect to need to see what was going on outside. My people are trying to rig up some eyes, but we do not know what happened after the Kozun attacked.

"We might need to consider reducing our power consumption to conceal our presence. For the moment, *Carpenter*'s wreckage is covering us...we hope."

Sylvia nodded, then winced against the dizziness that followed. Her network let her ignore the concussion to a point...but only to a point.

"We need those eyes," she agreed. "Eight days...should be enough."

"Enough for what?" Trosh asked. "If we cannot hide, we are doomed. If we can hide—"

"We will be rescued," Sylvia interrupted. "There was a plan for this. There is a relief force hidden nearby. Once they do not hear from us, they will come."

She shook her head and glanced over at where the Kozun Voice was standing against the wall, the woman waiting calmly for some sign of what was going on.

"There will be a war over this," she told them. "The UPA will have to act, to show that their ambassadors are untouchable."

Even if she died here, the UPA would act. The only way the Initiative could ever work was if everyone knew the UPSF would crush anyone who stepped too far out of line when dealing with the forces the Peacekeepers could deploy.

Civis romanus sum had been deadly words to conjure with during the Roman Empire, even beyond its borders. "I am a citizen of Rome." Fear and respect were the real weapons the United Planets Alliance needed to keep their people safe beyond their borders. The death of an accredited ambassador at formal peace negotiations could *not* be tolerated.

"We are-were-will appreciate the aid of the UPA," Rising Principle told her. "Fate-time will see us to safety. If-when we live."

"We will," Sylvia assured them. "Now, I think I need to speak to the Voice. I have questions."

ORAN AVAL'S bodyguards tried to step in front of her as Sylvia approached, even in the face of the leveled guns of the La-Tar soldiers.

"Peace, children," Aval told them. A second phrase followed in a language Sylvia didn't even recognize. The bodyguards hesitated for a moment, and Aval spoke again, more sharply, in a *third* language. This one was the Kozun main language, and the young men finally retreated.

Sylvia knew that calling the language *Kozun* was as accurate as calling English *Terran*—which, to be fair, she suspected more than a few people in the former Kenmiri Empire did.

"They are tasked to protect me," Aval said in Kem. "The situation makes them uncomfortable, regardless of my choices or commands."

"Someone's choices and commands led you here," Sylvia agreed. "It appears your people believe you expendable, Oran Aval."

Aval said something in that strange language the UPA ambassador didn't recognize, then sighed.

"I am a Voice of the Seven," she said in Kem. "I Speak for those who cannot be heard but who control all. If it is Their will that I fall, it shall come to pass...but no mortal hand of the Kozun would betray me."

"Really," Sylvia said. "So, Mal Dakis did not order the murder of our fleet despite the fact that you would be aboard?"

"No," Aval said simply. "I do not deny the evidence of your sensors and my own eyes, Ambassador Todorovich. But I can assure you that we did not plan this. This was not the order of the Voices of the Seven. This was not the order of Star Voice Kalad.

"Kozun hands may have betrayed us all, yes," the priestess conceded, "but this was not the order of the Voices."

"How can you be so certain?" Sylvia asked. "Your ships fired on us."

"Because the Kozun can no longer afford this war," Oran Aval said flatly. "Or any of our wars. In a mix of arrogance, desire to help and desire to *rule*, we overextended ourselves and made enemies of too many of our neighbors."

Sylvia studied Aval. It was possible the other woman was lying. Both of them had been trained to read microexpressions and to at least partially control their own. It was *possible*.

But it didn't seem like it.

"You expect me to believe this?" she asked.

"It does not matter now, does it?" Aval said. "We realized our mistake, Todorovich, far too late to change our course. Now we have no choice but to solidify our borders and sign treaties and spend a *generation* rebuilding the trust we threw away."

"You only stopped because you *were* stopped," Sylvia noted. "If you expect sympathy from me..."

"You are correct," the Kozun agreed. "But our course *must* now change. This peace was to be the first step. I do not desire your sympathy or pity for my people, Ambassador. I desire your understanding that we would not have done this."

"Mal Dakis is no stranger to the concept of secret orders, Voice Aval," Sylvia said. "Henry Wong has told me much of him."

"There is a reason Star Voice Kalad commands my escort," Oran Aval replied. "Mal Dakis knows that she and Henry Wong were once lovers. We were relying on that bond to buy us every fragment of trust we could find.

"But the only secret orders were mine," she concluded. "And they were that I *was* to get a peace treaty. At almost any price La-Tar and the UPA could demand, we needed to end this war. Not expand it. Not enrage the United Planets Alliance and test just how far they could project power without the Drifters."

"And yet your ships fired on us," Sylvia pointed out, surprised by the flash of jealousy that Aval's description of Kalad triggered. She let that drive her anger and chill her words. "You can tell me a thousand reasons why you did not want this—but your people opened fire."

Aval bowed her head.

"I know," she admitted. "And I do not know why, Ambassador Todorovich. I do not know what happened or how to fix it. All I know is that you and I and Rising Principle are all supposed to be dead— and if there is to a be a chance of peace between our peoples, we *must* survive."

"And how do you plan on doing that?" Sylvia asked.

"I do not know yet," Aval told her. "But any skill or tool I have is at your disposal. We live or die together now, Sylvia Todorovich. And while I hope for Star Voice Kalad...I fear our fate rides on Colonel Henry Wong."

CHAPTER THIRTY-FOUR

"I've got good news, bad news and we're-fucked news," Song told Henry when Henriksson connected her.

"I'm hoping one of those is that I have a gravity shield," Henry replied grimly. "Those fighters are going to be in range far more quickly than I like."

"That's the good news, yes," Song replied. "The good news is that we've checked all of the breakers, they're all fine despite the power surge that blew them out, and that means that not only do you *have* a grav-shield, you're going to *keep* having a grav-shield. If the switches keep holding up, we're looking at a thirty-second reset if they take the shield down again."

"They can still kill us in thirty seconds, but that's better than I dared hope," Henry admitted. "What's the rest of the news?"

"The bad news is that the keel is completely irreparable," his chief engineer told him. "She's done, ser. Short of a complete rebuild of the core hull, *Raven*'s main batteries are history. You've got missiles and what's left of the defensive lasers; that's it."

That at least made the age-old game of power-balancing much easier, Henry supposed. Without the ability to fire the main guns,

Raven had *more* than enough power to run all of her systems simultaneously.

"If that's the bad news, what's the we're-fucked news?" he asked.

"I overestimated how much stress the keel could take," Song said quietly. "We can't sustain this pace for much longer, and the compensators are in rougher shape than I thought, too."

"What do you mean?" Henry demanded.

"If we keep the ship under any kind of subjective thrust for much longer, we're going to snap the keel in half," the engineer told him. "And the compensators aren't going to hold up against half a KPS-squared either.

"We need to cut to point three and we need to do it in the next ten minutes, ser."

Henry was silent for several seconds, studying the geometry. The three Guardians were still pursuing the last Kozun cruiser. Somehow, what he guessed was Kalad's flagship was intact as she drove for the skip line to Hierarchy space.

She'd lost enough acceleration that the pursuit had to be nearly over, but she was still fighting.

The Drifter starfighters, on the other hand, had now been chasing *Raven* for ten minutes. Almost forty minutes had passed since the beginning of the fight, and *Raven*'s desperate course had taken her almost two million kilometers from the original contact point.

The fighters were still almost another million kilometers past that, but they were now closing the distance at almost three times *Raven*'s acceleration.

"How long can we push it?" he asked, turning his attention to the broader map. He'd been counting on outrunning the Guardians for the next two days. If he suddenly went from having an acceleration advantage to a *dis*advantage, that wasn't an option.

"The closer you get to that ten-minute mark, the more likely we are to break the ship in half, ser," Song said bluntly.

"Right." Henry sighed and adjusted the settings for his virtual bridge. "Bazzoli, cut acceleration to point three KPS-squared and confirm with Engineering. Lieutenant Colonel Song has the call on our acceleration now."

"Ser, we're..."

"Going to get caught by fucking everyone at that accel," Henry agreed. "I know. Set your course for the comet swarm at sixty by forty-seven. Can we zero-zero at them before the Guardians are close enough to pick out our heat from the ice?"

"They're ten million kilometers away, ser. ETA is two hours, eighteen minutes. If the Guardians flip now...they'll still be at least two million kilometers away when we zero in," Bazzoli said slowly. "We might just make it."

"We'll have to take out every one of those starfighters," Henry noted. "Ihejirika? You get the new pattern?"

"I've got it," the tactical officer replied. "Weapons range in forty minutes for us...couple more for them. We'll get one unopposed salvo in, but they've only got one salvo aboard."

"What about internal weapons?" Henry asked. "They'll be over one percent of lightspeed relative to us at that point. They're not breaking off easily."

"Most Vesheron fighters are pure missile platforms," Iyotake said from CIC. "They'll probably break off vertically, pass around us."

"They'll stay close enough to pick us up if we try and hide," Henry concluded. "We have to kill them all."

That was easier said than done. Sixty starfighters...and he currently didn't even have *one*.

"Hopefully, we'll have starfighters by then," he murmured. He had faith in O'Flannagain's people, but at the same time...time was not their friend.

"Ser, the Guardians," Iyotake interrupted his thoughts. "They're breaking off... Oh."

Henry turned his attention back to the running battle he *wasn't* involved in, just in time to see the end. It turned out that it wasn't just the skip line to Ra-175 the Drifters had laid laser satellites at. The

Kozun cruiser had almost made it, but then dozens of weapons plat-forms lit up.

Iyotake had seen the first energy signatures, and now Henry saw them all. The beams weren't full heavy weapons, but they were also firing at ranges as short as fifty thousand kilometers, and there were almost a hundred of them.

The last ship of Star Voice Kalad's command came apart as the beams slashed through her hull, ripping the warship to pieces...and leaving the Guardians clear to come after *Raven*.

"That's it, then," he murmured. "Officers. We are now the only people who can counter whatever story the Drifters want to tell about what happened here. Somehow, I don't think those starfighters are on their way to save us."

"They could be," Iyotake pointed out. "Even if the Drifters are behind this, they haven't done anything outside their agreements yet. The Kozun fired first."

"Did they?" Henry asked. "Then tell me, XO. If *you* had managed a perfect alpha strike that had destroyed or crippled every enemy in the battlespace, would you have just *sat there* for ninety seconds until the Drifters started shooting at you?"

"Gods." Ihejirika's curse was soft. "All they need to do is cut that ninety seconds out of the sensor footage and there'll be no question, will there? It won't even be doctored footage, so almost no analysis would pick it up."

"Those ninety seconds aren't enough to prove the Kozun's inno-cence," Henry told his people. "But they're enough to create *doubt*. They're enough that we'd *talk* to the Kozun before going to war...and I have this sinking feeling that someone *wants* us to go to war."

"Or are we just jumping at shadows because we're afraid of the Drifters?" Iyotake asked. "You're stretching, ser. Stretching pretty damn far."

"The question, I suppose, is also why they aren't talking to us," Henry pointed out. "We could wait the extra few minutes to see if they fire first. But...we also have to consider that *Raven* is walking wounded at this point."

The channel was quiet.

"It's your call, ser," Iyotake told him. "It's my job to tell you that you're twisting for a chance to say Star Voice Kalad didn't shoot at you. But...that twist doesn't look wrong, either."

"I know," Henry conceded. "On all counts."

And he was angry. He was so *very* angry that Todorovich was dead. If he could blame Kalad, well...that would hurt, but his anger was targetless.

If Kalad wasn't at fault, somehow, then he *did* have a target—and two women dear to his heart to be angry over.

"We can't risk it," he said aloud. "Commander Moon, we will make an attempt to warn off the Drifter starfighters. If they do not break off...Commander Ihejirika, you are to fire as soon as they are in range.

"We can't give up that shot. It's the only chance we've got of reducing the odds."

CHAPTER THIRTY-FIVE

"Drifter fighter wing, this is Lieutenant Commander Lauren Moon aboard the United Planets Space Force Vessel *Raven*." Henry was leaving the whole message to Moon. He suspected his version would involve a lot more bloodthirsty threats than hers.

With everyone out of the acceleration tanks and back in their seats on the bridge, he could even hear her speaking instead of playing the message back.

"*Raven* is withdrawing to a safe skip line to fall back to friendly territory. While we appreciate Drifter intervention against the Kozun attack, we must act to protect our own safety at this point. Any fighter craft entering within seven hundred and fifty thousand kilometers of *Raven* will be fired upon.

"We are not in need of immediate assistance or escort. Fall back for everyone's safety."

The fighters continued on their course, though lightspeed delays meant they wouldn't get Moon's message for several seconds. They were moving at well over a percent of lightspeed relative to the initial battlespace now, accelerating hard to close the distance with *Raven*.

Most starfighters would carry between five and ten percent of lightspeed in delta-*v*. They had the fuel to burn for this, but Henry wished he knew if the Drifter fighters carried internal weapons. He wouldn't normally worry about the relatively weak lasers or plasma guns that could be mounted on a starfighter, but today...today he was going to worry about everything.

"Henriksson, let's bring the shield up," he ordered. "That should help scare them off if anything will."

"Yes, ser."

New icons flickered across his screen. It would be *very* obvious to the starfighters when the gravity shield came up. His ship would be harder to locate inside the bubble once the shield was up, buying her a small but useful amount of stealth and evasion.

He checked on the fighter-wing status and grimaced at the icons flashing under the spacecraft. Seven fighters were marked as red, offline. The eighth was *black*—destroyed. There was only one way that had happened.

"O'Flannagain, report," he ordered.

"I'm sourcing dark alleys for meeting that designer," the CAG said flatly. "We *almost* had everything aligned, and then one of the emitters broke free and fell."

"Through the starfighter," Henry finished.

"Through the starfighter at eleven subjective gravities," she confirmed. "And knocked a hundred-and-eleven-kilogram maintenance robot free in the process. *Raven*-One is offline, permanently.

"We've been working on the alignment since we cut to compensated acceleration, and it's slow going," she admitted. "At least ten minutes, ser."

"We'll be nearly in weapons range of the Drifter starfighters at that point, Commander," Henry told her. "Is that going to be the full wing?"

"No," she admitted. "I only have five pilots, ser, even if I'm down to seven fighters...and we're only going to have *two* Lancers ready for this. With the GMS and the grav-shield, I'll back them against sixty Drifter TIEs."

Henry swallowed his reactions. He hated that particular nickname for an unshielded fighter.

"We don't know enough about the Drifters' fighters for me to want to take that bet, O'Flannagain," he pointed out.

"I didn't say I wanted to take it, ser. But what choice do we have? I'll scramble as soon as I have planes."

"If we're only a little lucky, we'll still have a battlecruiser for you to scramble from," Henry admitted.

"RANGE IN NINETY SECONDS," Ihejirika reported grimly. "No response to our hails. Bringing up the targeting radar now and pinging them."

That was early, but Henry held his peace. It was the final warning the incoming fighters were going to get, and he'd let his people do everything they could to warn the Drifters off. It was always possible, after all, that this was some giant misunderstanding.

"Fighters remaining on course. Initial target locks acquired and downloaded to missiles. Launchers one through twelve armed and ready. Range in...sixty seconds."

"Courses are adjusting slightly," Iyotake's murmured in Henry's internal network. "Not enough to change the timing, but they're setting up for a wide pass. They're going to avoid our laser range."

"If only they knew," Henry replied. "They could fly right up to us and would be in the same danger they are at seven hundred thousand klicks."

"Our defense lasers would have *some* impact on fighters," his XO said. "But yes, they appear to be overestimating the threat."

Henry's answer was interrupted by two of the icons on his display flashing to green.

"Fighters up," O'Flannagain's voice barked in the command channel. "*Raven*-Three and *Raven*-Four, dropping in twenty seconds!"

"*Finally,*" Henry said under his breath. "Well done, CAG; pass my compliments to your people," he told her aloud.

"Missile range," Ihejirika snapped. "Firing."

They didn't even need to flip the ship to clear the launchers. They were decelerating toward the comet swarm, shedding their velocity to match the debris orbiting Lon, which meant their missile tubes and fighter launch bays were all pointed toward the enemy.

Twelve new green icons blinked into existence on the displays, missiles hurtling back toward the pursuing starfighters. Relative velocities were already over a full percent of lightspeed on launch, separating the weapons from *Raven* in a heartbeat.

"Twenty seconds to enemy range," Ihejirika reported. "Second launch ten seconds after that."

"Starfighters away," Iyotake declared. "Two birds in space, O'Flannagain in command."

Henry chuckled softly, probably quietly enough to be unheard. *Of course* Samira O'Flannagain was in one of the two starfighters they'd actually deployed. It was easily argued that the CAG's place right now was in Flight Control...but he'd never met a Commander, Air Group, worthy of their wings who wouldn't be in a starfighter in this moment.

"Lancers are breaking away toward the Drifters; acceleration is two point five KPS-squared," Iyotake continued. "I thought they had more than that."

"They do," Henry confirmed. "She's *also* carrying full-size missiles and doesn't need to close the range."

He watched O'Flannagain's starfighter fall behind *Raven*, closing with the enemy fighters at almost five KPS^2 with their combined acceleration.

"Trust O'Flannagain," he told Iyotake aloud. His attention turned back to the damage-control schematic he knew in his heart was going to get updated again soon.

There were clear red sections showing where *Raven* had been hit, but they'd avoided any hits from conversion warheads. The weapons that *had* hit them had been the disruptors, which apparently didn't have a warhead beyond their resonance systems.

Henry blinked.

"Enemy missiles launching," Ihejirika reported. "One-twenty inbound. They are preserving half their missiles, probably to see how our defenses hold up. If they only need to spend half, well..."

"Ihejirika, analyze those birds," Henry snapped. "Some of them are conversion warheads and some of them are disruptors, but the disruptors end up as pure kinetic weapons—most of which the gravity shield is going to tear to pieces.

"I need to know how many of each they've fired."

"I'm not sure we can ID that, ser," his tactical officer replied. "Not with two and a half minutes to do it in."

"Try," Henry ordered. "If we can prioritize our antimissile lasers, we can survive this. So, *try*."

More missiles blazed out from *Raven*'s launchers as he spoke, the battlecruiser's response pitiful compared to the tidal wave now sweeping toward her.

Still almost two minutes until the first salvo connected. The distances involved left even the fastest of weapons taking seeming ages to connect.

"Third salvo away," Ihejirika reported. "Drifters are continuing to hold on to their remaining missiles. Surely, they'll launch before we hit them."

"That depends on whether they think they've already killed us," Henry said grimly. "We might take some of them with us, but there's no point wasting missiles on an enemy that's already dead and just hasn't realized it yet."

"Ser." The tactical officer response was clipped. "We...think we've found a pattern in the incoming fire."

"Show me," Henry ordered.

Ihejirika took control of one of the big screens around Henry, zooming in on the swarm of missiles heading their way. There was nothing to the interweaving weapons that looked unusual to Henry.

"It's not much," his subordinate told him. "We wouldn't have noticed it if we hadn't been looking for it, but the trailing missiles have a different radiation signature. They're carrying plutonium-based fission devices—igniters for their conversion warheads.

"The lead missiles don't have enough plutonium aboard to flag at this range."

One hundred and twenty missiles blinked, suddenly acquiring a mix of orange and crimson icons.

"It's not a perfect distribution, but they tried to send the disruptors ahead of the conversion warheads, to bring our shields down *before* they hit us with the plasma bolts. Three-quarters of the salvo are disruptors. The last thirty are conversion warheads."

Ihejirika paused, as if running numbers in his head.

"We can probably shoot down thirty, maybe forty missiles," he noted. "Usually, I'd say we could take thirty conversion warheads, but…"

"But our last estimates say they only need fifty disruptors to knock out our shield," Henry finished. "Even the disruptors can hurt us, but we're not going to take many hits from conversion warheads if we don't have the shield.

"Target the conversion missiles, Commander," he ordered. "We can reset the shield and we can hope to dodge any un-warheaded missiles that make it through, but we can't survive conversion warheads. If the shield is going to come down either way, I don't want there to be a fusion bomb left out there."

"Understood, ser," Ihejirika paused. "We could use O'Flanna-gain's missiles, ser. What's she doing?"

"Her job isn't to save *Raven*, Commander," Henry said calmly. "That's our job. *Her* job is to make sure there are none of those fighters left to tell their motherships where we're hiding."

"First salvo impact in thirty seconds, sers," Lieutenant Ybarra told them both. "Enemy salvo in defense range in fifteen seconds."

"You have your orders," Henry replied. He leaned back in his chair, doing what he could to take in the entire battle. "Carry on, Commander."

IN THE ABSENCE of gravity shields or other passive defenses, most Vesheron fighters that Henry had seen over the last two decades had been true TIEs: since they couldn't take a hit, they were left with pure maneuverability as their defense.

They were expendable, lethal missile platforms manned by that seemingly universal cultural group of youths convinced of their own immortality. The UPA had never leaned into that standard, equipping its fighters with both gravity shields and antimissile lasers.

The Drifters, it seemed, were more in line with the UPA's policies. The incoming fighters opened fire as the UPSF missiles closed, rapid slices of coherent light glittering across the void.

"Enemy starfighters are equipped with rapid-tracking pulse lasers," Iyotake reported from CIC. "They're almost certainly intended as pure antimissile lasers—energy levels appear to be in the one- to two-hundred-megawatt range. They might cause our people a headache in a dogfight, but that's not what they're built for."

"Eight warheads survived to convert," Ihejirika reported. "Scans suggest seven kills."

"Ten percent in the first salvo, Commander, well done," Henry replied. They might just make it through this yet.

He turned his attention to the Engineering section.

"Henriksson, we're going to lose the shield," he told the young officer. "I want it back up as quickly as physically possible. We have at least a hundred seconds *this* time, but we need to get that time down."

"Understood, ser," Henriksson said, her voice shaky but level. "Song says thirty seconds, ser. We'll try and get it in less."

No one verbally reported when the enemy missiles entered the range of *Raven*'s defenses. Icons started waterfalling on one side of

Henry's displays as their defensive laser installations started reporting capacitor-drain and -recharge settings.

Without the main guns, they were dedicating an entire reactor to feeding the dozens of quarter-gigawatt lasers across the hull. Normally, they were often the poor sibling when it came to power draw.

Today, their capacitors were being kept at full power. There was a minimum-cycle time on the weapons, but Henry had never seen it tested.

"All conversion warheads destroyed!" Ihejirika snapped. "Disruptors impacting the shield!"

The scream of a gravity-shielded warship undergoing resonance disruption was familiar now. They'd probably work out a control or mitigation for that in the future, but at that moment, the piercing shriek tore through the bridge—and then the gravity shields flared out.

Henry held his breath for a second. Five. Ten.

Then he exhaled.

"Report," he barked.

"No impacts," Henriksson told him, sounding astonished. "I repeat, *zero impacts*. Shield will be back up in eighteen seconds."

"Ihejirika?" Henry asked.

"We shot down forty-two missiles," the tactical officer told him. "The shield ripped apart over sixty, and Commander Bazzoli *dodged* the rest."

Henry looked toward the front of the bridge, where his navigator seemed half-frozen, the woman nearly hyperventilating as she looked down at the emergency manual joystick in her hands.

"Commander, well done," he told her. She didn't respond. "Commander? *Iida!*"

Her first name snapped the woman out and she sucked in one final breath before regaining control of her breathing and releasing the emergency joystick. She looked back at him and nodded.

"Yes, ser," she said. "Thank you, ser."

"Ihejirika, kill me those starfighters," Henry ordered. Their second salvo erupted amidst the Drifter spacecraft as he spoke, wiping another half-dozen of the enemy from existence.

The rest opened fire a second time a moment later. Only ninety missiles this time—and their vectors changed dramatically, the formation splitting into five groups of nine fighters apiece as they tried to reduce the risk from *Raven*'s fire.

"Designate Bandit groups Alpha through Epsilon," Iyotake snapped from CIC. New icons appeared on the clusters of starfighters as their vector cones expanded. "None will enter laser range of *Raven*. All will be in position to see what we do in the meteor swarm...assuming they survive the next ten minutes to get out of our range."

"Epsilon is mine," O'Flannagain reported from her starfighter a few seconds later. "Delta is Turrigan's. Alpha through Gamma are your problem, *Raven*."

Henry smiled as he looked at the scattering starfighters.

"Commander Ihejirika, get me the split between conversion and disruptor missiles, please," he ordered. "Then start focusing your salvos. Do we have the time to put two salvos on each of those groups?"

"Yes, ser," the tactical officer confirmed. He paused. "We have five salvos already in space; retargeting one per group. New salvos will target in cycle."

The range was dropping *fast* at this point. If Henry had his main guns, the fighters would be doomed. As it was...they were still doomed. They'd wedded themselves too tightly to the pursuit and failed to keep their relative velocity low.

"Enemy salvo is seventy disruptors, twenty conversion warheads," Lieutenant Ybarra reported. "Focusing on conversion warheads."

"*Raven*, you're stealing my kills," O'Flannagain said over the radio. "I mark five more down in Bandit Epsilon, and my missiles are online. Fox Three, Fox Three, Fox Three, Fox Three."

Another report came in from Turrigan, and eight new icons appeared on the display. Launched at *far* shorter ranges and with even higher relative velocities, they slashed into targets that were clearly expecting the shorter-ranged fighter missiles the UPSF had equipped their older fighters with.

"Delta and Epsilon are down, and mark for the record, please, that both myself and Lieutenant Commander Turrigan just made ace," O'Flannagain reported.

Henry concealed a grin. The Kenmiri had never built starfighters, which meant that there were *very* few aces—pilots with five or more fighter kills—in the UPSF's FighterDiv now.

Today there were two more.

"They're running as best they can, but they aren't going to make it," Iyotake reported. "Situation is under control, Captain."

Henry nodded and exhaled.

"We'll remain at battle stations until we're in the meteor swarm," he ordered. "Then...we'll see how it looks."

Despite all of the excitement, any chance of reinforcements was still over forty-five hours away.

CHAPTER THIRTY-SIX

The sensors Trosh rigged up told a story far beyond the worst of Sylvia's worst-case scenarios. They weren't much more than automated telescopes linked to an optical processing program the Ashall had set up on a portable computer, but it was enough for them to watch the final death of Kalad's flagship.

And it was enough for Sylvia to watch the Drifter fighters attempt to swarm *Raven*.

"*Raven* is limping," she admitted as she looked at the data. "Point three KPS-squared? She has been badly damaged if Henry is only running at that."

"There is-was nothing we can-will do from here," Rising Principle told her. "I see no answers in this-that. Only fate-time of our doom."

"Please, let me see," Aval asked, projecting her voice from across the room. "I need to know what happened to my people as much as you do what happened to yours."

Sylvia looked at Rising Principle, the alien's mouth open to show their eyes. They closed their mouth and made an odd gesture with a tentacle, one she chose to take as *go ahead*.

She picked up one of the several tablets Trosh had linked to the computer and walked it over to the Kozun ambassador.

"The Drifters destroyed your ships," she told Aval bluntly, setting up a replay of the death of the last Kozun cruiser. "Exactly as their agreement with us both required them to."

"The Drifters," Aval repeated as she stared at the recording of the fate of her ships, and something in her eyes made Sylvia nervous. "I will hunt that Convoy across the stars. I will burn their Guardians and shatter their ships and scatter the ashes of their precious gardens into a *thousand Seven-cursed suns*."

Sylvia waited for Aval to regain her breath as the Voice glared at the sensor data.

"Why?" she asked.

"They were the ones who sold us the missiles we used against your ships," Aval replied. "I am sure you had guessed that. Much of our military buildup was based on technology and weapons they sold us.

"They called on that debt to get us to agree to a Drifter escort for this conference."

A chill ran down Sylvia's spine.

"They told *us* you asked for neutrals," she told Aval.

"Did they?" the Voice asked bitterly. "They told us you had suggested it, and they insisted, out of a desire to make certain the talks went well. We know the UPA, Ambassador. We may not *like* you, but we know the weight of your word.

"We would have taken your guarantee of safety, but the Drifters insisted on being here. And..." she gestured helplessly. "The disruptor missiles in our magazines, loaded and ready to defend us against potential treachery...those were Drifter weapons."

"Drifters bug everything," Sylvia murmured, remembering the extended process of removing the beacons from missiles they'd bought. "More so now than before, even."

"I would now guess that the bugs hid a remote-activation system," Oran Aval told Sylvia. "I do not believe Star Voice Kalad would fire on your ships without orders, Ambassador Todorovich. I do not believe Mal Dakis would give the order to kill *me*, if nothing else."

"Why are you so certain of that, Voice Aval?"

The Kozun woman was silent, then looked at her bodyguards.

"We will live or die together, I suppose, but there are secrets held closely even among the Kozun," she said. "I guess it does not matter as much now."

"Voice Aval?" Sylvia asked softly.

"I am with child, Ambassador," Aval admitted. "Mal Dakis's child. So, Ambassador, I am *very* certain my head of state, who is both my lover and the father of the baby I carry, did not order my death for a pointless betrayal."

Sylvia nodded slowly and then reached over to tap a new command on the tablet, releasing the lock that was keeping it to the recording she'd set up for Aval.

"I believe you," she told Aval, watching the other woman's reaction as the video of the attack on *Raven* played out on the screen. "So, what do we do about it?"

"I...do not know," Aval said. "We survive? We challenge what the Drifters say happened here?"

"We do not have sensor footage of the key moments," Sylvia pointed out. "*Raven* does. That the Drifters appear to have been willing to give up any protestation of innocence in the eyes of Henry Wong and his crew to make certain that footage is destroyed tells me it might be damning enough.

"Our footage of the attack on *Raven* is probably enough too, but the Drifters might start hunting escape pods once *Raven* is destroyed. We will not stay concealed forever."

"My people..." Aval sighed. "It will be weeks before anyone is truly concerned over my silence. There is nothing they *could* send, even if they did know there was a problem." She grimaced. "Every one of our cruisers was here, Todorovich. *Mal Toranis* is our only remaining capital ship, and we cannot afford to uncover Kozun.

"We sent everything here as a show of force, to try and end our most dangerous war on the best terms we could manage."

"And now you confess all of this?" Sylvia asked.

"Either we will die together here, Ambassador Sylvia Todorovich, or the Kozun, the La-Tar and the UPA will fight the Drifters together," Aval told her. "I do not believe honesty at this point will fail me."

"Probably not," Sylvia said quietly. "In that vein, then: There is a UPSF task force on the other side of the Ra-One-Seventy-Five skip line...this one." She indicated the skip line on the tablet display since she had no idea what the Kozun called the system. "If they have not heard from us in twenty-four hours, they will skip through to investigate.

"If we can survive the next forty-six hours, *Scorpius* will save us."

"You did not trust us," Aval said.

"We did not trust *anyone*," Sylvia replied. "You. The Drifters. We only mostly trust Rising Principle and their people. So, yes, we had a backup. But I have no way to reach that backup. Henry—Captain Wong—*might* have been able to reach them, but I have no way to know."

"And that he runs so desperately suggests not," the Kozun said. "You fear time."

"Time is not our ally. By the time *Scorpius* gets here, *Raven* will be dead. We will have been found. Your people's escape pods will have been destroyed. And the Drifters will have a story and sensor footage lined up to explain everything."

"What if there were a way for you to contact this *Scorpius*?" Aval asked. "A way I am...mostly certain the Drifters cannot intercept."

"Unless you have a miraculously-still-working subspace communicator, I am not sure what you could offer," Sylvia admitted.

"A skip drone," the Kozun told her. "One we prepositioned at a skip line we did not expect you to survey...to the star you called Ra-One-Seventy-Five. Our emergency report system, that only I can activate."

"Sending it through Ra-One-Seventy-Five..."

"Added forty-three hours to the flight time, but it reduced the chance that you would detect and intercept it to almost zero. We believed that if the drone was needed, avoiding interception was critical."

"How close to the skip line is it?" Sylvia asked. "If *Raven* did not get a drone through, the Drifters had to have done *something*." And if *Raven* had got a drone through, this was unnecessary.

"It is *on* the skip line, following a ballistic course through the outer system well away from anywhere you or the Drifters could see it," Aval told her. "I would need to send a tightbeam message."

"That could get us found and killed," Sylvia replied. "And that is assuming everything you are saying is true."

"Yes," Aval replied. "But these people killed Star Voice Kalad and twenty-four hundred of my people. I want them dead, Ambassador Todorovich. Every bone in my body and the voices of my Gods scream for vengeance.

"I will let you record the message. I will provide the activation codes for the drone. My estimate puts it far enough that the Drifters will not detect it."

"That means we will have a transmission delay," Sylvia noted. "But...we can cut twenty hours off the timer. That is worth it.

"Assuming you do not get us killed."

"I cannot promise that," Aval admitted. "That depends on what we end up using for a transmitter."

"IMPOSSIBLE," Rising Principle snapped. "She must-will betray us. We can-will die."

"The only transmitter we have is too wide a beam to be hidden, either way," Trosh admitted before Sylvia could argue with the Enteni diplomat. "All we really have is an emergency beacon. It can be used as a transmitter, but it is an omnidirectional system, designed to make sure we can be found."

"The exact opposite of what we need," Sylvia conceded. "Look, the Drifters just killed over two thousand of Aval's people. She is not going to betray us to them. Our worst-case scenario is, what, she has a secret fleet in the outer system? They would still rescue her and us.

"Right now, our only hope is over forty-five hours away," she continued. "If this drone exists and works, we cut that to twenty-five hours. I am not certain we *have* twenty-five hours," she admitted. "But I am entirely certain that even Henry Wong cannot buy us forty-five.

"How long do you think we will be able to hide once they start sweeping the wreckage for escape pods, Rising Principle?"

"That fate-time is-has not yet come," they replied. "You ask-demand too much. To trust this Kozun…"

"Rising Principle, we might yet survive if we have to wait for *Scorpius* to arrive, but…" Sylvia gestured to the tablets displaying the sensor data, "*Raven* will not. The Guardians are already in pursuit. They have higher acceleration than she does now. They will catch her, and she cannot defend herself. Not against three dreadnought-equivalents."

"I agree with you," Trosh admitted, looking carefully at his boss, "but we still lack a directional transmitter. Unless the hardware you humans have in your heads is more powerful than I think, we have no way to reach this drone. Even if we trust Aval enough to concede its existence."

"Our internal networks cannot do it, no," a new voice interjected. Sylvia looked up to see Leitz and Thompson joining the conversation, her chief of staff and the GroundDiv officer looking drained.

"There is a very distinct limit on how powerful a transmitter we can install in somebody's skull," Thompson continued. "Which is always a pain for GroundDiv operations, so our combat gear contains more powerful transceivers. One might not do it, but we have multiple sets of combat gear here, plus the La-Tar gear, plus the Kozun gear.

"Both of them are using Kenmiri systems that are more powerful but less precise than ours," he continued. "I think we can rig up a directional transmitter with enough range. But...it will probably only work once."

Thompson shrugged.

"Battlefield tech upgrades."

"This is your ship, Rising Principle," Sylvia said, turning her gaze on the Enteni diplomat. "But...we doom *Raven* and probably ourselves if we do nothing."

"I trust your heart-soul," the envoy finally said. "This fate-time must-will destroy us all if we do nothing. Do what you must-will."

Sylvia gave Rising Principle a firm nod, then turned back to Thompson.

"Rig up that transmitter, Commander," she ordered. "I think I have a message to record."

CHAPTER THIRTY-SEVEN

There was a general unconcealed sigh of relief across *Raven*'s bridge as they finally crossed into the meteor swarm. They were still, for the moment, visible to their pursuers—but the presence of the hundreds of chunks of ice in their fast orbit of Lon made them harder to find.

And Henry had plans.

Meteor was an understatement for many of the objects around them. Some were nearly large enough to qualify as planetoids, dozens to hundreds of kilometers across.

The largest ice chunks would be the focus of the Drifters' search when they arrived, but also presented the best chance to hide *Raven*. Without some kind of additional confusion, the debris field was still sparse enough that their pursuers would be able to follow them right to their hiding spot.

"All right," Henry said firmly. "Ihejirika, I'm feeding you targets.

"Alpha-One through Alpha-Three, I want you to park a dozen conversion warheads on," he ordered, highlighting three large chunks of ice on the edge of the swarm. "Fly them gently and wait for the order, but we're going to blow those pretty quickly here. I just want to make sure we aren't creating a trail for ourselves.

"Once those bombs are in place, do the same for the Bravo targets I'm marking," he continued, haloing another set of six meteors farther into the cluster. "We'll hold on to those until we're in place and the Drifters are closer."

Three more meteors lit up as his Charlie targets.

"Charlie gets the last missiles we're going to preplace," he told Ihejirika. "Rig them for proximity detonation at thirty thousand kilometers. They're not going to *do* anything to the Drifters, but they'll add more confusion and hopefully spook their sensor techs."

He studied the debris and then haloed three massive chunks of ice near the heart of the swarm. They weren't the first three the Drifters would search, but they'd be in the top ten.

"Thompson, I need..."

He paused and swallowed before anyone could say anything. Alex Thompson was dead. The GroundDiv Commander had been on *Carpenter*, being the over-ranked commander of Sylvia Todorovich's bodyguard. Like their ambassador, the man was gone.

"Lieutenant Commander Satine," he said quietly, pinging the senior company commander left aboard the ship. "I need you to prep three of your shuttles for remote flight," he told her. "I'm transferring the Delta-designated targets now.

"I want you to embed the shuttles in the designated meteors with a program to keep pulsing their engines and other systems to increase their heat signature. They're decoys and hopefully they'll drag the Drifters off-target."

"Understood, ser," the company commander replied. "I'll have people on it straight away."

Henry swallowed his anger again as Melissa Satine took up the task he'd intended to give Alex Thompson. It was never easy. He *knew* that.

Today was going to add to his nightmares, he could already tell. He could handle nightmares now, though. He had *lots* of practice.

"Bazzoli, set a course for what I'm flagging as Target Epsilon," he told the navigator. "Henriksson, I want you and Song to rig up a system to radiate all of our heat in one direction. Epsilon is a hundred-and-twenty-kilometer-long chunk of ice and rock; it can absorb our heat for a while before it'll start showing up on anyone's scanners.

"We're going to use Epsilon as a giant radiator. Bazzoli, once Henriksson confirms where our new radiator focus is, you're going to land us on Epsilon with that focus pointed into the target. We'll use the defensive lasers to excavate ourselves a nice hole while the chaos from the Alpha and Bravo charges covers us, then we'll radiate our heat deeper into the meteor and slowly sink our way in.

"Eventually, we're going to end up surrounded by a few billion tons of ice, and that is *perfect*," he concluded.

"Just like that corvette in Satra," Ihejirika said.

"Exactly, Commander. Are we good, people?" Henry asked.

"That's going to use up pretty much every missile we have left," his tactical officer warned. "I'm already issuing orders to the system to strip penetrator busses off the shield-penetrator missiles. Those are hard to replicate, and even without them, the missiles have five-hundred-megaton warheads.

"We'll be down to less than thirty missiles, ser, but they'll all be penetrators."

"Those busses are just as useful against energy shields as grav-shields," Henry noted. "They'll be handy against the Drifters, but let's get those explosives set as a priority. We *can* fabricate more missiles."

They could even, given the right materials, fabricate the one-shot skip drives their penetrator missiles used to bypass shields. *Raven*'s stockpile of those exotic elements was generally earmarked for repairing her *own* skip drive, and Henry would need a *damn* good reason to release it for missiles.

Missiles were already beginning to jet out from his ship's launchers. Their usual powerful gravity drivers were firing on minimum, sending the missiles into space with barely enough velocity to counter *Raven*'s own momentum.

They weren't evading or trying to hit evading targets this time, after all. The missiles followed gentle courses that nestled them into the surfaces of Henry's Alpha targets, a dozen five-hundred-megaton warheads per asteroid.

"Alpha targets are ready to detonate on your command," Ihejirika reported. "Bravo targets will be a bit longer."

"Shuttles are ready for the Delta deployments," Satine reported. "Should we be holding off?"

Henry considered.

"Give us a couple more minutes to get deeper, Lieutenant Commander," he told Satine. "Ihejirika, set your timers for two minutes. Satine—as soon as the Alpha warheads go up, send out your shuttles. We want them to be as invisible as us.

"Let's keep the Drifters guessing."

To his surprise, his plan unfolded like clockwork around him.

The Alpha warheads detonated on schedule. All three of their targets had been at least eighty cubic kilometers of ice and rock, and they made for *spectacular* plumes of debris as the fusion bombs tore them to pieces.

"We now have zero visibility outside the cluster," Ihejirika reported. "There is no way they can detect us."

"Good. Satine?"

"Shuttles on their way," his new senior GroundDiv officer reported. "They're operating on remote and preset programming. They'll do the job."

"Good," Henry repeated. "Bazzoli, set your course for Epsilon. Let's go dig in the snow."

BRINGING the crippled battlecruiser in to a landing required a deft touch that Henry knew *he* was capable of. Instead, he metaphorically sat on his hands and watched Iida Bazzoli do the job. They were missing over half of their maneuvering thrusters, and this wasn't an exercise he thought they could easily do with the big main engines.

She surprised him. His navigator took them right up to the hundred-and-twenty-kilometer ice meteor under the main engines, shedding the last of their velocity in carefully measured bursts with the main engine until they were less than *ten* meters away from Epsilon and finally hit zero relative to the big chunk of ice.

"I have the focal direction from Engineering," she said softly. "It could be an easier one."

"We didn't have a lot of choices," Henriksson replied. "Sorry, Commander."

"Don't apologize, Lieutenant," Bazzoli told the engineering officer with a chuckle. "I know you're not intentionally making my life harder."

Maneuvering thrusters flashed for a second. *Raven* started rotating, slowly turning until her main engines were parallel to the meteor's surface. The thrusters flared again, bringing her to a halt "upside-down" above the icy surface. It wasn't an easy position to get into, but it was required by the awkward angle the ship was now radiating all of her heat toward.

"Ihejirika, make a hole, please," the navigator requested in a distracted tone.

"Firing."

This was about as far from the intended purpose of *Raven*'s defensive lasers as possible, but they were high-energy coherent-light weapons. They slashed chunks of ice free, explosions of vapor marking their work.

The amount of debris this was creating was the reason for the Bravo warheads and the decoys. It was impossible to hide this kind of mess—except in vast quantities of the same kind of mess.

"Clear," Ihejirika reported as the guns fell silent. "Scanners mark sixty-seven meters to the bottom of the cave."

"Confirmed," Bazzoli murmured. "Don't hold your breath, people."

The thrusters flared again, more continuously this time, as *Raven* dropped into a roughly battlecruiser-shaped hole in the side of the meteor. Bazzoli kept adjusting their velocity and angle, and it took them almost a full minute to reach the bottom of the cave and settle, ever so delicately, into their hiding spot.

"We're down. External temperature one hundred fifty Kelvin and dropping fast," she reported. "Is this going to work?"

"It will," Henry replied. It *had* to, or *Raven* was going to die in the forty-three hours before *Scorpius* appeared.

"Satine?" he continued.

"Delta shuttles are digging their way into their own hidey-holes as we speak," she confirmed. "It's taking them a bit longer."

"Understood." He hesitated. They still didn't have visibility on the Drifters, but they *needed* that cover. He swallowed a sigh and nodded firmly.

"Ihejirika, detonate the Bravo warheads," he ordered. "And then we all get very, *very* quiet."

New energy signatures appeared on his screens as seventy-two five-hundred-megaton warheads went off, shredding another set of ancient ice floes into a protective screen around *Raven*.

"What now?" Ihejirika asked.

"Stand down to Status Two," Henry ordered. "Get some sensor probes up on the surface to give us eyes, but send at least half our people to their beds. The Drifters will close the remaining distance over the next few hours.

"Let's make sure at least some of our people have rested when they get here."

CHAPTER THIRTY-EIGHT

"We have a confirmation signal," Thompson told Sylvia. "Transmission received by the drone and a confirmation sent back by tightbeam. If I'm reading the automatic message correctly, it skipped thirty minutes ago."

"That was farther out than we expected," she noted. "I'm glad our transmission caught it."

They were speaking in English, though the same results were showing on all of the tablets scattered around the escape pod. Food wrappers crinkled as the handful of survivors dug in to the horrible-but-nutritious emergency rations the Cluster crew had supplied the emergency capsule with.

Sylvia was mostly just glad that they'd included a bathroom. That could easily have been the kind of oversight that added an extra layer of unpleasantness to a survival situation.

"Ambassador, I have lost track of *Raven*," Trosh told her, the Eerdish officer stepping over to join them. "Please look at the datafeed from the sensor."

She obeyed, but it took her a moment to process just what she was seeing.

"That is a lot of explosions for the Drifters still being two million kilometers away from *Raven*," she noted. "And a lot of debris."

"It appears Captain Wong is vaporizing large pieces of a meteor swarm to help conceal his exact position," Trosh told her. "I am uncertain if it will work, but it is impressive.

"The Drifters have better sensors than our hastily rigged telescopes. They may be able to hold on to his signature better."

"Even if they lose him, there are only so many meteors in a swarm like that that can hide a battlecruiser," Sylvia said quietly. "He is buying time—and we, hopefully, have bought even more. If the drone skipped on schedule, we will have reinforcements in under twenty-four hours.

"Captain Wong will not expect them for over forty." She shook her head. "He will do whatever it takes to buy his ship and his people time. I worry about the price."

"Surely, he will see the reinforcements before he does anything dangerous, yes?" Trosh asked.

"I am not concerned about what Wong will do after *Scorpius* arrives," she admitted. "I am concerned about what he will do when *Scorpius* is an hour away...and he thinks his reinforcements are twenty hours out."

Trosh nodded his understanding as Sylvia looked over at Thompson.

"Is there anything we can do for *Raven*?" she asked the GroundDiv officer.

"Stay alive," Thompson replied. "That is all we can do right now, and it is the most critical thing we can do. Right now, if *Raven* dies and we live, we can stand witness to the Drifters' betrayal. If we die and *Raven* lives, they can stand witness.

"But one of us has to live. Right now, they are probably better hidden than we are...but the Drifters know they exist, and so far, everyone still thinks we died."

"We need to lower our power curve," Sylvia told Trosh, turning back to the Eerdish. "They flew right past us twice now, but we cannot rely on that happening again. They have to come back and sweep for escape pods eventually if they want this deception to hold up."

"Everything we do creates heat the pod has to radiate," the Cluster officer pointed out. "Breathing, eating, walking...everything."

"We can lower the lights, turn off climate control...turn off the damn *gravity*," Sylvia told him. "Everything we do creates heat, yes, so we need to create less."

"Very few of us have any zero-gravity experience," Trosh admitted. "I am afraid of the risks, Ambassador. That is why—"

"There are three dreadnought-level warships out there with a critical interest in making sure we never tell anyone what we saw," Sylvia told him. "Turn off the gravity, Trosh. A few bruises and broken limbs are going to hurt us less than a plasma cannon. This pod was armored enough to survive *Carpenter* getting destroyed—but I doubt it can survive the full firepower of one of those Guardians."

Trosh nodded.

"You are not wrong," he conceded. "We will do what we must. May I impose on you to warn everyone? I do not wish to remove the gravity without warning."

SO LONG AS no one moved, they didn't drift off. By the time the gravity actually turned off, Sylvia had ensconced herself in the chair set up for her at the negotiating table, with carefully arranged tools and food around her.

Oran Aval had done the same, hooking herself into the chair carefully and hanging on to a bulb of water as she drank. Rising Principle joined them several moments after the gravity cut out, the Enteni's trilateral tendrils proving surprisingly graceful in zero-gee.

"We is-are trapped," they admitted. "Fate-time must-will come. I wonder."

"Ambassador?" Aval asked, her tone amused.

"If we is-are all trapped anyway, perhaps we should-could complete our discussions," the Enteni told them. "If we live, a fate-course for peoples can-will have been set. If we die, we will-can have distracted ourselves in our final fate-time."

The Kozun chuckled, a surprisingly warm sound.

"I think, Ambassador Rising Principle, that if we survive this, there will be far different discussions to be had," she told them. "The Drifters betrayed us all, I think. I cannot prove they fired the weapons in my people's launchers, but I know we came here for peace.

"This treachery will be answered, and I think both our peoples are better served if we answer it together. Do you not?"

"This can-will be a possibility, but peace must-will be established first," Rising Principle told her.

"The Kozun Voices will take formal responsibility for the invasion, recognize the Cluster's borders as we were discussing, and pay an indemnity of one hundred thousand tons of refined palladium," Oran Aval said flatly. "In exchange, we want a nonaggression pact for ten years, a good-faith attempt to negotiate trade rights and mutual defense against other aggressors.

"Does that suffice for the La-Tar Cluster to accept peace with the Hierarchy, Ambassador?"

Sylvia had a decent idea of what the La-Tar Cluster wanted out of the negotiations, and unless she was severely mistaken, Oran Aval had just offered Rising Principle's entire wish list.

The Third Voice of the Kozun was *angry*—and the Drifters were going to regret betraying her.

Which was fine in Sylvia Todorovich's books. The Drifters were going to regret betraying *her*, too.

"Sers, ambassadors," Trosh interrupted. "We have a problem. The Guardians are splitting up...and as Ambassador Todorovich predicted, one of them is coming *here*."

CHAPTER THIRTY-NINE

If the soft chime had been an external alarm, it probably would have failed to wake Henry up. Since it was in his internal network and had almost nothing to do with his physical hearing, it actually *couldn't* fail.

To his surprise, he'd managed the three hours of sleep he'd set the alarm for. Checking into the status reports as he quickly showered and dressed told him that the Drifters were being surprisingly cautious.

They'd spent hours positioning two of the ships to sweep the entire meteor swarm from the outside while the third swept back along the course *Raven* had followed to get there. Now he could see the search-and-rescue shuttles sweeping the debris cloud that *had* been sixty Drifter starfighters, and understood their mission.

From their vector, though, the Guardian was going to continue on to the original ambush site and likely sweep for Kozun escape pods from there. Somehow, he didn't think anyone they rescued from the UPSF, La-Tar or Kozun wreckage was going to be well treated.

"Ser, it's O'Flannagain." Her message popped into his network. "Do you have a moment?"

"I'm awake and the Drifters are only now vectoring into the meteor swarm," Henry replied. "What's up, CAG?"

"I need you on the flight deck, ser," she told him. "We need to talk about this mess."

"You can talk to me now," he pointed out.

"Props are necessary," his CAG replied. "Be here in five."

Henry arched an eyebrow at a blank wall. That was mildly inappropriate and insubordinate, but he was used to that from starfighter pilots. He pinged Iyotake.

"XO, any idea what's going on with O'Flannagain?" he asked.

"She wants you to sign on putting our last few missiles on our fighters; I know that much," Iyotake replied. "I take it she pinged you as soon as you were awake?"

"She did," Henry confirmed. "Wants me to meet her on the flight deck. Can't hurt." He shrugged. "Status?"

"We're embedded in a hundred-plus-kilometer ice cube, and someone is about to come hunting for us with a laser," his XO said. "So far, everything I see suggests we're well hidden and it will take them time to find us. I'm just not sure how much time we're going to have."

"I'm hoping for about thirty-eight hours," Henry replied, checking his network for the time. "That's why we laid a bunch of traps and distractions. Surprised they haven't triggered any of them yet."

"My read is that they think they have all the time in the world," Iyotake said. "It'll be four days before the last regular drone reaches La-Tar. Without knowing about *Scorpius*, they've got to think they have at least a week."

"And if they know about *Scorpius*, Admiral Kosigan is going to need to launch a bloody witch hunt," Henry said. "Nobody farther out than Zion knew anything except us. If that leaked, IntelDiv is going be very, *very* busy."

"Indeed. Do you want me to check in once you're on the flight deck?"

"Yes," Henry confirmed. "Just link in; there's no need for you to be physically present. She's probably right about arming the Lancers; they're the last real weapon we have."

THE FLIGHT DECK was a busy hive of activity when Henry stepped onto it. One of the largest open spaces on the battlecruiser, it played host to their eight starfighters in bays along each side. Lights glittered in those bays, highlighting the still-odd-looking form factor of the new fighters.

One of the bays was dark, but enough light crept in from the rest of the bay for Henry to see the massive hole torn through three-quarters of the length of *Raven*-One.

"There you are," O'Flannagain said, emerging from one of several robotic trolleys running around the deck. "Catch."

Instinct was enough for Henry to grab the package she tossed him with ease, and he stared down at the familiar colors and bundled shape of a freshly fabricated flight suit.

"What's this?" he demanded, suddenly completely off-balance. The flight suit was marked with *his* name. *His* rank insignia. Even the entirely non-regulation red-gold wings of an ace who'd flown in the first campaign against the Kenmiri.

"It's a flight suit," O'Flannagain said with exaggerated patience. "*Raven*'s fabricators have your size on file. It's synced with *Raven*-Eight, though you'll want to double-check everything."

"Stop," Henry ordered. The pilot stopped. Henry gestured. "Iyotake, link in," he snapped. A virtual image of the XO appeared between the two of them, presented to them both by their internal networks.

"Lay it out, Commander O'Flannagain," he told her. "Fast."

"We can't launch missiles from the bottom of a hole that's now twice as deep as *Raven* is high," the CAG told them. "We're barely clear to get the SF-One-Thirties out around the hull, but we are clear.

"But we fired off all of our missiles in the engagements with the Drifter starfighters, and the entire battlecruiser is down to thirty-six missiles total," she said. "So, the XO didn't want to approve loading the starfighters without your authority."

"Seven starfighters, twenty-eight missiles," Henry said aloud. "That doesn't even leave *Raven* with a full salvo, so I see the problem. Not following on the flight suit, though."

"Two of my pilots, Lieutenant Brankovich and Lieutenant Commander Phạm, are in the medbay," O'Flannagain told him. "Lieutenant Commander Gaunt is dead; his quarters were vaporized when we got hit.

"So, I have seven fighters and five pilots. Five fighters only need twenty missiles, but I don't want to trust a single twenty-missile salvo to take down a *Guardian*."

"*If* I give you the missiles, they'll all be full penetrators," Henry told her. "That will help."

"The odds are still better with twenty-four than twenty," she replied. "And as it happens, there *is* someone else on *Raven* qualified to fly an SF-One-Thirty. That someone is a double ace with more fighter-on-fighter kills than anyone in the fighter wing *and* is the third-ranked pilot on the ship for fighter-on-starship kill participation."

"No." Iyotake had finally caught up. "We cannot put the commanding officer of a United Planets Space Force capital ship in a goddamn *starfighter*. That's a violation of at least six different regulations."

"Enforcing those regs would fall on Commander Thompson," Henry pointed out. It was probably unfair of him, but it was true. "But...even putting that aside, Commander O'Flannagain, I only have virtual hours on an SF-One-Thirty. I've never flown one in real space."

"Which still puts you ahead of our shuttle pilots, who are not starfighter-qualified, *period*," she told him. "Ser, you've kept up your virtual and realspace hours to keep your wings. You're *qualified* to fly a One-Thirty.

"There are only six unwounded people on this ship I can say that of," she concluded. "And taking you out with us, if it comes down to it, might just save everyone."

"Or kill the captain," Iyotake replied.

"Iyotake, you're right," Henry told his XO. "But we both know you're perfectly qualified to command a battlecruiser of your own. If something happens to me, you can take over—and *Raven* isn't going to win this on her own.

"If we get a clean shot at one of those Guardians, it might be worth it," he allowed. "But it's still a terrible idea, O'Flannagain, and we have a lot of other arrows in our quiver first."

"I'm not planning on taking us all right now, ser," she said. "I just want to make it clear that *when* we go out, you go with us. So that we don't argue about it while there's a Guardian in weapons range."

Henry knew he shouldn't do it. It was a terrible idea, one that risked *Raven*'s commander...and yet, O'Flannagain was right. Six fighters were more likely to succeed in an attack on a Guardian than five. It could make the difference between a suicide run to buy *Raven* time and an actual kill that changed the tone of the entire situation.

And he *wanted* to kill these bastards. He'd never been so angry, so determined to exact a blood toll on the people who'd killed his friends and two women he'd loved, in his entire life. It might be wrong...but it might be right, too.

Either way, he was going to do it.

"You're right, XO," he repeated. "But so are you, Commander."

He looked down at the flight suit.

"You have the con for the moment, Iyotake," he told his XO. "I'll be in the loop...but I'm going to go suit up. Authorize the missiles for six Lancers. That still leaves *Raven* with a full salvo in the launchers —and Song is to start fabricating new missiles ASAP. She's authorized to draw our materials stockpiles all the way down."

"It's dangerous," Iyotake said after a moment. "But it might be worth it. Whatever happens, I guarantee you the Drifters are *not* going to see it coming!"

CHAPTER FORTY

The first Charlie charges went off almost an hour later, a testimony to both the slowness of the Guardians' approach and the thoroughness of their search. The entire meteor swarm was almost half a million kilometers long, but getting within thirty thousand kilometers of the larger asteroids shouldn't have taken that long.

Henry was leaning against a wall in *Raven*-Eight's storage bay, linked into a virtual simulacrum of his bridge while still in position to jump aboard the fighter in minutes if they'd missed something.

"Charlie-Four just blew," Ihejirika reported, unnecessarily to anyone watching the tactical feed. A dozen five-hundred-megaton fusion explosions made *quite* the display, even before they tore a three-hundred-kilometer-long meteor into shreds.

"I almost feel bad for what we're doing to the real estate," Iyotake said. "If anyone lived in this system, this meteor swarm would be part of their astrology. Maybe even their religion."

"And if anyone *lived* in a barren hypergiant star system, I'd actually have considered that," Henry agreed. "As it is, there isn't even anything here for people to live on."

The Guardian he was watching dodged away from the explosions, engines pushing hard to fling the big ship clear of what they clearly thought was a trap...and right into the detonation radius of Charlie-Six.

"I wish we had our guns," Henry told Iyotake as another meteor blew apart, sending the Guardian flinching back toward the edge of the meteor swarm. "I think they're a bit spooked, *and* Bandit Two's new vector would leave her out of support range from Bandit One."

"We could send the fighters?" his XO suggested.

"No, that's not just our Sunday punch, Iyotake; it's our *only* punch," Henry said. "We'll hold it for when we have no choice." He considered the display. "Ihejirika, can we manually detonate Charlie-One and -Five?"

"Yeah, we have a relay on the surface with a tightbeam transmitter, but... Oh. I see."

The tactical officer's confusion faded before he could even ask. Charlie-Five would create a false sequence, an apparent vector of explosions that might guide the Drifters in the wrong direction. Charlie-One would both look like they were trying to distract from that sequence and be the closest set of charges to Guardian Bandit One.

"Detonating."

A few seconds passed with lightspeed coms and delays, and Henry nodded to himself as Guardian Bandit Two continued to accelerate away from the center of the swarm—but adjusted her course along the "path" laid out by the detonation of Charlie-Four through Charlie-Six.

Bandit One, on the other hand, was adjusting her course to arc around the bombs...which would bring her quite close to Delta-Two.

"Satine, do you have the data on Bandit One?" he asked.

"I do. I'm thinking I order Delta-Two to pulse up the heat levels a bit—low enough to look like they're hiding, high enough to look like it's us hiding badly—until they definitely show interest, then cut everything out. Make them dig."

"I like it," Henry agreed. If the Drifters had to dig deep into one of the massive meteors to try and locate a signal that had looked like *Raven*, that could buy him hours.

"Guardian Bandit Two's course is going to buy us some time," he told everyone. "She's headed along a route that'll take her to the wrong end of the meteor swarm. If we can get Bandit One to slice up one of the big ice chunks looking for us, that buys us *more* time."

He was playing for minutes and hours. He was down to just over thirty-six, but that still meant they needed to play matador for a day and a half.

"Pulsing up Delta-Two engines for a heat signature," Satine confirmed. "Let's see if they take the bait."

TAKING *the bait* turned out to look a *lot* more impressive than Henry had expected. Based on the Guardian's slow approach into the meteor cluster so far, he'd been expecting a detailed examination of the meteor and potentially digging into it with lasers to extract *Raven*.

Instead, the moment Bandit One flagged the heat signature at Delta-Two, the Guardian dove toward the asteroid at full acceleration and spun in space to bring her full broadside to bear. Ten heavy plasma cannon aligned on the ice chunk and went to full rapid fire.

Plasma bolts designed to hammer down energy shields and vaporize meters-thick armor went through ice like it wasn't even there. Each hit vaporized thousands of cubic meters of ice and exploded tens of thousands more into the void.

Even so, the scale of the meteor they'd buried Delta-Two in meant it took several minutes for Bandit One to reduce one of the largest objects in the star system to debris and vapor. *Raven*'s shuttle was vaporized somewhere in the middle of the chaos; even Henry wasn't sure where.

"Maybe we should have put the grav-shield up," Iyotake murmured. "I wasn't expecting that."

"The shuttles don't have them," Henry replied. "Our grav-shielded shuttles were on *Carpenter*, though I wish we'd rigged up something now. Even a faked gravity shield might have made the Drifters think they got us." He shook his head. "They definitely *don't* think they got us there."

The Guardian was slowing to a rendezvous with the new debris cloud, pulsing it with their sensors as they tried to resolve what had drawn their attention.

"Bandit One is poking through the debris," Ihejirika reported. "With a bit of work, I think we can definitely draw her over to Delta-Three when she's done there. Assuming she takes the bait, that will draw her farther away from us and buy time."

"And Bandit Two?"

"Bandit Two is clear of the swarm; I think they've detected something along the path we laid." Ihejirika paused. "I don't know what, because I don't have enough resolution from the scanners we left on the surface to ID anything outside the cluster that isn't under power."

"At their current velocity, that gives us lots of time, though," Henry said as he pulled the detailed information on Bandit Two. The Guardian was up to a solid velocity away from *Raven*, a vector that meant *Raven* now had at least four hours before they had to worry about Two—and every minute they accelerated away from the cruiser was roughly three minutes more before they could threaten his ship.

"Bandit One is looking extremely lonely," Iyotake said. "If we take her out..."

"We remove any question of whether we're in the meteor swarm," Henry noted. "And while Two is headed away from us, what's Three up to?"

"Bandit Three is shedding velocity," Ihejirika replied. The tactical officer paused thoughtfully. "I thought she was heading for the original rendezvous, but the vector is wrong. She'll hit zero velocity almost a million kilometers short of where *Carpenter* and *Glorious* died."

Henry nodded.

"Protector-Legate Half-Blue-Third-Red sees the same vulnerability on Bandit One that we do," he said. "Assuming she's coming right back, how long until Three can reach us?"

"Three hours minimum, ser."

"My money says One spends most or all of that time sifting through the wreckage of Delta-Two and that whatever Bandit Two saw is far enough away that they'll only be reaching it around then," he guessed. "If we can use the Deltas to distract One and Three after that...that gets us some breathing room."

He shook his head, glad that none of his officers could see it. His best-case scenario said they could play enough games to buy about eight hours. Then they'd be completely out of tricks and relying on their giant chunk of ice to hide them.

CHAPTER FORTY-ONE

"There goes the last Delta."

Satine's soft report was probably redundant, but Henry slumped on the bench on the flight deck anyway. There wasn't much of a point of him being on the bridge...and they were out of everything anyway.

This shuttle had been pulsing their engines and maneuvering, buying it enough attention from Guardian Three to draw sustained fire for almost fifteen minutes, even *after* the shuttle had been vaporized.

"I mark the time at twenty-seven hours," Iyotake said quietly. "All Delta decoys and Charlie charges have been expended, ser. Orders?"

"None," Henry admitted on a private channel with his XO. "I'll check with Song and Henriksson in a moment, see if they can lower our heat signature any more, but...we bought fifteen hours we might not have had, Tatanka. I'm not sure what else we can do."

"I'm guessing that six Lancers can't take on three Guardians," Iyotake said.

"With perfect surprise, we might be able to take down one," Henry said. "Against two or three, they'll just be a distraction." He sighed. "I almost wish we had gone for Bandit One when they were alone, now."

Two of the Guardians were still in the meteor swarm now. Bandit Two had gone a surprising distance off into the void, chasing *something*, but was now on her way back.

"Any clever ideas, XO?" he asked.

"If we turned off *everything*, we'd asphyxiate before we boiled," Iyotake told him in an uncharacteristically grim tone. "I'm told that's a better way to go."

"We're not that far gone yet, XO," Henry snapped. "We might not make it out of this, but we are by God coming through as officers and spacers of the UPSF."

"Yes, ser," his XO said crisply. "Should I loop Song in, ser?"

"Yeah, let's make this a conference." Henry gave several mental commands, linking the chief engineer into a three-way private channel.

"Song, what's our status?" he asked.

"Aren't you supposed to harass Henriksson for those questions?" the engineer asked with a sigh. "We're about what you'd expect. I've stepped all four reactors down to ten percent, minimum safe levels. Every weapon capacitor is drained; every system I can think of to shut down is shut down.

"I've got drones and people all over the engines still, but it's not good." Henry felt as much as saw her shrug. "I suppose I have *some* good news."

"I could use good news. What have you got?" Henry asked.

"Compensators are realigned and fixed," Song told him. "The ship can't take any subjective gees, it's just not going to happen, but we can get back up to point five again."

"That *is* good news," Henry agreed. Irrelevant, unfortunately, since the Guardians could get up to point *six* KPS^2, but good news. "Any ideas on reducing heat signatures or escaping this mess?"

She snorted.

"If it can be turned off, I've turned it off," she told him again. "I've got *one* last trick to play, but we can't sustain it for long."

"That's one more trick than I've got, Colonel Song," Henry admitted. "What are we at?"

"I can shut down the radiators and hold all of our heat in the hull," Song said. "We won't have zero heat signature, but it'll be low. *Real* low."

"And how fast will the interior air heat up?" he asked.

"Little over a degree centigrade every two minutes," she said. "So, we'll have about thirty minutes, and even *that* is going to send people to medbay. It's all I've got."

"It might buy us some critical moments, Colonel," Henry told her. "Get it ready for my command. Or Iyotake's, depending."

"Oh, it's already ready," Song said. "Give the word and we'll be sweating in no time."

"I look forward to it," Iyotake said grimly.

"Thank you, Colonels," Henry told them both. "I expect I'll be talking to you both before this is over, but...before we're down to the wire...it has been an honor to command you both. Thank you."

There was no response from either of his senior subordinates. There was no point. They knew as well as he did what the odds were looking like.

"Ser!" Ihejirika's voice suddenly echoed in all of their minds on the main command channel. "Bandit Three!"

BETWEEN THE DRIFTERS vaporizing three of the largest meteors to destroy the decoy shuttles and the dozen ice floes Henry's people had blown to pieces with fusion bombs, the meteor swarm was a *far* more active and confusing place than it had been when they'd first arrived.

Bandit Three had been sweeping just past the debris front from one of the Charlie explosions, ignoring the harmless debris field while they searched for signs of *Raven*, and missed the intact meteor that had been caught up in the pattern.

The Guardian was a modular ship, built of a dozen smaller sections and over a kilometer long all told. Her energy shields were more powerful than anything else in space, capable of standing off the full firepower of a Kenmiri dreadnought.

They were *not* capable of stopping a five-hundred-meter spike of ice traveling at several hundred kilometers per second.

Henry's attention was on the ship in response to Ihejirika's report, in time to watch the shield slowly cave in and collapse under the impact. The meteor was slowed by the defensive bubble, but it was still traveling with enough force to collide with the Drifter capital ship.

For a moment, Henry even dared to hope that the confusion and chaos they'd created in the meteor swarm might have managed to destroy the Guardian by pure fluke. Then plasma flared as Bandit Three's engines flung her away from the meteor.

She left a trail of atmosphere and debris as she moved, her shields flickering back up after a few moments, while several plasma cannon blew the meteor apart in illogical revenge.

"Three is bleeding atmosphere but appears to be functional," Ihejirika reported. "I had a moment of hope there."

"I think we all did," Henry said. "Looks like she might be down a few turrets, too. Nature was definitely feeling helpful."

"She's adjusting course and burning for open space," Ihejirika said. "Bandit One is maneuvering to support. In case we were feeling aggressive, I suppose."

"I'm feeling very meek at the moment, in fact," the captain replied. "They're leaving?"

"Vector is for open space," his tactical officer confirmed. "Unsure of when they'll turn over, but they're headed in the direction of the original summit location."

Henry nodded grimly. They might be planning to sweep for escape pods to make up for time, but their main concern was clearly getting Three out of the meat grinder *Raven* had accidentally assembled.

"Don't hold your breath, people," he told the command channel, "but fate may have just handed us a few hours I wasn't expecting to have."

"Maybe not as many as it might have been, ser," Iyotake told him, back on their private channel. "Bandit Two is still headed our way… and I make her most likely vector practically right for us."

Henry closed everything and exhaled a long sigh as he closed both his physical and virtual eyes. Then he opened the tactical feed to confirm Iyotake's assessment.

Bandit Two could still change their vector, but if they didn't, the largest meteor on their course and their likely destination was Epsilon, *Raven*'s hiding place.

The asteroid had taken two of the Guardians out of the immediate situation, but it was only four more hours until Bandit Two arrived right on top of them.

"Well," Henry said quietly, "then I guess it will shortly be time for O'Flannagain and I to demonstrate the UPSF's latest starfighter technology."

CHAPTER FORTY-TWO

"The tunnel is going to be a nightmare for everyone," O'Flannagain said bluntly as she looked around her pilots.

Henry sat slightly off to one side from the four regular members of the squadron. He was senior to O'Flannagain, but he wasn't so arrogant as to assume he was better at commanding a fighter wing than she was.

If nothing else, he'd never actually *done* it. After the initial Kenmiri invasion and the Red Wings campaign had wiped out ninety-five-plus percent of FighterDiv, he'd done one tour as a training officer and then transferred into the tactical track of SpaceDiv.

He'd seen too many pilot friends die to stay in the cockpit then.

"The area around *Raven* herself gives us a bit of room to maneuver," the CAG continued. "There's about fifteen meters of space above the cruiser. Not a lot of leeway, but more than enough for one of the Lancers, *if* we're careful.

"The problem is that we had a nice neat battlecruiser-shaped hole through the ice crust...fifteen hours ago. Scans suggest it's refrozen down to less than five meters across at the tightest point," she said. "That *should* be plenty of room, but we absolutely *cannot* open up the path. At minimal acceleration, the GMS drives are almost invisible.

"Our lasers are not."

"Two meters of spare leeway," Turrigan announced with a broad grin that Henry easily recognized as forced. "What's the problem?"

"*Less than* five meters," O'Flannagain repeated. "Educate me, Turrigan, what's the minimum bubble size for your grav-shield? The grav-shield *we can't turn off* if we want GMS drives?"

"Five meters... Oh."

"Gravity is almost nonexistent here," Henry noted. "We go up the chimney on thrusters. Even now it's only ninety meters high. We go up at one *meter* per second or less. We don't need the GMS drive till we're in space."

"Got it in one, skipper," the CAG agreed. "It is going to suck. But if the job was easy, anyone could do it, and then we wouldn't need battlecruisers."

Henry had to join in the shared chuckle at the joke.

"We're under a time limit, people," she continued. "We go up one at a time. Colonel Wong first, myself last. Once we're out of the meteor, we have a bit more flexibility, but we need to get the planes into space, intact, with missiles.

"Anyone who has a problem with doing that on emergency thrusters is welcome to tell the rest of the crew they're going to die because you lack fortitude."

MEMORIES FLOODED BACK in as Henry stepped into the cockpit of the Lancer. It was entirely different, of course. The last time he'd flown a fighter, he'd been immersed in an acceleration tank at the heart of the spacecraft.

And yet.

The controls were still the same. The screens and internal-interface datafeeds were the same. He'd trained in a virtual simulator for each of the generations of starfighters since he'd left FighterDiv, and spent time in each starfighter on training flights, but somehow, stepping into one intending to go to war was very different.

He strapped himself carefully into the seat, its acceleration-cushioning gel molding to his body. It was the same style of chair used on starship bridges—probably exactly the same and drawn from the same manufacturer. They hadn't needed fighter cockpit chairs in a few generations, after all.

More displays slid in around him as he brought the Lancer to life. Energy levels, missile status, shield status...the heat-radiation level that would betray him if it got too high.

The engine status was missing, merged into the display for the shield. The gravity shield and the gravity maneuvering system were inextricably linked.

He checked everything over one last time, running down a literal checklist, and then nodded silently and activated the squadron channel.

"*Raven*-Eight, confirming green."

Status reports for the rest of the fighters rippled in over the network as his command codes gave him the same data O'Flannagain had. He was, unsurprisingly, the last pilot to check in—but only by about five seconds. That was better than he expected.

"All right, Eight, you've got the lead," O'Flannagain's voice told him. "I'm in Seven. Two, you go second, followed by Three, Four and Six. I'll bring up the rear.

"Let's keep it nice and steady, people."

"Eight, this is Deck Control," Chief Anja, the cruiser's deck officer, said in his ear. "Are you good to go?"

"I'm clear, Control," Henry replied, years-old habits waking in answer to the old challenge and response. "You have the bouncing ball."

"I have the ball," Anja replied. "On the bounce, Eight... and...*bounce*."

Normally, the deck's systems would have flung him into space with a significant starting velocity. Today, he was gently tossed out the end of the deck, and he already had his thrusters firing to reduce the minuscule velocity *Raven* had given him.

There was almost no space around the cruiser, and he inhaled sharply as he carefully tucked the saucer-shaped starfighter up and around his girl. From there, he could actually *see* the damage the hits had done.

He had intellectually believed Song when she told him *Raven* was dead, but it was something else to *see* it. His ship was a wreck, her spine visibly bent around the impact points. A battlecruiser's spine was supposed to be a straight line, not have a fifteen-degree turn in the middle.

More important right now was the gap above the cruiser, the remains of the hole *Raven* had cut to get this deep into the meteor. The heat radiators had kept the ship sinking deeper into the block of ice, but there'd been nothing to keep that cut open.

"Exit is eleven meters at the entry point," he said on the squadron channel, feeding his sensor data back to the other five pilots. "Easy to get in, but we'll see how narrow it gets."

The maneuver thrusters answered his commands easily, aligning the Lancer with the bottom of the chasm leading toward the surface. Half-consciously holding his breath, Henry tucked his ship into the opening.

Slow and steady, he began his ascent. His proximity alarms blared warnings at him, but he was using the same sensors to guide his course.

"Channel is down to seven meters," he reported. "Continuing to shrink as I approach the surface." He checked. "Sensors show a clear path still. But...*five meters* was definitely overstating it."

The opening at the top of the chimney wasn't the narrowest part, if only because most of the melted material there had escaped into space. The narrowest part was ten meters below the surface, and he watched the scans carefully.

"Narrowest part of the tunnel is three point two two meters," he said calmly. "Watch your scanners and your alignment. This is..."

He exhaled.

"This is a tight fit," he concluded. "I'm through; exiting the surface *now*. Bringing up the GMS and holding position."

Shield icons flicked from black to orange to green as he waited, his primary defense and engine coming online at the same time. Motionless, the small bubble around his starfighter would diffuse the tiny amount of heat he was giving off. *Raven* might be able to see the Lancer, but nothing else would.

Grav-shielded fighters were the closest thing he'd ever seen to invisible in space. That invisibility traditionally disappeared as soon as they fired their engines, but it had still allowed the UPSF to pull off some nasty tricks in the war.

And now the GMS let them keep that invisibility while they moved. Only at low acceleration, but that was going to be enough.

"This is *Raven*-Two; I'm clear," Lieutenant Commander Turrigan reported. "That was a snugger fit than I like, ser."

"You're here, aren't you?" Henry asked. "It's fine."

Four more fighters rose up out of the ice after Turrigan, each of them drifting clear of the shaft and bringing up their GMS.

"Everyone clear?" O'Flannagain finally asked. "Did we lose any sensor dishes or critical components on the way up?"

"I think I might have frozen off some critical body parts," one of the Lieutenants quipped.

"Shut it, *Raven*-Three," O'Flannagain ordered. "All right. We have the last location of Bandit Three from *Raven*'s sensors. We take it nice and easy, point three KPS-squared, people."

"Be vewwy, vewwy quiet," Turrigan quipped. "We's huntin' Guardians."

CHAPTER FORTY-THREE

T HE CLOUDS OF ICY DEBRIS THAT HENRY'S PLAN HAD LEFT filling most of the empty space in the meteor swarm were both a blessing and a curse. They'd cover the starfighters' movements at a distance, but as his people approached their enemy, the trails the spacecraft left in the dust would give them away.

Assuming the Drifters looked for them. Even Henry was surprised by how small the heat signatures the other Lancers left on his sensors were. The six of them combined were putting off less heat than a single old-style fighter at the same low acceleration.

"We are on our own for sensors now," O'Flannagain reminded them all. "We have a loose contact on Bandit Two. Computers mark her at forty-five minutes from the edge of the meteor cluster and ninety from close contact with *Raven*."

The CAG paused for a moment.

"If the Guardian finds *Raven*, she'll kill her," she said bluntly. "*We* are carrying almost all that's left of *Raven*'s missiles. If we don't take down that Guardian in the next ninety minutes, your bunks are history, folks."

And so was Henry's crew. He doubted he was *much* more motivated than his pilots—they were good people and he trusted O'Flannagain completely—but he remained responsible for all of this.

He was so very, *very* angry. A quick run-through of his screens confirmed O'Flannagain's assessment.

"What's the plan, ser?" Turrigan asked. With Gaunt dead and Phạm in the medbay, Turrigan was the only Lieutenant Commander left in the squadron. He was the official second-in-command, since no one was quite sure how Henry fit into the chain of command.

"Bandit Two is reentering the swarm through the debris cloud from the Alpha-Two charges," O'Flannagain replied. "We're thirty minutes from there if we're careful. We'll cut our accel at five hundred KPS and coast into the cloud.

"The grav-shields will draw attention eventually, but we'll get as close as we can."

"How close are you planning, CAG?" Henry asked. It wasn't a challenge. He was out of practice at this.

"What's the skip range on the penetrator busses?" she asked drily.

"It's a half-second skip, and without a gravity line, they only carry their regular three-dimensional velocity in," he said. He knew she knew the answer, but the other pilots might not. The old-style fighter missiles couldn't fit shield-penetrator missiles.

"With just the launch velocity from the disposable cells, five hundred klicks," he concluded. "We're not getting that close."

"No, we're not," O'Flannagain agreed. "But we're getting as close as we can. Into laser range if they let us, people—and awful as a Guardian's armor is, that's still only ten thousand klicks with our onboard beamers."

A stunned silence filled the squadron channel, but Henry simply nodded. This wasn't a normal operation, where the Lancers would be primarily missile platforms extending the range and firepower of their mothership.

"This is do-or-die, people," he reminded them. "Either we take out that Guardian or we and every member of *Raven*'s crew dies...

and these *assholes* get away with blowing up the peace conference and our ambassador.

"They don't get away," he said flatly. "And if that means we fly right into that Guardian's guts and rip it apart with our lasers, that's what we do. The missiles should cripple her. If it's down to the knives, we're just finishing her off."

He hoped. Because if it came down to trying to kill a capital ship with the lasers of six Lancers, they were doomed.

"TARGET IS at one hundred thousand kilometers and continuing on course," Turrigan said calmly. "Velocity is five hundred KPS relative to the swarm, one thousand relative to us."

"Watch all threat sensors, stand by anti-radiation systems and prepare to fire," O'Flannagain ordered.

ARAD systems in this case were counter-targeting systems, sensors that would detect incoming sensor beams and temporarily jam them. They'd also alert the fighters when they were detected.

They were well within missile range, and Henry could only hold his breath as the big Drifter capital ship continued on, seemingly oblivious to the six starfighters lurking amidst the chaotic debris field.

"Passive locks suck," Turrigan muttered. "Even at this range, we could lose missiles."

"No, we won't," O'Flannagain said with a chuckle. "Seconds count, but my sensors are ready to pulse the radar. We'll have active targeting data."

Henry was silent, his focus entirely on the hostile capital ship. The other two Guardians were now at least three hours' flight away. If they took out this Guardian, that bought them time.

It wasn't going to be enough—Battle Group *Scorpius* was still twenty-one hours away. It would be another ten hours before Rear Admiral Cheung Jian Chin even declared them overdue.

But every trick, every victory, every game, bought them another handful of hours. One of the Guardians was damaged—probably not as much as he hoped, as the collision had almost certainly spooked the Drifter crew more than it deserved—and if they took out another, maybe...just *maybe*, the remaining intact ship would leave them alone.

He didn't buy that, though. They *needed Raven* to die, to cover any evidence that they had destroyed the peace conference. The Drifters hadn't even been prepared to accept the *chance* that he'd doubt the Kozun had betrayed him.

Just like, it seemed, they hadn't been prepared to accept the chance that the UPA would become competitors or enemies. Or that the Kozun and the UPA would come to an agreement. All of this had been done to protect the Convoys—but not from a real threat. From a *potential* threat.

"Sixty thousand kilometers," Turrigan reported. "Velocity thousand-twenty-four KPS. Missile flight time twenty-five seconds."

O'Flannagain didn't respond. The seconds crept forward.

"Fifty thousand. Flight time *twenty seconds*."

"Eighty percent of detection threshold, O'Flannagain," Henry murmured. "We're out of time."

He heard the CAG exhale sharply.

"Firing radar pulse," she snapped. "Fire all missiles on confirmed target and take GMS to full power."

At fifty thousand kilometers, it was less than half a second before the targeting systems on the Lancer confirmed one hundred percent lock. Henry took another moment to confirm alignment with the rest of the squadron and then fired.

Twenty-four missiles blasted away from the starfighters, disposable launchers providing hundreds of kilometers per second of additional velocity while their own drives lit up behind them.

At three KPS^2, the strange invisibility they'd enjoyed at lower accelerations vanished. Each of the six starfighters blazed like full-size starships as they charged forward, falling into carefully calculated gravity wells inside their defensive shields.

The Guardian might have been oblivious to their presence, but the Drifter crew had been prepared for an attack of *some* kind. Defensive lasers flared to life in the first ten seconds, targeting the incoming missiles—but they had never expected fire to come from that close without warning.

But it was still a *ten-million-ton* warship the best part of a kilometer long. A hundred lasers opened fire, filling the void around the Drifter ship with coherent light. A third of their missiles disappeared from Henry's scanners...and then the rest disappeared a thousand kilometers short of the Guardian's shields, shifting into a different level of the seventeen dimensions humans couldn't perceive.

Half of the weapons rematerialized around the shield, barely inside or outside the defensive energy bubble. Several others completely missed—and three five-hundred-megaton warheads exploded amidst the modules that made up the massive vessel.

Between the explosions directly on the shield and the damage to the Guardian, the shields went down—and the Lancers were there, twenty seconds behind the missiles.

"Target is still active," Turrigan snapped. "Engines are damaged but still operational. Shields are down but I'm reading at least three still-active plasma turrets."

The squadron XO didn't even need to report the lasers. The defensive systems that had targeted the missiles now turned on the charging starfighters. Gravity shields distorted and deflected the beams, but more and more lasers were coming online as the fighters closed.

"Plasma turrets firing." It took Henry a moment to realize the calm voice reporting the massive plasma weapons activation was his. His own fighter drew the short straw, with one of the big guns aimed directly at his craft.

The GMS allowed him to easily dodge the incoming burst, and then they were in range. There was no detailed plan for how to attack a capital ship with six starfighters' defensive lasers. The lasers were occasionally used for this—but usually with closer to a *hundred* starfighters.

Henry targeted the turret that had fired on him, blazing a beam of coherent light down its barrel as it tried to track him. The laser gouged through the armored barrel, and for a second, nothing happened.

Then the turret tried to fire again, and its containment failed. A multi-hundred-megaton explosion tore apart one of the weapons modules, sending other pieces of the big warship flying as the starfighters dove in again.

"*Raven*-Two is down," O'Flannagain said flatly. "Guardian turrets are down. All turrets are down. Target the power pla—"

Henry wasn't sure if it was a hit on one of the power plants or backlash from the destruction of the turrets. One moment, the broken-but-still-formidable Guardian was rotating in space, trying to bring intact defensive lasers to bear on the mosquitos killing her.

The next, two fusion reactors and an engine containment vessel failed in less than a second. Three massive new explosions tore through the modular ship...and then there was silence.

"*Raven*-Three is down," O'Flannagain reported in the quiet.

That was Lieutenant Commander Turrigan's bird, Henry realized. The odd-numbered starfighters were the wing commanders, the senior half of the squadron. That meant they had Four, Six and Eight left alongside O'Flannagain's own Seven.

All of the CAG's senior pilots were gone. Phạm was at least in sickbay, but *Raven*'s squadron had been cut in half.

"We need to get out of here, CAG," Henry told her. "Fall back to *Raven*. We should be clear enough to use lasers to open the chasm up a bit to get back in."

Whatever happened now, the starfighters had *more* than done their part.

CHAPTER FORTY-FOUR

"And here they come," Iyotake said calmly.

Henry was back where he belonged, on *Raven*'s bridge. He hadn't changed out of the flight suit. It had his proper rank insignia, the steel oak leaf emblazoned on the right side of the collar, and he didn't have much time.

"Time?" he asked.

"Admiral Cheung will likely declare us out of contact in just over eight hours," Moon reported. "Twenty to twenty-one hours before relief, ser."

He nodded; his eyes focused on the screen.

Bandit Three was definitely damaged. She was accelerating at point five KPS^2, blood in the water if he'd had *any* ability to engage her...and if she weren't being accompanied by the clearly completely undamaged Bandit One.

The two Guardians might have been a match for an undamaged *Raven*. In her current state, well...

"I don't believe I have ever been quite so appreciative of ice in my life," he murmured.

"You, I see, do not vacation in the Caribbean," his XO said with a chuckle. "When you're on those beaches and there isn't a cloud for five hundred kay in any direction…you *really* appreciate ice.

"But you're right; today I might appreciate this chunk of ice more."

It wasn't going to buy them twenty hours, Henry suspected, but it had bought them almost thirty already. More than he'd had any right to hope for, really.

"Any clever ideas, people?" he asked. "According to the fabricator reports, we are up to twenty-four total missiles."

He supposed they could fill one or both of the pilots in the medbay with painkillers and stims and send out a five-fighter strike. It was *very* clear from their maneuvering, though, that the remaining Drifter ships knew roughly what had happened to Bandit Two.

"Bury our heat signature as they get close and hope," Iyotake told him. "That's Song's option. We still haven't needed it yet."

"It might buy us a few more minutes," Henry conceded. "I just don't think it will buy us enough for them to completely bypass our hiding spot."

"Ser… No, that can't be right."

Henry turned to look at Ihejirika, the tactical officer rubbing his eyes with the back of his hand. None of the senior officers had taken any breaks since they'd embedded themselves in the meteor. Even with internal networks regulating fatigue toxins, it was starting to show.

"I confirm, ser," Ybarra said quietly. "Multiple skip signatures at the Ra-One-Seventy-Five skip line. Drifters are turning, sers."

"Ihejirika?" Henry demanded.

"Guardians are turning; course is for Kozun space," the big African officer replied crisply. "I make the new signature three capital ships and seven escorts, high probability that the central capital ship is a *Crichton*-class fleet carrier.

"It's *Scorpius*, ser," Ihejirika said wonderingly. "We're too far and using sensors without enough resolution to be certain, but I believe I'm picking up a full deck launch."

Henry stared at the data as it appeared on his screens. A *Crichton*-class fleet carrier had a hundred and twenty SF-122 Dragoons aboard. At this point, having flown a Lancer into combat, he knew the Dragoon was obsolete—but it was still the *second*-most powerful starfighter he knew of.

"Maneuver cones, Commander, please," he said, his tone distracted.

They were already flickering onto the screen, and they told him everything he needed to know: the Guardians weren't going to escape. They only had a third of the acceleration of the starfighters pursuing them. They couldn't make it to the skip line. They couldn't make it to *Raven*.

"Ser, incoming transmission," Moon reported. "Two transmissions," she corrected. "One is on Vesheron protocols; one is encrypted on UPSF protocols."

"Play them both," Henry ordered. "Vesheron first."

"This is Rear Admiral Cheung Jian Chin," the familiar-looking short Chinese Admiral said in rough but clear Kem. "To the Drifter forces in the Lon System. We are fully aware of your treachery, of your betrayal of both the United Planets Alliance and the Kozun Hierarchy.

"By the time you could reach Kozun space, the Hierarchy will be fully aware of your crimes...but you will not reach Kozun space. Surrender, or my fighters will run you down like the rabid dogs you have proven yourselves to be."

The message ended and Henry grinned. He *knew* it was a cruel and vicious grin, but he had no sympathy for the people who'd wrecked a peace conference—and he knew that Cheung was correct.

There was no way the Guardians were escaping the Lon System.

The second message started playing a moment later, this one showing the tall blond features of Commodore Peter Barrie. Henry's ex-husband looked worried.

"Captain Wong, *Raven*, this is Captain Barrie on *Scorpius*," the Commodore declared. "We received an update on the system from

Ambassador Todorovich. *Jackdaw* and two destroyers are headed to your rough location now.

"Stay concealed until they reach you. We have the situation under control. I repeat, the situation is under control. Stay where you are. *Scorpius* and *Rook* are also en route to retrieve the Ambassadors from their survival capsule. Everything is under control."

The world fell out from under Henry.

Todorovich had told them what had happened. *How?* She was dead...except the UPSF contingent was picking up a survival capsule with the ambassadors. Had they *all* survived?

"Ser?" Moon said after a moment. "What...what do we do?"

"Stand the ship down to Status Three," Henry ordered. "We stand by until *Jackdaw* is closer to us than those Guardians, then we establish communications."

He looked at the expanding cluster of green icons on his display.

"We did it, people," he told them all. "We did it."

CHAPTER FORTY-FIVE

The rescue shuttle settled onto the immense flight deck at the heart of *Scorpius* with a gentle *thud* audible throughout its passenger compartment.

Scorpius was a squashed cigar shape six hundred meters long, and her flight deck ran the full length of her hull. As Sylvia slowly stepped down the ramp, she could see the rows of single-fighter bays that held the carrier's "main battery."

Those bays were empty, their usual inhabitants flying search and rescue through the wreckage of the two Guardians that had refused to surrender in the face of overwhelming firepower. Not all of those starfighters would be coming home—but the only Drifters that would see their homes again would do so through the mercy of the UPSF.

A formal greeting party was waiting on the deck, with files of immaculately turned-out GroundDiv troopers lining a long blue carpet. Rising Principle had already reached the end and was now standing beside the tall blond officer waiting for them.

Sylvia instead stayed at the bottom of the ramp, waiting until Oran Aval and her escort made it down to join her. Several people in the crowd clearly seemed to be expecting the Kozun Voice to emerge as a prisoner, but they'd get to be disappointed.

"Come, Voice," she told Aval in Kem.

"I was expecting a different welcome," Aval told her.

"Whether the UPA is at peace with the Kozun is *my* call, Voice Aval," Sylvia reminded the other woman. "And you and Rising Principle made a deal. That means we are at peace.

"So, we should go."

Aval smiled thinly and joined Sylvia as they walked down the long blue carpet together, their bodyguards and staff trailing a few steps behind. GroundDiv soldiers snapped to attention as Sylvia passed them, and there was something ever so slightly different in their posture.

It wasn't that Aval was with her. It wasn't even that these troops didn't know her and she was used to *Raven*'s troops. It was... *Respect* was the wrong word. GroundDiv troopers had always been respectful of her.

It was *awe*. She'd survived the destruction of her ship and then orchestrated the defeat of the Drifters' plot from inside a glorified escape pod, and that story had clearly already spread.

"Ambassador Sylvia Todorovich," *Scorpius*'s commander greeted her with a bow. Barrie wore the standard black slacks and turtleneck uniform of the UPSF. His sweater had the white collar of a starship captain with the gold oak leaf of a Commodore pinned to the right side of it.

"Voice Oran Aval," he continued, turning to the Kozun and switching easily to Kem. "I understand that the La-Tar Cluster now has a peace treaty with the Hierarchy."

"We do," Aval confirmed. "And given the treachery here, the beginnings, I believe, of a potential alliance against an enemy that has attacked us both."

"It is not my role to speak to the place of the United Planets Alliance in that conflict," Barrie said calmly. "That duty lies on

Ambassador Todorovich, who I trust will handle the affairs of our nation with her usual skill."

"Thank you, Captain," Sylvia told him. "For the moment, the UPA will be operating on our defensive treaties with La-Tar and others...but the Drifters have clearly demonstrated themselves a threat to everyone.

"I hope that threat can be defused by discussion and negotiation," she admitted, "but if they prove as paranoid as their actions here suggest, I have the utmost faith in the courage and skill of the United Planets Space Force."

Enough of the crew would understand Kem that her words would be communicated throughout the ship and the battle group within hours.

"You must all be exhausted," Barrie said after a moment. "I have medics standing by to check over all of your people. They are trained on Kozun and other Ashall physiology, I promise."

Aval almost unconsciously touched her stomach.

"That strikes me as a good plan," she agreed.

"We are at your disposal, Voice Aval," the Commodore told her. "Please, this way."

SYLVIA FELT MORE than a little silly, hesitating outside Barrie's office a couple of hours later. *Raven* was now on her way to join the battle group, which had both good and bad elements.

Good was the confirmation that Henry Wong had survived. A lot of his crew hadn't, though, and it was clear that the battlecruiser would never fight again. *Raven* was a wreck, mobile under her own power but no longer a functioning warship in any sense.

It also meant that they had the full copies of *Raven*'s telemetry of the Drifters' betrayal, the ninety seconds of Kozun shock that might have been critical if the Drifters hadn't proceeded to blow any pretense in their hunt to destroy those records.

She was outside Commodore Peter Barrie's office, though, for entirely selfish reasons. It was uncharacteristic of her to hesitate—but she didn't like leaning on her position and the contacts it gave her for personal matters.

On the other hand, well...

She buzzed for admittance.

"Come in," Barrie replied. "Ambassador?"

The questioning tone in his voice carried over to his face as she stepped into the office. The degree to which the office mirrored Henry Wong's on *Raven*'s was fascinating to her. The spaces were laid out identically. The only difference was that where Henry's office had *Raven*'s bird-with-quill seal on the wall behind him, Barrie's office had the ancient astrological constellation the ship was named for.

"How may I help you?" he asked, gesturing her to a seat.

"It's nothing critical, if you're busy," she admitted. "It's a personal matter, though somewhat time-sensitive."

Barrie eyed her for a moment, then chuckled.

"I am the commander of a capital ship with forty-five hundred souls aboard, Ambassador, I am well familiar with creating time for time-sensitive matters when I'm busy. I'm not sure how I can help with personal matters, though."

Sylvia paused for a few moments, then took a sharp breath and dove in.

"Henry Wong," she said bluntly. "You're his ex-husband. May I ask what happened?"

"That's...*very* personal," Barrie admitted, clearly surprised for a moment before his eyes narrowed in suspicion. "But you've been aboard his ship, on and off, for almost a year now, haven't you?"

"About that, yes," she confirmed.

The Commodore sighed, laying his hands on the table and looking down at them.

"The short version is that practically every other couple I knew had an *understanding* about the nature of wartime relationships and their requirements," he said bluntly. "Rather than actually talking to Henry, I assumed. Given what I knew about Henry's own nature as far as romance and sex go, that was, in hindsight, spectacularly stupid.

"Our divorce was reasonably amicable, but I'm not going to pretend it wasn't my fault," Barrie said. "I regret it, but it is far from the worst sacrifice the war demanded."

"I wondered," Sylvia admitted. "He seemed surprisingly un-bitter about it, for all that he didn't talk about it, either."

"He's a better man than I am," the Commodore said. "I am far more upset with my younger self than I think Henry is." He shrugged. "I don't think that's what you need to know, though, is it?"

Sylvia had the self-control required to be a key ambassador of a nation of seven star systems and over forty billion human beings. She still flushed at Barrie's blunt assessment.

"How the hell did you even get him to notice you?" she finally asked.

Barrie laughed.

"I beat him with a metaphorical stick for six long, frustrating months," he admitted. "Once I decided I was interested, I *told* him. We were already friends and I knew he was as interested in men as women...but I also knew the *level* of his interest.

"I didn't push him; I just kept gently reminding him, week after week, month after month, while we ran peacetime operations in the old FighterDiv. Eventually, his brain flipped a switch and things worked out." Barrie sighed. "I don't know quite what to suggest, Em Todorovich. Tell him, I guess? Let him make up his own mind."

"That's more helpful than you might think," she admitted. "Thank you."

She rose from her seat and he made an airy gesture.

"It's nothing, Ambassador," Barrie told her. "Just promise me one thing, all right?"

"Captain?" she said carefully.

"Make him happy, if you do make it work. A good chunk of me still needs to see him happy."

"I hope I get the opportunity," Sylvia said.

CHAPTER FORTY-SIX

Raven LIMPED HER WAY INTO THE REST OF THE FLEET, WITH her younger sister hovering around her like an overprotective puppy. The two destroyers circling the battlecruisers broke off as they entered the defensive perimeter of _Scorpius_'s slowly returning fighter wings, joining the rest of the escorts.

Henry was on his ship's bridge as they reached safe space, and he allowed himself to finally relax as ten SF-122's swung around behind his ship, a physical barrier between _Raven_ and the system where she'd been so badly mangled.

Only a tiny watch was on the bridge, with over ninety percent of his crew unconscious in their bunks. What damage could be repaired had been fixed under the ice. Only a shipyard could do more at this point—and even most shipyards couldn't do much about his poor ship's broken spine.

Or Henry Wong's exhausted soul. Sylvia Todorovich and Alex Thompson were alive. Those were powerful balms against his mental wounds, but the toll of the Drifters' betrayal continued to stack up.

Few of _Carpenter_'s or _Glorious_'s crew had survived. They'd been fired on at close range without warning. There had been no chance for anyone to make it to escape pods or safety bunkers. Of the four hundred and twenty-three UPSF officers and spacers aboard *Glorious*—all of them under Henry's command, hence his responsibility—*seventeen* had been found alive.

The Kozun had at least been at battle stations, and many had made it to escape pods. The survivors' stories there were the worst wound of all, though. Star Voice Kalad's flagship had lost her bridge early in the action, and Kalad had taken direct command of the cruiser, fighting her to the last.

She'd still been aboard and in command when the ship ran into the minefield no one had anticipated. There was no evidence that anyone aboard the heavy cruiser at that last moment had survived.

Henry Wong had sent Star Voice Kalad away in defeat once, but she'd survived both her battle with him and the consequences of that defeat in the Hierarchy. The Drifters had changed that fate, orphaning her child in a single moment of violence.

"Ser, *Scorpius* reports they're sending a shuttle for you," the Chief holding down the com console told him. "ETA is ten minutes. There's apparently going to be a command meeting including all three ambassadors in two hours."

"Understood," he replied. He glanced around the sparsely inhabited bridge and sighed. "Chief, can you get a team to pack up Ambassador Todorovich and her staff's things? They'll be far safer aboard *Scorpius*, and while I don't know where they're ending up, well..."

He shrugged. He didn't even need to tell the Chief. No one aboard *Raven* had any illusions about the battlecruiser. A surprisingly large portion of the crew had survived, but only through the sacrifice of the starship herself.

"I guess I'll go find a dress uniform," he said, glancing around. "Lieutenant Henriksson!"

The engineering officer looked up in surprise. She'd been entirely focused on her console and the task of finding anything still repairable aboard the battered ship.

"Ser?" she asked.

"You have the con, Lieutenant," he told her with a grin. *Engineering officer* wasn't a watch standing role, though any officer who wanted to advance to command would volunteer to backfill the watch standers to get experience.

"Ser!" she confirmed, her voice concerned.

"We're in the middle of a friendly fleet with our engines off, Lieutenant," Henry told her. "I *know* you can handle *Raven* in that situation—and you're the only other officer on the bridge. So, yes, Lieutenant, you have the conn."

"Yes, ser!" she said, straightening slightly and tapping commands to transfer central control to her console. "I won't let you down."

"I know."

Not only did Henry have full faith in the junior officer, there was basically nothing she *could* do to let him down in *Raven*'s current state.

HENRY'S DRESS uniform was his normal slacks and turtleneck with an additional white-piped and short-tailed black jacket. The jacket was collarless, allowing the white collar of his turtleneck to showcase his rank insignia above it.

A four-soldier fire team of GroundDiv troopers hovered behind him as he waited for the shuttle to land. They had the cases of Todorovich's people's gear on trolleys. All of them would fit easily on the spacecraft they were waiting for.

He could have taken one of his own shuttles. *Raven* had two of them left, after all, but he couldn't really argue with a superior officer sending a ship for him. Plus, those shuttles might be needed. The battlecruiser didn't seem *likely* to acquire any new trouble in the next few hours, but it might. She'd been battered hard enough.

He was half-expecting Alex Thompson to be aboard the shuttle, so he wasn't surprised to see a figure at the top of the ramp after the shuttle settled to a stop.

He was *not* expecting Sylvia Todorovich to walk down the shuttle's ramp alone, dressed in one of her sharply conservative suits but moving with renewed purpose the moment she saw him—and he hadn't expected the instant decision that the deck was quiet enough that propriety could be *damned*.

Before Henry Wong even realized what he was doing, he'd wrapped the Ambassador in a bear hug. He had just enough time to process just how thoroughly he'd broken *every* rule of military-civilian decorum before Sylvia's arms wrapped around him in turn.

"I thought I'd lost you," he murmured.

"I thought I'd lost *you*," she told him, leaning her head back to study his eyes for a seemingly eternal second. Then her fingers were on his chin and she was leaning in.

Henry was reasonably sure he was blushing like a teenager when he finally came up for air and looked around. The GroundDiv troopers and the scattering of techs in *Raven*'s shuttlebay had apparently found something *spectacularly* interesting on the wall opposite.

"I'm supposed to report aboard *Scorpius*," he admitted. He hadn't let go of her. She hadn't let go of him. His escort was still studying the wall.

"I know. I just hitched a ride on the shuttle," she told him. "Thompson is also aboard, but he thought he'd give us a moment."

Henry coughed. He was pretty sure he was flushing harder now —but Sylvia was clearly not letting him go.

"Everyone seems to think we should have that moment," she whispered in his ear. "But I think we should continue this...*conversation* later. In private."

"We've got work to do," Henry agreed. He slowly, reluctantly, released her. A moment later, she let him go.

"Somehow, I don't really want to do the work today," she said with a wicked spark in her smile. "But you're right. Let's let poor Commander Thompson off the shuttle and get aboard ourselves."

CHAPTER FORTY-SEVEN

There was, in Henry's mind, no subtlety about the way he and Sylvia arrived at the meeting. If any of the UPSF officers in the conference room thought it strange that the ambassador had flown over to *Raven* to fly right back and enter the meeting side by side with the battlecruiser captain, though...they didn't show it.

Henry very carefully did not meet Peter Barrie's gaze as he took a seat across from Admiral Cheung. Another man and woman in identical uniforms to his, the Colonels commanding Cheung's two battlecruisers, sat at either end of the table.

It was one of the carrier's midsized meeting rooms and would have been easily capable of handling the negotiations that had taken place aboard *Carpenter*. Right now, though, it had three Colonels, a Commodore, a Rear Admiral and the UPA Ambassador.

"I thought we were meeting with Aval and Rising Principle," Henry asked.

"We will," Sylvia told him. "This is a preliminary meeting for us to all get on the same page." She turned her attention to the Admiral at the head of the table.

"As I understand, Rear Admiral Cheung, Colonel Wong is not under your command?" she asked.

"That is correct," Cheung said in English that carried the tones of his home country. "Colonel Wong is the senior ship captain of the Peacekeeper Initiative and reports to Admiral Hamilton. While his ship is the entire Initiative presence here, he does represent an independent command.

"Though I think he and I will agree on what *Raven*'s next step is," Cheung admitted. "What is her status, Colonel?"

"*Raven* is no longer a functioning capital ship," Henry said quickly, before he could think about it. "Her spine has been broken. She is no longer capable of withstanding subjective thrust, and her primary batteries are offline.

"I do not believe that Zion's repair yards will suffice to restore her to function. She will require scrapping or a complete rebuild."

The words hung in the room like the Sword of Damocles—or the end of Henry's career. He'd commanded one of the UPSF's most modern starships to an unquestioned defeat and her destruction. Only paranoia on the part of High Command had saved his people.

"Understood," Cheung replied. "I believe, then, that your next stop is Zion, yes?"

"Yes, ser," Henry confirmed. "Admiral Hamilton will decide whether I accompany *Raven* back to more substantial shipyards."

"If you will permit, Colonel, I would like to detach *Rook* and two of our destroyers to escort you back to Zion," the Rear Admiral told him. "It would be a poor reward for the heroism of *Raven*'s crew to leave them vulnerable."

"It would be appreciated, ser," Henry admitted.

"In general, I believe we have no choice but to divide up Battle Group *Scorpius*," Sylvia said after that was resolved. "Voice Oran Aval has no transport back to the Hierarchy.

"It will serve everyone's interests if she is returned to Kozun and the rest of the Voices as safely and as swiftly as possible. I would like to borrow at least one of your destroyers, Admiral, to make certain she makes it home."

"She agreed to the peace treaty, didn't she?" Barrie asked.

"She did. The Drifters made an enemy of the most powerful woman in the Hierarchy," Sylvia told them. "She has already asked the La-Tar Cluster to consider a treaty of mutual defense against the Drifters.

"Both Rising Principle and Aval will need to get authorization from their home governments to continue that particular line of discussion—as will I," she admitted. "But we will want everyone to make it home safely to make sure the war ends."

"Then I think we will want to send more than a destroyer to Kozun," Cheung said. "I believe *Jackdaw* will make an impression— of both the UPA's power and of our willingness to protect their Voice. A destroyer companion—*Brachiosaur*, I think—will make the point in strength."

"I had intended to ask if I could borrow *Jackdaw* to deliver Ambassador Rising Principle," Sylvia admitted.

"*Scorpius* will be heading to La-Tar with the escorts I am retaining," Cheung replied firmly. "We can easily transport the ambassador home. To honor our commitment to secure La-Tar's defense, I feel that the presence of a proper fleet carrier will be needed."

He grimaced.

"The Drifters have lost their chance to keep us and the Kozun at war. I do not know what their next step will be, but we must be ready to honor our promises."

"I agree," Sylvia said. "My understanding was that Battle Group *Scorpius* was only out here for Operation Yellow Bicycle."

"That is correct," the Admiral confirmed. "But since we no longer have an instant communication cycle with High Command, a flag officer *must* act on their discretion—and like you, Ambassador Todorovich, I am bound by the honor and the promises of the United Planets Alliance.

"To keep those promises and protect La-Tar, my battle group is going to need to stay out here and keep watch."

"Thank you," she murmured. "Like Aval and Rising Principle, I need to return home and consult with our government. I believe that there must be consequences for attacking our ambassador, but that is not truly my decision to make."

"If they come for the Cluster, we will stop them," Cheung told her.

Henry felt a load leave his shoulders at that promise. He'd left three destroyers at La-Tar. They could *probably* fight a Guardian for the locals, but if the Drifters sent a real fleet—and even a single Convoy could muster a real fleet—they could never have held.

"I will return to Zion aboard *Raven*," Sylvia continued, and Henry tried not to blush like a schoolboy caught plotting. He'd been *hoping* that she'd be returning with him, but he hadn't been sure it was the best plan.

"We wanted to avoid entanglements outside our borders," she noted. "We wanted to secure peace with the minimum possible level of force and resources. I now don't believe that will be possible—but we *also* now have proof of the economic value of opening up these markets to UPA trade.

"We have made promises out here, promises that the Initiative alone cannot keep. For the honor of the UPA, we must act as one nation with *all* of our resources."

"I agree," Admiral Cheung said. "We will hold the line while you convince the Security Council. I hope your return trip is fruitful."

Sylvia nodded, her gaze meeting Henry's across the table.

"We'll be fine, I think," she said. "I just hope...that Blue Stripe Green Stripe Orange Stripe was working in isolation. If anyone had the ability to gather allies over the last year, it was the Drifters. The Convoy is a dangerous-enough threat on its own.

"If their arming and manipulation of the Kozun is representative, though...we could be seeing the birth of a new foe, potentially more focused on our direct defeat than the Kenmiri ever were."

"We will be ready," Henry promised, looking around at the other senior officers in the conference room. "I have solid guesses what the Drifters wanted out of wrecking the peace conference, but they're only guesses."

He smiled thinly.

"Unless there's something in play I didn't see, they're going to realize the risk was *never* worth what they stood to gain."

CHAPTER FORTY-EIGHT

Zion again. The seemingly delicate structures of Base Fallout stretched out as far as the eye could process and beyond. A corner of Henry's vision was occupied by a video feed of a camera above *Raven*, watching the repair base's teams swarm over the bent cruiser.

He knew what their conclusion would be. Song had left him in no doubt about the state of his command.

"Get in here, Wong," Hamilton's voice barked.

Flinching slightly, Henry stepped forward through the door to his boss's office. The last week of traveling with Sylvia aboard *Raven* had proven a surprisingly effective balm to his mental and emotional wounds, but this was the end point. This was where he learned what was going to happen to him.

He instinctively crossed to stand in front of Admiral Sonia Hamilton's desk and came to a crisp attention.

"When, Henry, have I *ever* wanted that mickey mouse bullshit?" she demanded. "Sit down."

He sat.

"Yard is still surveying *Raven*," Hamilton told him, the gray-haired and steely-eyed Admiral studying him. "You know what they're going to find, though."

"It'll be cheaper to rebuild her than build an entire new battlecruiser, but not by much," Henry said. "She needs a year—maybe more—in a major yard, like the one that built her."

"I saw Song's report, yes," the Admiral confirmed. "She and I will be speaking shortly. She'll take command of *Raven*'s passage crew and deliver her and Ambassador Todorovich to Sol."

Hamilton shrugged.

"There's a Colonel's billet and a mobile dry dock waiting for her there, anyway," she noted. "You weren't going to keep Song any longer, I'm afraid. She'll get her steel leaf before she leaves Zion, though."

"That's good, ser," Henry said. "She deserves it, even if she isn't a line officer."

Even Colonel Anna Song, with a steel oak leaf instead of a copper one on her collar, could never command a battlecruiser. A mobile dry dock, though, that was a fitting command for a UPSF engineering Colonel. They didn't have many of them, either, so that was one *hell* of a cookie.

"Promotion board sat while you were gone," Hamilton told him. "No news, I imagine, that you were going to lose a lot of your senior officers anyway. Iyotake's another one with a steel leaf waiting for him, though finding him a command is going to be a pain now."

"Ser?"

"He was *supposed* to get *Raven*," the Admiral noted. "Since she's going in for repairs, that won't happen."

Hamilton shook her head.

"*You* weren't staying on *Raven* any more than Song was," she noted. "Sadly, *Raven*'s loss doesn't change my plans for you at all. Or Commander Ihejirika, for that matter."

"I'm confused, ser," Henry admitted.

Admiral Sonia Hamilton laughed aloud.

"You wrote glowing reports for every one of your officers for their actions at the Great Gathering and La-Tar," she reminded him. "I don't think there is anyone on *Raven* who isn't getting bumped a grade right now. There are plum assignments waiting for most of your officers, though some of those assignments were intended to still be aboard *Raven*."

"And despite all of that, *you* expected to remain *Raven's* captain?"

"Yes, ser," Henry admitted. It sounded silly when she phrased it like that.

"Well, I apologize, Henry, but you're losing the white collar," she told him. A jewelry box appeared out of nowhere. "You get a new leaf, though. The last one you'll ever wear, one way or another."

The gold oak leaf of a United Planets Space Force Commodore somehow wasn't a surprise. Henry stared down at it as he touched the white collar of his turtleneck, the mark of a starship captain.

"So, you don't have a command for me?" he asked.

Hamilton laughed again.

"I just told you you're keeping Ihejirika," she pointed out. "*Lieutenant Colonel* Okafor Ihejirika will be transferred off *Raven* before she leaves, along with his physical orders. He'll be assuming command of the destroyer *Paladin*. *Cataphract* and *Maharatha* brought captains with them, but *Paladin* was slated to be Ihejirika's command before they left Procyon."

He looked down at the oak leaf as he began to catch up.

"I don't recognize those names, ser," he admitted.

"They're why your stunt flying a Lancer is probably a good thing," she told him. "You'll be taking command of DesRon Twenty-Seven. She's understrength, but all three of her ships are the brand-new *Cataphract* class."

Henry finally recognized the name. Even more than the Lancers, though, he'd regarded the *Cataphract* class as a fable, a pipe dream he never expected to see realized.

"Congratulations, *Commodore* Wong," Hamilton concluded.

"We'll probably hang some medals on you in the end, too, but the reward for a job well done is another job. Welcome to command of the first and currently *only* formation of GMS-equipped warships in the United Planets Space Force.

"Believe me, Henry, I have work for you to do with them."

JOIN THE MAILING LIST

Love Glynn Stewart's books? To know as soon as new books are released, special announcements, and a chance to win free paperbacks, join the mailing list at:

glynnstewart.com/mailing-list/

ABOUT THE AUTHOR

Glynn Stewart is the author of *Starship's Mage*, a bestselling science fiction and fantasy series where faster-than-light travel is possible—but only because of magic. His other works include science fiction series *Duchy of Terra, Castle Federation* and *Vigilante*, as well as the urban fantasy series *ONSET* and *Changeling Blood*.

Writing managed to liberate Glynn from a bleak future as an accountant. With his personality and hope for a high-tech future intact, he lives in Southern Ontario with his partner, their cats, and an unstoppable writing habit.

VISIT GLYNNSTEWART.COM FOR NEW RELEASE UPDATES

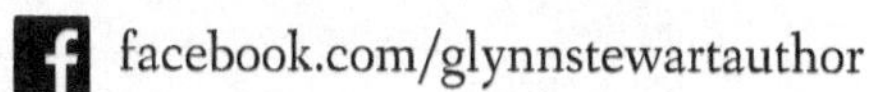 facebook.com/glynnstewartauthor

OTHER BOOKS
BY GLYNN STEWART

For release announcements join the
mailing list or visit **GlynnStewart.com**

STARSHIP'S MAGE

Starship's Mage
Hand of Mars
Voice of Mars
Alien Arcana
Judgment of Mars
UnArcana Stars
Sword of Mars
Mountain of Mars
The Service of Mars
A Darker Magic
Mage-Commander
Beyond the Eyes of Mars
Nemesis of Mars *(upcoming)*

Starship's Mage: Red Falcon
Interstellar Mage
Mage-Provocateur
Agents of Mars

Pulsar Race: A Starship's Mage Universe Novella

DUCHY OF TERRA

The Terran Privateer
Duchess of Terra
Terra and Imperium
Darkness Beyond
Shield of Terra
Imperium Defiant
Relics of Eternity
Shadows of the Fall
Eyes of Tomorrow

SCATTERED STARS

Scattered Stars: Conviction
Conviction
Deception
Equilibrium
Fortitude
Huntress
Prodigal *(upcoming)*

Scattered Stars: Evasion
Evasion
Discretion
Absolution *(upcoming)*

PEACEKEEPERS OF SOL

Raven's Peace
The Peacekeeper Initiative
Raven's Course
Drifter's Folly
Remnant Faction
Raven's Flag *(upcoming)*

EXILE

Exile
Refuge
Crusade
Ashen Stars: An Exile Novella

CASTLE FEDERATION

Space Carrier Avalon
Stellar Fox
Battle Group Avalon
Q-Ship Chameleon
Rimward Stars
Operation Medusa
A Question of Faith: A Castle Federation Novella

Dakotan Confederacy
Admiral's Oath
To Stand Defiant *(upcoming)*

VIGILANTE
(WITH TERRY MIXON)
Heart of Vengeance
Oath of Vengeance

**Bound By Stars: A Vigilante Series
(With Terry Mixon)**
Bound By Law
Bound by Honor
Bound by Blood

TEER AND KARD
Wardtown
Blood Ward

CHANGELING BLOOD
Changeling's Fealty
Hunter's Oath
Noble's Honor
Fae, Flames & Fedoras: A Changeling Blood Novella

ONSET
ONSET: To Serve and Protect
ONSET: My Enemy's Enemy
ONSET: Blood of the Innocent
ONSET: Stay of Execution
Murder by Magic: An ONSET Novella

STAND ALONE NOVELS & NOVELLAS
Children of Prophecy
City in the Sky
Excalibur Lost: A Space Opera Novella
Balefire: A Dark Fantasy Novella